BORN OF BLOOD AND FLAMES

AND FLAMES

GRAVESTONE BOOK ONE

AMBER DARWIN

CONTENTS

DEDICATION

FOR MY FATHER, WHO made his journey to the other side before any of us were ready to say goodbye. You always told me I'd be an author someday. Hope you're smiling! Oh, and if you can somehow read what's in this book from the other side? Avoid Chapter 25. Please.

Love you, Pop!
Dwight Darwin 4.7.08

WELCOME TO THORNFALL

"She may be going to hell of course, but at least she isn't standing still." – E.E. Cummings

Author's Note

I WRITE GRITTY, RAW, sometimes disturbing gothic/dark fantasy/paranormal romance. The heroes do villain-type shit, and the villains are not always what they seem. Some find redemption, some never will. These characters are not human and won't always behave as you or I would expect, but I hope you see something in each of them that speaks to you. And through their struggles, I hope you find those jagged pieces of yourself and learn to love them for what they are.

Are there errors in this book? Probably. I'm human, and I'm pretty sure my editor is too. Although magic can't be ruled out with her.

This is the first installment of The Gravestone Trilogy. An adult gothic fantasy romance (18+)
It contains scenes that may depict, mention, or discuss: abduction, animal death, anxiety, attempted murder, blood, death, emotional abuse, fire, kidnapping, murder, occult, PTSD, torture, war, graphic sex, gore, foul language, dysfunctional relationships, miscommunication, and cliffhangers. If any of these themes are

damaging to your mental health, turn back now. This is not the book for you.

- If that just made you want to read it even more? Congrats. We're besties, and I need to know your favorite color. XO – Amber

PROLOGUE

UNDER THE COVER OF night, my mother runs her hand along my tiny cheek with tear-soaked eyes. "It's time." Her voice shakes as the walls of my childhood home echo with violence and death. "One day, you will understand why, and you will forgive me, my sweet one. Until the day comes, know that everything I've done is for love."

She places her hand on my temple, and fiery agony rips into my soul. I don't understand what tears through my mind's eye, leaving carnage in its path. Faces I don't recognize, places I've never been, events that pass, and visions not yet set into motion. Her power terrifies me, consumes me, breaks me, and then abandons me to darkness.

I wake up as a Blood Seer and an orphan.

Love is a transient thing. A thought, a goal, a verb, an idea, an action. It can be so real, and yet... not. To some, it's the ultimate high, an all-consuming obsession. For those who have been love-starved, it's something else entirely. A bitter poison, a weakness.

I thought I knew my definition of love until it destroyed me, and, in the wreckage I was remade. Born of Blood and Flames.

CHAPTER ONE

PRESENT DAY THORNFALL

THE RAUCOUS SONG OF traffic horns is deafening below my second-story window. Cool, salty sea air breezes through my window, along with rumbles and crashing of enthusiastic wyverns digging glass out of a dumpster, searching for shiny treasures to line their nests. Wild Elphus–a type of humanoid hummingbird–flutter near the edges of my sheer curtains, looking for sugary treats.

Loud, it's too fucking loud. I crack open one lavender eye and sweep a thick section of unruly midnight hair from my face, glancing at the alarm clock. 8:03 am. Ugh. With a tired sigh, I gather a thin strand of wispy electricity with my fingertips; the air shimmers crimson around me, like heat rising off the horizon. Lifting my arm, I flick the enchantment toward the racket, and a comfortable blanket of silence descends upon my apartment.

I am not a morning person.

Calypso lounges in a pile of fluff on our bed, cleaning herself. Stretching her dagger-like claws into the skin of my thighs. I wince at the sting. "You could help." I roll my eyes as

I communicate through our mental bond. Not interested in conversation, she jumps down from the warm bed and saunters across the wooden floor toward the front door, swishing her tail violently.

"Okay, fine, I'm getting up," I mumble as I untangle myself from my silky sheets and place my feet on the soft rug.

Calypso, "Lippy" for short, is a total diva. A short-haired, coal-black, large, and in charge force of nature. Although she is my familiar, she doesn't answer to me, even on a good day. It's a personality trait deemed undesirable by the elder witches. It makes familiars "difficult to control" in their eyes, but I admire it. That's why she chose me. We're both outcasts with unpredictable magic and a penchant for finding trouble.

I stumble across the floor as I wipe the sleep from my eyes, knocking my departed mother's ring under the bed. My heart sways as I drop on all fours, trying to recover it. I stretch my arm beyond its limit as my fingers search the neon green rug, roaming through the long fibers until my fingers touch metal, and relief washes over me. I cram the plain silver band back on my finger, shaking my head. Maybe taking it off at night isn't such a fantastic idea.

I have a sock dangling from my foot, a banging headache from too many shots last night, and the last thing I need right now is another rerun of 'fireworks in the apartment.' I'm not kidding, by the way. My magical cat blows shit up when she's annoyed. The colors are pretty, I'll give her that. But can we say fire hazard?

With that memory in mind, I hot-mess myself down the hallway to the front door before she detonates. "At your service, my queen," I grumble as she slips through the crack in the stainless-steel door and out into the foggy morning.

I crack the heavy door a little wider to remind her for the thousandth time, "No more snacks in the house, Lippy. I mean it!" she wanders down the alleyway, shape-shifting to the size of a massive jungle cat.

"I swear if I find one more lizard, rodent, or anything with feathers under my bed, I'll give you store-bought cat food for a week! The chunky kind!"

No response, as usual.

My mind returns to its present state of exhaustion. Last night was a train wreck. I barely slept a wink, and I cannot function without my daily latte and lemon muffin; so, the first order of business is to finish dressing and do something with this crow's nest called a hairdo. Then, I'll wake Marlow and find Lincoln. My two best friends. Never mind that they're my *only* friends.

Marlow will expect to hear from me after I hightailed it out of The Gravestone last night like a kelpie with my gills on fire. I'm surprised she wasn't on my stoop at midnight with twenty questions and a lousy attitude about it, but my guess is she's waiting to grill me today. I'm not looking forward to that at all! Nevertheless, we have a pact. Caffeine is life, and we worship at the espresso altar together.

I grab my phone off the disheveled kitchen counter and press the speed dial. Staring at my dingy cupboards and thinking about how I should strip then paint them black instead of looking at the current atrocity. After several rings, a groggy voice on the other end grumbles. "Vivi Graves, if this call does not include some serious dishing about Mr. Smokin' Hot Sex God at work last night, I will be so pissed."

Shuffling noises...

"I swear he tried to burn a hole through your top with his eyeballs. He reminds me of Drake's character from the last book I read. He's a dragon shifter, and let me tell you, those guys really know how to... Wait, what time is it?"

More Shuffling noises. A 'thump' echoes through the speaker.

She's looking for her glasses.

"It's freaking 8:15, Vivi!" Marlow shrieks in my ear as I hold the phone at arm's length.

I can't help but smile at her derailed train of thought. Marlow, Lowe for short, is a total genius. A walking encyclopedia, a book addict, and a shameless pervert. Sometimes the genius takes over, and when that happens, the common sense? Well, that takes a back seat. She's the brains of our trio. Lincoln has the lady-chasing comedian role covered. So, I guess that makes me the brawn?

Marlow and I were just kids when I stumbled upon her being mean-girled in our school foyer. "Halfling, halfling. Daddy's little science experiment. You don't belong here, crossbreed!"

They taunted her like a pack of hyenas in gaudy designer clothes. She was a stranger at the time, but it pissed me off, so I froze their panties to their thighs in a flurry of sweet retribution. Side note: they also sent me home for three days for the infraction. My guardian was not pleased, but I never had any regrets. I'd do it again in a heartbeat. Only this time I'd be much more creative now that I'm older and have more practice in witchy bitchery.

'Poor impulse control' is what my official records stated. I prefer to describe it as a low tolerance for assholes. A difference of opinion, I suppose. Marlow and I have been inseparable ever since.

"Morning, Lowe. Sorry, blame Calypso and the dumpster diving quartet for the rude awakening. Coffee? Baked Goods? 20 minutes?" A moment of silence hangs on the other end as if she needs time to think about this no-brainer.

"Fine, but you're buying! I'll find Linc." she huffs as she hangs up.

I set my phone down, spotting the growing stack of mail I'd left unopened. A gaudy envelope with a red wax seal stares back at me, mocking my existence. I already know who it came from and where they can shove it. Underhill Academy of Magic, my old alma mater.

The Council of Elders has been trying to entice me back into their clutches for years. Even though I am explicitly uninterested, they continue to send me offensive envelopes and long-winded voicemails I have to delete.

Vivi Graves, Thornfall's youngest Blood Seer extraordinaire. Blood Witch, meaning I can dabble in your blood to see how shitty your future will be, or rip it from your veins if I'm in the mood. Seer meaning that I pick up on a lot more than the average witch. I'm the youngest because I was forced to ascend over a decade too early. Most witches and warlocks spend their entire academic and magical career at Underhill Academy, preparing for ascension in their sixteenth year. I'm the exception; the only one in history.

Which is just a long-winded way of saying I'm a freak of nature.

Either way, ascension was thrust upon me before I ever stepped foot into the building. A five-year-old who had come into her powers was quite the miracle. Or, as it turned out, a commodity. I was their weapon, a promise of darkness and death to anyone who dared disobey. They molded me into their weapon and stripped me of ever having a normal life when I was too young to understand what it meant. To say I'm not a fan of The Academy or its Elders is an understatement of epic proportions. Five years ago, I graduated from that hell scape and walked away without looking back.

Funny thing about creating your very own five-foot-nothing boogeyman is that in my absence, faith in their administration continues to decline. The citizens of Thornfall are thinking for themselves. Questioning the rules. Realizing the beast has no teeth. It must suck to lose all that psychological control, but ask me if I give a shit? Newsflash, I don't. I hope one day this entire city rises against them and burns the fucker down, preferably with the Elders inside it.

"Junk mail is what it is," I speak to the empty room as I toss the insulting envelope in the trash and grab water from the fridge.

EVERY TIME I VENTURE onto the rickety metal steps leading down from my apartment, it feels like a gamble with my life. One of these days, I'm going to fall to my demise in a pile of wrought iron bullshit.

"I need to talk to Deacon about these death traps." I remind myself. Again.

The chill in the air nips at my neck as I step down to the cobblestone alley; Mabon is approaching. Soon the leaves will turn, and the frigid winter will set in. Every year is a reminder of the freedom I've gained, real or imagined.

Strolling along, lost in my own thoughts, a tingle skitters across the back of my neck. I'm always on edge. They molded me that way: an unassuming monster. So, I turn to see what's lurking behind me as 'Spirit Frank' tips his Styrofoam cup in greeting. Jeez, I'm jumpy. It's something in the air.

I suspect Frank died years ago- hence the 'Spirit' part. If Frank is even his real name. It could be Ragnar or Sparkle Barbie, for all I know. Maybe he was an Elven Knight in his days on this side of the veil. Or perhaps he was an operative for the Rune Force, our Preternatural Peacekeepers. He doesn't speak, so I don't have a clue. I could dig around for answers, but I use my gifts sparingly these days.

So, yeah, I see spirits like the creepy kid in the movies. Except I do my best to ignore them. I can't help them, anyway. Not with the myriad of restrictions the Academy puts on the use of magic, so what's the point?

Plus, when you spend most of your childhood as a living torture device, magic doesn't seem all that great. I've damned hundreds of souls to the Repentance Halls because of magic. I've debased myself and corrupted my soul with it. Not by choice, but does it absolve me of my actions if it wasn't my idea? Not really.

Absolute power corrupts absolutely, right?

ENCHANTED BREW IS A bright spot in our otherwise depressing seaside city, where overcast skies are the rule and sunshine is the exception. If you like rain, ice, assholes, and the smell of fish? Thornfall is the place for you.

Muffled music echoes as I grab the rose-shaped door handle and yank hard. The wood frame sticks if you don't use some elbow grease. 'All part of the eclectic downtown charm,' Lincoln would say in his I'm-a-charming-comedian voice.

The familiar whimsical tables and mismatched chairs welcome me like old friends. My small slice of ordinary, whatever that means. Herbs and tinctures suspend from the rafters and line the walls.

A cozy reading nook is tucked away in the corner. The makeshift stage is deserted; however, Marlow, Linc, and I have spent countless hours watching acoustic and spoken word artists honing their craft with second-hand audio equipment. Marlow is a fan of 'Nerd Night'- aka Tuesday night book club, and Lincoln enjoys messing around with his vintage Gibson at the open mic. Singing husky ballads, attracting crowds of admiring females.

There's something quirky and peaceful about this place, but it's not flawless. Customers should be aware of their drinks, for starters, with Rowena's concoctions and the trio of mischievous sprites in the kitchen. Things can get awkward around here. Bron, Bairn, and Baela are notorious for "altering" recipes with hilarious but catastrophic results.

For example, Marlow once had her brown skin turned neon pink for three entire days because of a pinprick of the finger, a full moon, and Bairn's idea of comedy. Ordering the "Pink Rose of Beauty" can be interpreted in multiple ways. Technically, they weren't breaking any rules. Sprites are tricksy that way. Be extremely specific with the fae-folk or suffer the consequences.

"Good morning, my darling Vivi!" a cheery voice calls out as I pass through the heavy door, bells tinkling like a delicate song as I pull it tight behind me.

Rowena Fairchild is the sage-green-skinned proprietor of this establishment. As my mother's spell weaver and personal attendant before her death, Rowena is sort of like a fairy grandmother. No, not the godmother. A fairy *grandmother*. Fairy godmothers grant wishes. Fairy *grandmothers* do a little too much meddling in your love life and hound on about what you ate for breakfast. There's a difference.

"What's on the menu?" I reply with a grin, browsing the handwritten chalkboard sign hovering over the gilded antique register.

It reads:
'Cup of the Day.
Autumn Spiced Tea:

Cinnamon for abundance and love.
Ginger for when push comes to shove.
Nutmeg for good fortune and wealth.
Ordering our tea will bring you good health!'
No, thank you. I've already learned my lesson about "abundance and love." Another one of Rowena's half-cocked attempts at enhancing my sex life. She is something, but I love her with all my shriveled heart.

"Got anything for lots of tips tonight?" I smile.

"I have just the thing!" She glides over to the shelf and grabs a mug with a death's head hawkmoth painted on the side. She hums to herself as she brews up a masterpiece, adding this and that in a whirlwind of shimmery cream-colored dust. There's a faint smell of violets, and something mossy fills the air.

"Grab a seat. I'll send Bron over," she calls across her shoulder, busy at work.

Tinkling bells and the distant sound of wood grinding against metal draw my attention. As I turn to investigate, everything in the café darkens into background noise - everything except him. To say he's beautiful is an understatement. I've never witnessed someone so blindingly attractive up close. Intricate tattoos of wicked-looking birds flow up and down his arms. His inky dark hair tinted blue in the daylight. Pair that with intense turquoise eyes, a chiseled jawline, and cheekbones I would murder someone for.

Everything about him captivates me. He's the kind of man who's made of lightning: mesmerizing and deadly. Something you want to touch, but you know there's nothing but pain waiting for your fingertips. Pain, but also power.

I'm powerful even without the blood. That's just a bonus. I was also "blessed" with the Sight. Auras call to me. It's challenging to hide emotions from me. I sense tainted souls and foul deeds. I see the rank shades of dark greens and shit browns that slither through the energy fields of the wicked. Not his, though. When I search for something from him? There's nothing. No color, no sound, no taste, no impressions. I don't know what it means, but my gut tells me that's not a good thing. He's like a palm pit viper. The beauty lures you in for their kill. But let me back up. I'm getting ahead of myself. Because this isn't the first time I've seen those stormy turquoise eyes...

Last night, I worked my regular shift at The Gravestone Bar & Grill when he blew in like a category five hurricane of trouble. He took one look in my direction and glared like I'd murdered his entire family or something. I mean, this guy had pure hatred for me written all over his sexy as sin face.

He sat at the corner table near the front window with what I can only assume was his entourage. Three large men who looked like they could all be Olympians. There was something 'other' about all of them, though I couldn't put my finger on what it was.

After his initial rudeness, I caught him staring. Studying me intently. Those stormy eyes were mesmerizing, intense, and quite terrifying. Warmth radiated throughout my whole body. Emphasis on the lower half - which was beyond disturbing, if you're wondering. After several minutes of his intense gaze, I dropped a bottle.

Listen, I practically live in that bar. I grew up on a barstool. No, not drunk. But my guardian sleeps in his office at The Gravestone Bar (don't ask), and my apartment is above it, for Goddess's sake. I'm the girl who can mix a drink blindfolded on one leg in high heels. I don't make mistakes, and I do not drop bottles.

The dusky amber glass hit the cement floor and shattered, making a sticky fucking mess everywhere. Breaking whatever unholy trance he had me in, and as fast as I bent down to pick up the shards, he was gone. Whatever he is, he'd shaken me like no other man ever has, and I wasn't appreciative of it in the least. After the toxic bullshit I've been through, this is the last thing I need.

I had rushed past Marlow with no explanation. I ended up fleeing to my shithole apartment to burn the memory of his beautiful chaos from my mind with tequila, salt, and lime. It wasn't my finest moment; I'm not known for being emotional. Usually, I'm the monster under your bed, the girl you don't fuck with, and I guess I pride myself on that. For no other reason than I inspire fear and respect. It's my armor, and I'm still pissed he got under my skin without having to say a damn word.

"Earth to Vivi!" Marlow hums in my ear, bringing me back to reality. "Mmm, Mmm. Yummy... Tall, Dark, and Dangerous found our hideout?" she tosses me a saucy wink as she brazenly eyes him up, spending extra seconds near his zipper.

Oh, my Goddess, I might die of second-hand embarrassment. This is why we can't have nice things.

Leaning sideways to elbow her in the ribs, I end up stumbling into her arms instead. Knocking one of her books to the floor in a heap of twisted paper. "Oof, I'm so sorry, Lowe!" my cheeks flush pink. "I need a latte more than I thought ..."

Marlow arches her brow in amusement. She's not buying what I'm trying to sell at all, so there's no point in even finishing that sentence. Why am I acting like a fucking idiot in his presence, anyway? It's not like I've never seen a pretty douchebag before.

"Yeah, okay. Must be the coffee you need, but I think you might need something else more," Marlow says with a knowing smile.

A giggle escapes her lips as she bends down to pick up her disheveled manual on Candle Magic. Her flowy boho skirt swished with the movement. "Why don't you go over and say hello? Strange he's standing here, don't you think?"

"Sure, and then I'll warm up hot pokers and shove them under my fingernails while I'm at it. That man has at least seventeen felonies written all over him. And didn't you just call him dangerous?" I cock my head.

"Don't forget tall, dark, and staring at you right now." She grins, leaning her head in his direction.

I realize too late he's already been to see Rowena, and she's finished with his order. How convenient. She never fills mine that fast! So, with a to-go cup in hand... Mr. Tall, Dark, and Dangerous is headed straight for us.

My heart hammers in my chest, palms sweating. *Please do not let him come this way. Please, Universe...* but that's just wishful thinking. He makes a slight turn to avoid another customer and it puts him smack between us and a rack of magical herbs for sale. Something tells me that's intentional.

I'm standing wide-eyed and unmoving like one of Medusa's victims when he makes direct eye contact. The kind where I have to look back, or I'll seem even more awkward than I already feel. So, I raise my eyes to him, nod, and... grunt? It was supposed to sound noncommittal, but it came out kind of like a wounded animal.

Smooth one, Vivi. Goddess, help me. There's not enough coffee in the Universe for this.

"Good morning, ladies," he speaks in a deep, silky-smooth voice, holding his gaze to mine for a fraction longer than necessary. A complete one-eighty from the menacing scowl last night. And I swear, internal combustion never felt like a real thing until this exact moment.

Stupid, drunken, worthless butterflies.

"Have a wonderful day!" Marlow half-shouts as he makes his way past us. He gives her a confident nod and struts off toward the sidewalk.

Marlow levels her gaze at me. "What is your problem? He's smokin' hot! And he's eye-fucked you into oblivion twice now. Who cares if he's a demon fuckboy or a walking mistake? It's been so long I bet you've got cobwebs growing between your legs. What are you waiting for? Do you need a written invitation? Chase his fine ass down the street and hump his leg! Or maybe I will." Her eyes glitter.

I swear if Marlow spent even a fraction of this energy on getting herself laid, she wouldn't be the most inappropriate virgin I've ever met!

She's right about one thing, though. It has been a while. Not that I mind. My dating life is more of a cautionary tale than a guidebook. Unless it's like a 'What Not to Do' manual. Then I'd be a bestseller.

I've collected a string of self-absorbed bad boy clichés that could wind around the block. Healthy and functional aren't in my vocabulary. Plus, the last shithead ruined it for the entire male population. He, too, had all the right things to say and the looks to back everything up. I got caught up in him, and the next thing I know I'm the basic bitch crying in the break room and lurking around corners, trying to catch him doing goddess knows what. Turns out I didn't have to look far. I'd gotten off work early one day and found him railing some random girl on my kitchen counter. When I threw his ass out, he took some liberties with what he considered his things. Like, three hundred dollars out of my cash stash and a bunch of my vintage records.

So, am I interested in men right now? That's a negative.

"Let's just get to our table." I'm distracting Marlow before she can develop any wilder ideas. Next, she'll be talking about picket fences and mystical babies. Too many raunchy sexcapades and fairy tale endings floating around in that dirty bookworm's head.

Once we're seated and my brain is functioning again, the familiar tendrils of rage wrap around me like a security blanket. Blood Seers are prone to anger. You know, the whole *seeing red* thing? Yeah, that's got my name all over it. But I think it's justified. I mean, who the hell does he think he is?

Waltzing into our sanctuary all Vampire Diaries' hotness and looking at me like I'm next on the menu. After he was just in my workplace acting like he wanted to burn me at the stake.

My palms vibrate with fury.

"Tone down the fire show, Killer. Someone's going to notice." Marlow warns as I glance down at the wisp of smoke drifting from my clenched fists.

Shit! I shake my head at the burst of wild magic. *Cool down, Vivi, focus.*

Panic seizes my mind, which makes it so much worse. Finally, Marlow grabs my hand and infuses water into my pores. I inhale a deep breath, willing the heat to disperse. With her help, an icy film of snowflakes travels over my fingers, drifting toward the floor, and evaporating.

"What's that all about?" Marlow continues the conversation like I didn't almost sign my own death note. "First, he comes into Gravestone, and you bust a two-hundred-dollar bottle of bourbon. Now he's in our coffee shop, and you nearly burst into flames? You're so into him."

"We've seen his type before. The poster boy for unwary females with no sense of self-preservation. Nobody is that smooth unless he's had years of practice in breaking hearts and crushing souls. He looks like he gets off on it, too." I chew the inside of my cheek, close to saying something stupid about his sinful lips, when Linc slides into the chair next to me. All quirky smiles and boyish charm.

Whew, saved by the shifter.

"Sorry, I was, umm... handling some stuff. What did I miss?" When Linc notices the scowl on my face, he adds, "You look like someone pissed in your oatmeal, Viv."

"Handling some stuff?" I roll my eyes. That's awfully vague. Wonder what her name is? Poor girl.

Marlow erupts in a fit of laughter, "I don't know about any piss, but why don't you ask Vivi how our shift went last night? Someone's panties melted over a hottie with a body, and now we're missing a bottle of bourbon - because she dropped it! Deacon is going to flip shit when he finds out, and I'm bringing popcorn to the show!"

Linc flinches at Marlow's words. A mask of cheerfulness falls over his face just as quickly, but I saw it. Shit, he remembers the drunken attempt to kiss me last week. I dodged him hard, but he would have regretted it when he woke up the next day. I was trying to do him a solid. Then he took off like he always does, hooking up with randoms and wandering the forests until he's good and ready to come back and pretend everything's fine.

It's not my idea of a healthy coping strategy, but what do I know? There isn't a therapist in this realm that could take on my issues. I've got no room to judge over here.

Bron approaches with our heavenly smelling lattes and muffins, but I've lost my appetite.

"So, I hear we've got a new coworker starting tonight." I change the subject. "I'm going in early to scrub the sticky mess before Deacon catches it. So, you can save popcorn for another time, Assholes."

Deacon will be all over me if he catches wind of my shitty closing job. I'm already in a heap of trouble for assaulting my piece of shit, cheating, thieving ex "whatever" when he had the balls to walk in and sit at my bar a few days back.

He who-shall-not-be-named wanted to get touchy-feely all over my new leather pants. I was more interested in the three hundred dollars he liberated from my secret cash-stash and the satisfaction of my fist meeting his face. Whoops! It made me feel better, but Deacon, not so much.

I'm sort of on a 'keep my hands to myself' probation now.

By the grace of the Goddess, Marlow was moving on from the subject of my train-wrecked love life. Twirling her chestnut curls around her finger, somehow something was already enthralling her between the pages of the book she brought with her.

"I'm on at 6 tonight," she replies, taking a sip of her raspberry mocha.

"I'm in the kitchen at seven," Linc adds. His voice is hard to understand with a mouthful of muffin, but his dimples make up for it.

An ear-piercing shriek startles me from my thoughts as a spoon whizzes past my ear. The table beside us is a flurry of activity. Someone's face is sprouting spikes. Total chaos unleashes while Baela giggles like a psychopath. Soaking up the screams as her bat-like wings carry her back to the safety of the kitchen.

I can't help snicker. Sprites are wicked little beasties with interesting feeding habits, but they sure are entertaining. We spend a few hours at The Brew, people watching and chatting about the upcoming festivities.

THE FESTIVAL OF LIGHT happens every year in
Thornfall; it celebrates the three witchling
bloodlines forming an alliance after centuries
of conflict. Basically, the Bloodgoods wanted
the gift of persuasion. The Moonfalls wanted
access to earth magic. The Darkmoors wanted
concentrated mind magic. They all wanted access
to blood magic. And nobody learned how to
share. After years of violence and nonsense, I
guess they are tired of trimming each other's
family trees. Or did they find a common enemy?
I believe the latter, on account of the fourth
witchling bloodline nobody dares speak of.

Our historians paint a picture of the Shadowfax
line wandering off to new lands, just disappearing
into the night. Taking their shadows, dark magic,
and gruesome experiments with them.

I think it's unicorn shit. We all know The Rune
Force wasn't created for fun. They're policing a
lot more than illegal contraband in Fairy Folk
Alley, that's for sure.

So, back to the festival. This year is a
big spectacle with Underhill Academy as the
crowning jewel. *'At Underhill Academy of Magic,
children of all magical bloodlines learn to hone their
unique skills and coexist under the watchful eyes
of our Council of Esteemed Elders.'* We've heard
this bullshit PR line a million times before and
nobody buys it but them. In reality, Underhill
Academy is an elitist hellhole with a deceptively
pleasant face and powerful pockets.

Soon, their students and staff will overtake our
side of town in droves. They'll hold a parade,

shop, listen to the street bands, and most likely try
to ditch their chaperones to find the back-alley
vendors who don't check for identification, just
like Marlow and I did when we were students. A
little Pegasus dust can have you feeling euphoric
for hours, and dried Minotaur horn? Well, let's
say you and your partner won't be needing pants
for at least two days.

The point being, in a few days, students would
be free of the Academy walls and crawling over
everything like little magical cockroaches. *I can't
wait.* After some quick errands, I head home to
get cleaned up and ready for my shift. Calypso
comes barreling to my side in full jungle cat form
as I round the corner. Fur standing on end, ears
back, fangs bared.

"Danger!" She hisses through our mental bond.

I place my fingers around the moonstone
dagger concealed under my jacket. My eyes comb
the filthy alleyway, looking for threats. Instead,
I find Meredith Bridgewater, Head Mistress of
Underhill, standing beneath my death traps.

"Oh, this is fantastic. Can this week get any
better?" I mumble under my breath as I cross
the distance between us, pushing my dagger back
into its hidey-hole.

"What can I do for you today, Mistress?" I
address her with contempt because I literally hate
her, and I'm hoping my irritated tone is enough
to ward her off, but I already know it's unlikely.

"Hello Genevieve, I'm sorry to intrude on you
in this manner, but we need to speak," she replies,
lips a thin white line.

"I can't imagine why we would need to speak.
I've made it clear I am not interested in your

offers. You can pass the message along to the Elders, too. I'm not helping any of you with shit." When my mouth opens, the sarcasm pours right out.

"I'm not here on official business, Miss Graves." her voice cracks, "May I come in?"

Not on official business, huh? Doubtful.

Pushing my way past her, I head up the steps. She follows closely behind, disgust etched on her face at having to touch my banister. I'm sure it burns her ass having to be on this side of town for any reason... but especially because of me. The feeling is beyond mutual. Who knows, maybe today is the day my death traps give out and send her tumbling to the muck-filled cobblestones because that would make my entire year!

"Can't we have this discussion over the phone? Actually, I don't enjoy talking on the phone either. Oh, I've got one better... a text?" I shoot a barbed glance in her direction, making one last-ditch effort to blow her off.

The Head Mistress levels her eyes at me, unimpressed. "That would require a reply, Miss Graves, which we both know you have been less than cooperative in providing."

Okay, fair enough.

When it becomes painfully clear Bridgewater won't be taking no for an answer, I open my door and usher her in. I can tell she's uncomfortable in my unorganized living space, with her crisp khaki-colored trench coat and plum-colored tea-length dress. Not a honey blonde hair out of place. I'm ashamed to admit that makes me a little happy. I'm not a total asshole or anything. I just want her to experience even half the misery she watched me endure. This isn't half, but something's better than nothing. Was she the one who traumatized me for life? No, but she stood by and did nothing to stop it, which might be worse.

She wanders around the apartment, inspecting my things like she's visiting a museum. No doubt taking full advantage of the opportunity to quench her curiosity. Her footsteps slow in front of the only picture I have of my mother, and I watch in disbelief as she runs her manicured fingernail across the frame. She's got some real lady balls touching that picture. The urge to rip her fingers off and feed them to her is powerful right now.

My mother is a sore subject. Most decent people would leave it alone, but not Bridgewater. Nope, she likes to poke at open wounds to see what oozes out. She's her own type of monster in that way. From overhearing hundreds of conversations not meant for my ears, I learned she voted against my entrance to Underhill Academy at five years old. This wretched twat argued with Deacon when he asked the Council to conceal my identity too. So yeah, she's a monster, alright. Just a different breed.

My magic bubbles to the surface, begging to lash out, but I'm not in the mood for a run-in with the Rune Force today. So, I grab the skeleton key hanging from my neck and take a deep breath. "I have things to do. So, if you have something to say, how about we cut to the chase?"

"Very well, Miss Graves," she says with a deep sigh. "I believe this will come as a shock. Have a seat."

"Thanks, but I think I'll stand." I smile, all snark.

She makes an exasperated noise as she straightens her dress for the third time. What comes out of her mouth next, I never expected in my wildest dreams... "Genevieve, you have a sister."

On second thought, maybe I should have taken that seat.

CHAPTER TWO

VIVI

A SISTER? I CAN'T help but stifle a snort of amusement. It's not the most appropriate reaction to have after someone drops a bomb in your lap, but I've watched the Elders pull some truly bizarre rabbits from their hats in the past. They've proven time and time again they'll do anything to further their agenda. But this? This is impressive.

"You've lost your mind, Bridgewater. Let me spell this out for you in kindergarten letters. I. Will. Never. Step. Foot. In the festering shithole you call a school ever again." a sinister smile spreads across my red lips. "And nice try, but I don't have a fucking sister."

Should I be speaking to the Head Mistress this way? No.

Do I give a shit? Also, no.

Every terrified expression when I was brought into the Halls of Repentance. Every agonized face, begging me not to break their mind. Every drop of blood that flowed from their eyes, noses, and ears by my hand. Every tear I shed in private. Every time I felt helpless to do anything to save them. Or myself. That's what I see when

I look at her face. My skin hums. Goosebumps fill with wild, untamed magic as Calypso stalks back and forth across the apartment. She senses my emotions and acts accordingly, which means this situation will go South. I'm talking "grab the handbasket" because we're going to the hell dimension in gasoline underpants. South.

"I assure you, Miss Graves. We have credible information that suggests otherwise. You must come to The Academy and answer some questions." She taps her clean heel against my wood floor, waiting for me to respond. When she doesn't receive what she's waiting for... she adds, "The Council demands it."

Did she just say the Council demands it? Well, that sounds like a threat I'm used to hearing. So, she's not official business, but the Elders sent her like a lapdog to fetch me? Not suspicious at all. Too bad they don't own me anymore.

"How about no?" I snap at her. "Deacon never mentioned this, and I trust him a shitload more than I trust you!" The room temperature rises. Calypso warns in a low growl. I need to calm down before I land myself in some serious shit.

An expression of concern passes through her eyes before she resumes the facade of cool perfection. "Very well, Miss Graves. You need some time to come to your senses. I'll take my leave."

She's afraid of me. Her emotions bleed into the gray walls of my apartment. *Good, she should be.*

"Time is of the essence. We will expect you." An air of superiority leaks into her voice as a shimmer between her fingertips produces a tarot card. The Tower. Also known as 'shits about to hit the fan' card in astrological terms. Great! Just great. "Present this to the attendant at the main security gate. It will grant you entrance." She nods and exits, slithering back to whatever dark hole she crawled out of.

What in the fuck is going on around here? I've spent years putting as much space as possible between myself and Underhill. I lie low. I don't use my magic often. The little that I do use isn't enough to draw attention. I don't like to draw attention to myself. Not on purpose, anyway. I have done everything in my power to fly under their radar. I work, train, and make the best of this half-life they've strapped me with. They'd go to great lengths to keep me tethered to that house of horrors. I know it pisses them off, but this is a little rich, even for the petty Elders.

Glancing at the clock on my nightstand, I release an audible sigh. I don't even have time to process this walking nightmare. I'm going to be late for work.

Although I hate the tainted blood in my veins most days, being a witch has its slight advantages. Like, how I'm about to enchant my stereo because I'm too damn lazy to walk across the room. Who needs Bluetooth when you have a bewitched surround sound? All magic has a cost, of course. I have the scars to prove it, but minor spells are harmless and untraceable.

The haunting melody of Radiohead dances through the air. I sway my hips, chanting the lyrics, calming my tense muscles. Digging through the chaotic pile of clothes next to the bed, I find my cutoff tank and lacy red bra. Don't judge - when you work for tips, a little cleavage never hurts. I get a little extra attention; they get tasteful side boob. See? Mutually beneficial.

Still in jungle cat form, Calypso hops on the bed as it groans under her weight. She licks her paws and swats at her fuzzy pink bunny toy, which hangs from the beat-up headboard. "You look ridiculous."

The Queen of the Jungle likes dainty pink toys.

I chuckle to myself as I head to my rusty, old claw-foot tub.

DEACON HARWELL OWNS THE Gravestone Bar & Grill. A brick-faced, rundown fossil of a building with eccentric charm pouring from every corner. Dark surfaces, worn over time. Cream-colored walls are littered with vintage bar signs, hand-painted seaside art, lighthouses, and storm scenes. Thick beams span the ceiling, giving it a rustic vintage music venue vibe. It's unique; it's cozy; it's home. Over the years, we've grown a reputation as the place for supernaturals who have nowhere else to go.

I guess it all started when Deacon found Lincoln Blackwood on the doorstep not long after relocating to Thornfall - filthy, injured, hungry, and cast out of his clan. Deacon took him in and cleaned him up. He became my family and my first real friend. It was easy when we were young. We wrestled and climbed trees; we had picnics and pretended everything was a grand adventure. As we both grew into our teens, things got weird, as they do. I remember the first time my friend looked at me like I was tempting. My heart fluttered, and my skin warmed.

First crushes, they're so innocent.

Linc isn't a witch, so he wasn't welcome to attend Underhill when we were kids. Instead, he spent his days with Deacon learning how to control his beast, training in our basement, and helping run the bar while Marlow and I were away. I think Deacon secretly loved having a boy around to mentor. Shocker! I'm a handful sometimes.

Speaking of Linc, where is he? I swear I've spent a quarter of my life asking myself that question. I want to set us right before the night begins, but one thing never changes about Lincoln. He wanders. Sometimes he answers his phone, sometimes he doesn't. It's part of his wolf nature. Oh well, I'll have to catch up with him later.

So, Deacon. How do I explain? Deacon was a warrior long ago, the commander of my mother's personal guard. When she died, he gave that up to take on a five-year-old mini-witch with temperamental magic and an uncanny ability to find trouble. Thank the Goddess he had Rowena to help him. If she had left him to his own devices, I would have ended up feral.

He's all business, no bullshit, with a protective streak a mile wide and a mean mug that'll make you piss yourself. He's an asshole for sure, but he's our asshole. Deacon has never been the fatherly type, but in his own way, he loves us. He shows love by making us tough. He trained Linc and me to hone our senses from a young age, to fight with our wits. He pushed us to fight with weapons and fists. "Magic can fail. Skill will never leave you unprotected."

That's his motto, and he repeats it until our ears bleed.

"Genevieve Evanora Graves. I've told you a thousand times, you do not leave this bar until you've stocked the coolers and you mop the floors. Do you have gravel between those ears?" Speaking of my pleasant guardian, "And you broke a bottle?"

I tried to make it to work early, hoping to beat him to the punch and avoid his wrath, but I failed. The bath was too relaxing, and I was still a little mind fucked and having a hell of a time paying attention today.

"I'm sorry, Deacon. I'll fix it before we open, I swear." I made my eyes wide, batting my lashes, adding a little razzle-dazzle.

"I don't know what kind of screw-up you've gotten yourself into this time, and I doubt you're going to tell me. But whatever it is? Unscrew it!" he barks, his voice sounding gravelly and tired. I wonder if he's been getting enough sleep. He's been gone a lot with mysterious meetings he doesn't share details about. When I hint around at what he may do, it's always "none of my concern." But I know him better than that. Something's happening.

"I will. I promise."

"I've got some business over in Rockvale. I need to be on the road if I'm going to make it before sundown. I'll be back in the morning. Is that going to be a problem?" he asks, forehead wrinkling in concern.

"Marlow and I have it under control. Plus, Linc is back." Judging by the way his face changes, that seems to appease him. Lincoln can do no wrong in Deacon's eyes. Not that I blame him for the perception; it's one we share. Linc's kind of perfect, minus the string of broken hearts he leaves scattered around Thornfall, but that's none of my business.

Deacon lumbers toward his office as I trail behind, hoping he might want to divulge some details about this trip, but no such luck. He packs up a few things, pats my shoulder somewhat lovingly, and asks again if I need him. He's uncomfortable leaving, I can tell. But I'm not ready to talk anyway, and he has a sixth sense for fishing the truth out of people.

Besides the laundry list of fuckery from the last twenty-four hours, I was avoiding some serious conversation I don't have the balls for right now. As much as I love Deacon and this bar, this isn't where I want to spend the rest of my life. I'm sure he has plans for me to take over someday, but this city is a constant trigger for me. I want out. Am I going to straight-up ask if he's been lying to me for my entire life about a sister? Nah, I think we'll wait.

I just want to find a peaceful place, somewhere beyond the reach of the Academy. If I go far enough, maybe the nightmares will lose my address too.

Marlow is plotting her escape as well. She wants a little occult shop and bookstore to run. Somewhere green with lots of sunshine and fresh air. It's gloomy here, foggy, and almost always raining. The brine and fish scent lingers on everything, so I don't blame her for wanting to go inland.

Plus, Marlow's family is even more screwed up than my ragtag situation. Her parents are the literal worst. An overbearing scumbag tyrant and a human Stepford mom who does anything she's told, without question. Part of me is jealous, although I know I shouldn't be. But even with her monstrous prick of a father, she still knows her roots. She even has a decent relationship with some of her extended family.

I have very little memory of life before my mother died. But in my dreams, I see her. I know things. I just can't remember them after I wake up. Deacon tells me stories sometimes when he dives too far into the whiskey bottle. His face softens, and he speaks of her beauty; her unconditional love for me (I have my doubts about that). He knows how I feel, but I let him have his bias with minimal pushback. Regardless, the mood always sours when I try to breach the subject that hangs between us.

What really happened?

Here's what I know: High Priestess Evanora had badass power. The type of power that threatened people. She could create or destroy, heal or punish. My mother didn't need a sword, only a thought, and they all fell to her feet. She had raw magic, untethered and limitless. Some say we were descended from an actual goddess. I doubt that, but I can't confirm. I know she was ruthless, and I know whatever she did to me the night she died was irrevocable.

At one point, the Bloodgoods were the most formidable of the bloodlines, which made us walking targets when the war broke out. They hunted down and systematically erased us. We destroy what we don't understand. Right?

Technically, I am heir to the Bloodgood line. I have a handful of distant relatives left, but very few of us remain. And the ones who do? Their blood is diluted to barely a drop. We can trust none of them with the truth about me. As far as society knows, I'm an exceptional Blood Seer, touched by the Pools of Starlight. I am Vivi Graves, a distant relative. Not Evanora's heir. Not a Princess. Not the last royal Bloodgood in existence. Deacon assures me it's for my safety, and I have no reason to doubt him. So, I've lived my life in disguise.

Marlow strolls in at six o'clock on the dot, distracting me from my tumultuous thoughts. Tonight, she's wearing a sleek black mini skirt with a leopard print tank top and a red belt. Bangle bracelets tinkle with every move she makes. After taking inventory of her fantastic fashion choices, I noticed the girl who walked in behind her. This must be our new hostess. What's her name again? Oh yeah, Bronwyn.

At first impression, Bronwyn is tiny and adorable, with shoulder-length lilac-colored hair, delicate facial features, and big round icy gray eyes. She reminds me of an anime character. All she needs is a sword and a villain to cut down. I note her pointed ears and an iridescent sheen on her skin. Barely noticeable unless in the proper lighting. She must be part fae.

Marlow walks over to introduce us, and Bronwyn smiles. I pick up an air of sadness and distrust underneath her bright exterior. It's not surprising. Everyone who finds their way to The Gravestone has a story, and I'm sure she's no different. If she's here? She needs us. What has she done to find her way here? Not my business.

We settle into our routine. In between the antiseptic scent of glass sanitizer and pine-scented water, I enlist Bronwyn's help. Starting with scrubbing the dark counters and pulling down the well-worn bar stools while I cut limes and stock bottles. The bar is quiet, and the work is menial, so my mind wanders. I can't help thinking about all that transpired since I woke up yesterday. Twenty-four hours feels like a lifetime.

Once again, I find myself fixated on stormy turquoise eyes that stare right through me, past my skin, and into my soul. Then in the same breath can deliver a glare like I am his personal nemesis, or maybe his salvation? A memory dances at the edge of my mind. I've seen those eyes before, but when I try to conjure the time and place, any details at all, there's only haze. Nothingness. It's like a déjà vu. Sometimes I have visions I can't recall. That's got to be it, but something doesn't feel right. It doesn't feel authentic.

I don't know why I'm even thinking about this infuriatingly sexy beast that crashed into my life with a wrecking ball. I should focus on the Academy and what the hell they're up to. Instead, uneasiness settles in my stomach; there's something I'm missing. I know it's calculated, like everything with the Elders' stench on it. But after so many years under their thumb, why now? My thoughts file through the possibilities.

A sister. I just don't see how? I don't know
who my father is, but that's not uncommon
in our matriarchal society... err, I mean
former matriarchal society. The High Priestesses
consorted with whomever they pleased; their
female offspring were royal by their mother's
blood, not their father's. So, I guess men were
kind of expendable? That changed after the war.
Everything did. The title of High Priestess means
very little now.

Bronwyn continues to shadow me as I
work, deep in thought. She's pretty observant.
Something about this girl pulls at my
heartstrings.

"New to town?" I inquire as we set up shop.

"I haven't visited in many years." She replies, but
doesn't offer details.

Being closed off is not unusual for a
supernatural who's found their way to Deacon
and The Gravestone. However, I remind myself
to scan her over with my Sight when it gets a little
quieter. I like her vibe, but one can never be too
sure.

When everything seems to run according to
plan and our first few waves of customers
thin out, Marlow pulls me aside. "Girl, you're
distracted tonight. And don't think I didn't notice
the lacy bra popping through your shirt. Nice
titties, by the way! Is this about TDD?"

My eyes bulge. Tall, Dark, and Dangerous has
an official nickname now? Leave it to Marlow,
always appointing alternative names to help her
remember people. We especially enjoy assigning
them to unsuspecting customers. The nicknames
are helpful, but I thought we reserved them for

people who are a regular part of our lives, and as far as I can tell? TDD doesn't qualify.

"Lowe, he is not even on my radar at the moment." *Lie.*

"Then what is it? Did someone see your flames?! That's it, isn't it? Okay, we can run. I've already researched places outside the city where we can hide out. What about Dark Falls? That's far enough away. Rowena can whip up some glamor for us in no time, and I can find a location blocker spell. Linc will protect us. We can pack up before the Rune Force even hears about..." She's panicking now. Sometimes anxiety gets the best of her, and when that happens, she talks faster than a priest caught pants down in a bordello.

"We can't talk about it here." I need a quiet space and a sedative to talk to Marlow about what Bridgewater said today. "I'll fill you in tomorrow. Let's find something on the jukebox and forget about it for now."

I saunter over and pick a few of our favorites. Stevie Nicks, Rob Zombie, and a little Doja Cat to spice things up. Swaying my hips all the way back to my spot behind the bar. Marlow and I dance wild and free, singing along and shaking our asses to the beat. Customers smile and sing along, tossing a few dollars in the tip jars. After a bit of coaxing, Bronwyn even hopped up on the bar and joined in, swinging her lilac hair around and giggling.

Okay, this one has friend potential.

I was about to ask her if she wanted to do another shot with us when Luca, our bouncer, motioned to me. "Hey, Vivi. You've got another one!"

As much as I want to stay hidden, being Thornfall's former 'golden threat' has some unexpected consequences. Most of the population gives me a wide berth. Underhill's Blood Seer turned Monster isn't something they want to tangle with, but every once in a while, a desperate soul finds the balls to search me out for my talents. Of course, they bring in extra cash here and there when I'm in the mood to oblige them, so I guess it's okay. However, most know better than walking in and requesting me like a circus sideshow. That's a sure-fire way to get on my ugly side. You come in, you sit down, and if you're lucky? I'll call you over and ask you to hold out your hand for my dagger. Those are the rules.

I try to hide my irritation at being summoned like an employee. I can't say I'm not tempted to become the thing that goes bump in the night to prove a point. But I could use a distraction, and the cash will help the 'get the hell out-of-town fund.' So, I wander over to the corner of the bar and address the mysterious hooded figure who asked for me by name.

"What can I do for ya?" I wipe my hands on a dry rag and plaster a sweet grin on my resting bitch face.

"Are you her? Princess Genevieve. Daughter to the High Priestess Evanora of the Royal Bloodgood Line?" The hunch-backed gentleman asks in a gravelly voice from underneath his charcoal-hued cloak. I can't see his face through the dim lighting, just a vague outline of a misshapen head and murky eyes.

"Who's asking?" I bristle, suspicion rising with his use of my title.

That's not public knowledge. Deacon took every precaution. The only people who know my true identity are Deacon, Rowena, Marlow, Linc, and the Elders. As far as the Earth Realm knows, there are no more Royals. Just a council of former royal-blooded dickbags who think they're better than everyone else. I wait for some kind of sign he heard me speaking, but he sits in silence from the protection of the hood concealing his face.

"Is there something I can help you with, or are you here to stare at my breasts and take a selfie?" I play the nervousness off with my famous snark. They have trained me for this. Show no reaction to my rightful title. Practice the poker face.

He sticks out a sickly pale arm from under his cloak and grabs ahold of me. My power comes roaring to life as my eyes glow a blinding white. *A night creature?* What the hell? They don't exist on the Earth Realm. Or at least they're not supposed to. A night creature is a blanket term. They're dark beings of all types, belonging to the Netherworld. They are the grotesque nightmares that crawl and slither within its confines. The lowest of the low. Nightmares made flesh.

What is he doing here? The portals are closed. His grip is tight enough on my wrist to cause a painful pinching sensation. Blackened nails dig into my skin, piercing through. What the fuck? Is he trying to bleed me?

"I suggest you remove your hand from my arm before you learn what I'm famous for." I hiss through my teeth in a stern warning.

Yet he draws closer, tightening his hold on my skin. My power surges from the deep well inside me, ready to strike. I could rip the blood from his veins with one thought if I wanted to. I could shred his leathery skin to ribbons and tie them in a grizzly bow. But I prefer hand-to-hand combat. Deacon didn't whip my ass in training for nothing.

Besides, using my magic for anything other than parlor tricks is dangerous.

The signature it leaves might as well be a tracking device outside the wards of Underhill Academy.

Rattling noises vibrate his chest as he moves closer. "Beware, Genevieve. He is coming, and when he arrives, you will cower at his feet." Okay, this thing is bat shit crazy; I don't cower for anyone.

"Run, Little Princess. Run if you can. He will flay the skin from your bones. He will drain the essence from your soul, and your power will be his once more." He yanks me closer to his pock-marked face, where I can smell his putrid breath.

I'm seconds from decking this abomination when the aroma of sweet smoke and night-blooming jasmine fills my nose. Tingling stirs in my stomach, unfurling and pulsing lower. If I wasn't so angry, I'd have a hard time not dropping to my knees.

"I don't believe the lady is interested." a dark timbre caresses my neck through my midnight hair. Close enough to my ear, I feel his warm breath.

How did he sneak up on me like that? Goosebumps raise along my spine. Back away, don't even look at him. Ignore it, Vivi. Don't you dare turn around... curse the stars; this man makes my brain short-circuit, and his intoxicating scent pulls at something wild inside me. As if I have no other choice, I turn toward him.

Mr. Tall, Dark, and Dangerous is standing behind me in all his sinful glory with a chilling glare in his stormy eyes, the kind that promises violence and... something entirely different. I suppress an inner shudder, pulling myself (and my lady bits) back together. I mean, how messed up does someone have to be? I'm being attacked by something from the Netherworld, yet my panties are soaked from his voice? I don't have time for this.

"Are you fucking kidding me?" I aim my finger at TDD. "You have serious stalker tendencies. Has anyone ever told you that?"

"You're my first." He smiles, unbothered. Something about the way he says it feels dirty, forbidden, exciting. Ugh. Does he not see I'm kind of in the middle of something?

"Look, I have no use for a dollar store Prince Charming, right now. I'm a little busy." I hiss between frustrated teeth.

He curls his lip in a smirk, bowing low in a mock gesture, "Then, by all means, proceed."

What the hell is that? I stare defiantly as I whip my dagger from the holster under my skirt with my free hand. Spinning without warning, I slam the night creature's face into the bar, the point of my dagger piercing the skin of his bumpy throat. Swampy liquid pools at the tip of my blade, and it smells like straight-up roadkill.

Gross, even his blood is rotten.

I growl at this sack of excrement struggling under my dagger. "I have had a long day. If you value your wretched life? You will unwrap your disgusting fingers from my wrist and walk out that door. You have five seconds. Now four... three."

He turns his head a fraction, digging my dagger deeper into his skin as he meets my molten stare. "A word of warning, Princess. You've been marked."

The Night Creature glances at TDD with a knowing smile and then disappears in a billow of russet-tinged smoke. My wrist burns, and the beginning of a strange symbol rises against my ruined skin. I'm contemplating which season of Punk'd I'm starring in when I recall the intoxicating sensation rolling up and down my legs.

I spin back on TDD with lightning speed, ready to rip into this dirtbag when I slam into a rock-hard chest. My hands land on impressive abs as I stumble forward. His strong fingers grip my hips, steadying me on my feet. On contact, my head spins with a primal desire. I want to climb this mystery man like a tree, and I do not know where that's coming from.

Shit, this is not what I had planned at all! Does he bathe in aphrodisiacs?

Lifting my face to meet his, my knees buckle. He's peering over my shoulder, searching for threats. The look on his face is murderous. No hint of the panty-dropping vibes he was throwing around moments ago. Now, he looks like an avenging angel. No, not an angel. Something much darker, and it's startlingly hot.

Is he supernatural, like me? Something else? Friend or foe, I can't tell. What I can tell you with certainty is that he's an asshole.

"How dare you use your magic on me? Turn it off." I shove him, and his eyes widen.

"It's not on," he replies, confusion etched in his brutally handsome features.

"Oh, bullshit! Shut off the 'I wanna sex you up' right now. Or I'll punch you in the dick."

That aggravating smirk forms across his lips again. "It's not me who's doing it."

I stand up taller, lifting my shoulders, planting my feet firmly, and look directly into his eyes. Expecting to see intense turquoise under his dark lashes. Instead, I find indigo flames dancing inside inky black depths that remind me of galaxies. Well, that's horrifying! What kind of supernatural creature has serious sexy mojo and fireball eyes?

"Stop looking at me like that."

"Like what?" He looks pleased with himself.

"You know what! You're showing up everywhere. No concept of personal space. I don't know if you're a skinsuit-wearing serial killer or if you're trying to fuck me? But I'm not interested in either. Would... would you back up?" I'm keenly aware of the distance he's closed between us as I'm rambling like a psycho.

By this point, the entire bar is deathly quiet. All eyes are on us. And that's when I notice his three lackeys, brothers, entourage? Whatever they are. With all the commotion, I hadn't realized they were here too. The hulking, dark-haired one is leaning against the end of the bar, tattooed arms holding him up, a pair of golden eyes glinting.

He's grinning as if he heard a hilarious joke.
He must be the cocky friend; every group has
one. The other two are twins. They're eerily still,
like statues with silver hair. Not blonde, silver.
Their black eyes watch me with cold, snakelike
intensity. Talk about some horror movie shit!
These two belong in a museum of oddities.

Another ruinous half-grin lifts the corner of
TDD's lips as he watches me assess his buddies.
Our faces are closer than I'd like them to be, but I
can't help myself when I look him up and down,
running my tongue along my bottom lip.

What is wrong with me?

He makes a show of removing his hands from
my waist, trailing his fingers across my skin
lightly as he backs away, "I'll be seeing you soon,
Kitten."

What the fuck did he just call me? "My name is
not Kitten!" is all I can blurt out before he makes
his way across the building, opens the back door,
and swaggers into the night. Kitten? Real original,
Asshole.

Ugh, why do all the good comebacks show up
after you've already said the dumb thing? I place
my hand on my forehead, speechless. If I don't
walk away right now, something will catch fire,
and that something is me. This cannot happen
under any circumstances. I didn't explain this
before, but we have specific abilities rooted in
Earth's magic as a member of the Bloodgood line.
We're Blood Seers, Mystics, Diviners, Animal
Communicators, etc. Most of us have an affinity
for plants in some capacity, usually poison. The
most ancient of our line could move the earth...

as in mountains and shit. But one thing is firm;
we do not possess the ability to harness fire.

That's considered dark magic, and it's explicitly
forbidden. If the Elders or the Rune Force ever
catch wind of my possessing it I'll be toast.
Thrown into the dungeons under The Academy
as a meal for the things that go bump in the night.
Or worse. I shiver at the thought.

Marlow must've watched the entire scene
unfold because she motions for Luca to shut it all
down as she grabs Bronwyn by the shoulders and
points behind the bar, as in - get your ass back
there and away from any danger.

"Vivi, are you okay?" she approaches me
apprehensively. Linc rushes over to stand behind
her. While working in the kitchen he missed the
action, but they're both looking at me like I've
grown an extra limb.

"I'm fine. I just need a minute. Can you wipe
their memories on the way out, Lowe?" she nods,
already building the baby blue clouds between
her hands. We can't have anyone in this building
remembering what the night creature called me.

Linc leaps into action, helping Luca round up
the customers. Apologizing for the disturbance
and herding them towards Marlow, who's waiting
for them to pass through her spell. As I'm
struggling to pull myself together and head to
the back office, Linc adds, "Calypso is creeping
around the kitchen door, by the way."

Shit! She must've felt my distress and couldn't
get in. That snaps me out of my haze. Calypso is
nothing to mess with when she's in fuck-shit-up
mode. She'll tear someone to shreds to get to
me. I head for the back entrance with a silent

prayer on my lips. As I grab the latch to step into the alley, oddness creeps into my bones. Immediately, I search for Spirit Frank, thinking maybe he's trying to warn me of trouble? But all I see are the janky old streetlights that flicker off and on with no real consistency. My feet move of their own accord, pulling me forward. As I turn around the brick ledge, I'm dumbfounded. There she sits, calm as a cucumber. My merciless familiar is being stroked like an ordinary house cat, and she's purring... PURRING?

Lippy invades my thoughts before I have the chance to lose my temper, *'Smells good,'* she presses through our bond, looking very content with herself, rubbing her whiskers across TDD's leg as he scratches her behind the ear.

"You get away from him, right now." I scold her telepathically.

"Why are you still here?" I roll my neck from side to side, exhaustion leaking into my voice.

"Your pet required reassurance." TDD smiles at me, his expression open and friendly.

This must be his third personality. I can't keep track.

"First, she's not a pet. She's a well-oiled killing machine who's gone temporarily insane. And second, I would appreciate it if you'd take your hands off her."

He doesn't seem to hear me, so I suck it up and use my manners. "Please?"

His eyes soften as he gazes at me behind dark lashes, stepping back from her and throwing me for a loop. All I had to do was say please, and suddenly he's the perfect picture of a gentleman? I call bullshit.

"I believe we've gotten off on the wrong foot, Genevieve." he grins seductively.

Shit, so he heard that part. I wonder what else he heard. When I was dirty dancing on the bar in a mini skirt, was he there? Kill me now.

"Allow me to properly introduce myself. My name is Killian, and I assure you I am not here to wear your skin as a Serial Killer Suit."

I stifle a snort; he totally butchered that reference. Serial Killer Suit. Like a bad Halloween costume? I thought about pointing it out, but it was kind of cute. Is he always this stuffy in an actual conversation? It clashes with the dark clothes, sex mojo, and supervillain hairdo.

Another captivating grin forms on his lips and all thoughts of him being cute flee the continent. He is not cute. He's devastating, and I suspect he should come with caution tape. "I have orders to watch you, Princess. It seems I've arrived on time."

CHAPTER THREE

Tanglewood Manor

Two things. He just said they sent him to watch me, and he called me Princess. This is bad, like unbelievably bad. Did he hear the night creature say it, and now he wants to glean my reaction? School your face, Vivi. Maybe he's testing you. It takes a moment to gather my wits through the fog of exhaustion threatening to take me under.

"I don't know what you're talking about, and who issued those orders?" I glare at him, tapping my foot impatiently.

"That's not something we need to discuss at the moment."

"The hell it isn't!" I'm practically screeching as I sway on my feet. My reserves are depleted, and I'm feeling faint.

His brow creases, "You've had a difficult evening. Perhaps now is an appropriate time to get some rest. I will see you soon, Kitt ..." he pauses mid-sentence. "May I call you Vivi?"

"Well, it's gotta be better than Kitten or Princess, right?" I prod a bit with the wording, judging how much he heard inside earlier. But he shakes his head in agreement, no sign either way.

So, we're playing dumb then? Alright, I can play.

He studies me for a moment before he adds, "I don't want to presume I can use the name reserved for friends." He said the word 'friends' like it was foreign to him, filling me with an odd sadness. Does he not have any friends? I imagine what a lonely existence that must be.

Baby Cerberus on a stick. I should get my head checked. He's not a puppy, for star's sake. Why do I feel sorry for him? He's fucking with my head again; he has to be. Is this good cop, bad cop? Except he's both? I don't trust it.

"Don't go buying us matching pajamas. We're a long way off from friends." I bite out, but it doesn't translate as viciously as I'd hoped.

One look at his face says he took it literally. Bringing his knuckles to his chin as though he imagines us in matching underthings and friends is the furthest thing from his mind.

"I'll be in touch." he nods as he turns on his heel, a playful grin on his sexy mouth.

"Just what I need. My very own stalker." I call out as he walks away.

I STUMBLE INSIDE MY apartment, lock the deadbolt, and slide down the heavy door until my backside smacks the tiles. Holy emotional overload. I'm just going to throw myself a pity party on the floor quick. Five minutes tops, and no tears. I'm too exhausted to cry, anyway.

Wiping sweat from my forehead with the back of my hand, I try to wrap my brain around the twilight zone my life has become. Calypso pads over and arches against me, rubbing her silky head on my shoulder. I lean into it, scratching behind her ears. "I'll always have you, though, won't I?"

Shrinking before my eyes, Calypso morphs back into the size of a house cat and leaps up to the counter, batting old mail and an empty soda can onto the floor. I shake my head in frustration and slight amusement. I must be the only witch alive with a familiar who is this problematic.

Fifteen minutes later, I'm in my favorite band tee and a pair of boy shorts. Ready to climb into my bed-fort and impersonate a blanket burrito. But the grotesque hand around my wrist and the wrongness of it play on repeat inside my mind. All the scalding water in the world couldn't wash away the foulness. Not to mention the inferno growing inside me, smoldering under the surface like a beast looking for a way out.

My skeleton key amulet barely holds the forbidden flames at bay. Why is it failing now? I make a mental note to talk to Rowena. She spelled the amulet when I was a child. I'm sure it's something easy. I need to be more careful, especially with my anger. Strong emotion seems to affect my control.

The dull stinging pain in my wrist is troubling; this strange symbol solidifies on my skin by the hour. At first, I thought it was a circular burn, but now that the redness is fading, a spiral shape is forming. I get up to hunt down a notebook and pen, intending to draw the symbol. But as I walk over to the shelf, I'm disrupted by a soft knock on the door.

Lincoln stands on the dilapidated metal stoop, his muscular arms leaning up against the railing. "Hey, Viv. Thought you could use some company." He holds up a bag of chocolates and winks.

What can I say? Chocolate is the way to my heart. I unblock the space between us and allow him through. As soon as I close the door behind him, he embraces me in an affectionate hug, smiling down at me as we make our way over to my bed.

Before you get the wrong idea, I don't own a couch. First, because I can't afford one. Second, the thought of grabbing a used one weirds me out. Who knows what spells could linger in the cushions? So, my bed is the community hang-out space with my whopping two friends.

Linc and I both hop up and collect the blankets and pillows, arranging them in a comfortable pile like we've done hundreds of times before. Neither one of us speaks for what seems like an eternity, but it's a comfortable silence.

"Marlow is taking care of everything downstairs." Linc breaks the silence, glancing at the notebook in my lap. "I wiped everyone. They won't remember. I had Luca stay and make sure Marlow got home, too. I think her dad is on her case again." he smiles. "She mentioned some kind of monster threatened you and then went poof?"

"Yeah, something like that." I peek up from the blanket I'm picking at. It's a bummer Lowe didn't come to the apartment with Linc, but I understand. I'm sure her father found yet another reason to keep her from me.

"He grabbed me, Linc. I think he branded me and said I was marked." I lift my wrist to show him.

Lincoln inspects the raised skin and the spiral design that's setting in. His brows furrow for a moment before returning to lighthearted and calm. "Hmm, I know what happened. You're secretly a Hobbit! And this is the beginning of your quest to find meaning in a new life or something? You know, I've always wanted to meet Gandalf!" He chuckles as he slides a reassuring hand across my shoulder.

"Yeah, and we're going into the fires of Mordor. I don't want to be Sam, though. That's too much responsibility. Can I be Frodo instead?" I reach over to mess up his deep brown waves, snatching the bag of chocolate from his olive-tinted hands and pulling them into my lap, belly laughing.

"You're way too cute to be Frodo, Viv. You don't even have hairy feet, do you? Let me check." He reaches toward my foot, knowing they're ticklish. I jerk back, and he laughs even harder. "No, I think you're Arwen."

That's him in a nutshell. No matter the mood, Linc is blessed with an uncanny ability to lighten it. It's unusual for his species; male wolf shifters carry a reputation for being possessive asshats, especially the alphas.

Before finding his way to the steps of the Gravestone, Linc had been next in line to take the position of alpha in The Blackwood Clan. The Big Dog- pun intended. He has the power to take his rightful place. The issue is he doesn't want it. We've spoken about his clan more than once over the years; he finds most of their practices unpleasant, if not downright barbaric.

The Blackwood Clan forced his mother to mate with his father by law. Not because she loved him, but because she was his property. Shifters take arranged marriages to a whole new level of disturbing if you ask me.

So, my friend spent his entire childhood watching his Alpha father order his mother around like a servant, all while taking multiple women to his bed. If his mother expressed displeasure, he punished her by allowing other clan members to have her. It must have been traumatizing for Linc, having to stand by while the only person who cared for him was treated like a possession.

Sadness tugs at my heart, thinking of how he must have felt. So powerless, helpless to change it. The mommy issues must be astronomical. No wonder he's so hesitant to find a nice girl and settle down.

When Linc came of age, he pushed back against his father. Unfortunately, the only option after that was to issue a challenge and fight to the death or leave. They fought, and Linc had the upper hand, but he refused to kill his father, so they cast him out. I can't say I'm disappointed. If it hadn't happened, he wouldn't be here with me now. But there's always a pang of guilt that he doesn't have his mother with him. I'd give anything to speak to mine. I have so many questions.

"I know you're trying to cheer me up, and it's working... but something bizarre is happening in Thornfall, Linc. I don't like it." I admit, and he nods.

I tried to ignore Killian, saying he's been ordered to watch me. If that's even true? Which I doubt. Watch me do what, grow wings? There's nothing to watch. And then there's the other matter. This unreasonable attraction that I don't understand. My head says run far and fast, my heart has zero clue what to think, but my vagina? She's insane and has poor listening skills.

I can't trust Killian; he pushes me to a level of rage I can't put into words. I also can't stop thinking about him (*and me, without clothes*). I know this will end in disaster, but here I am, thinking about him again. Like I don't have more important shit to deal with right now. I peer over at Linc's sympathetic face. He's been messing around with the controller, straightening the pictures on the cream-colored wall behind him, petting Calypso, and allowing me to run through my conflicted feelings without interruption. Is he even real? Sometimes I wonder if his mom snuck off and mated with an angel. This world doesn't deserve him. I certainly don't. His forest green eyes watch me, waiting for me to speak.

Knowing that I can't keep it quiet forever, I take a deep breath and open the floodgates. "Bridgewater came here today. She gave me a card and said I needed to come to the Academy and answer some questions about my sister. I don't have a sister, Linc. Do you think they found out about this?" I lift my palm and allow a small flame to dance upon it gracefully. I close my fist as promptly as I'd opened it, snuffing out the growing flame. Tendrils of smoke waft into the air.

His eyes crease, "It would be pointless for her to come herself when she could dispatch the Rune Force to snatch your adorable little ass off the street, though. It makes little sense." his hands move through his wavy shoulder-length hair.

"Yeah, this is a problem. Did you tell Deacon?" My expression tells him I haven't. "You're a magnet for chaos, Viv. Someone should slap a warning label on your forehead."

Someone should, indeed.

Exhaustion seeps into my bones, making my limbs feel heavy. We settle into the blankets and turn on a comfort movie. Linc plays with my hair as I lean against him, listening to the steadiness of his beating heart. It calms us both. With Linc by my side and Lippy curled near my feet, I yawn, eyes heavy.

"Find some sleep, warrior princess. You can conquer the world tomorrow," he whispers to the top of my head as he places a gentle kiss on my messy hair. His woody spiced apple scent surrounds me in a safety net as I drift into a fitful sleep.

The nightmares start off the same. I'm in the hallways of my childhood home at Bloodgood Manor...

Terror courses through my veins as a shadow creeps over the threshold to the throne room. I search for a hiding place, but all the doors are locked. The hallway turns into a dungeon as the walls close in. Screams echo down the corridor. The smell of piss and decay burns my nose. I'm standing in front of a chair, with a frail form settled in the seat. My hands glow. I try to pull back; I don't want to do this. No, no, I don't want to hurt them. If I could use the light to heal this man...

Bitter laughter behind me sends ice up my spine. He won't let me walk away. He won't spare me. I lift my hands to touch the man's face. But he's not the hundreds of nameless anymore... It's Killian, and I scream.

"Viv, wake up. You're burning the sheets!" someone is shaking me. "Viv, VIVI!! You need to wake up!"

My eyes pop open, and my first instinct is to fight. Kicking, flailing, screaming and burning.

Strong arms hold me in place, whispering calm words. "You're okay. It's a dream. It's only a dream." I release a shaky breath as my eyes open. Relief fills me when Linc's green eyes search mine. It always happens like this. Forgotten memories about my childhood morph into the trauma from Underhill and then transform into Goddess knows what else.

"Linc," I choke out of my ravaged throat as I throw myself into his arms.

He holds me close until the shaking stops, like he's done so many times before. Chasing the dark visions away.

———◆———

THE FOLLOWING MORNING, LINC and I head to the training pit in the Gravestone basement. Deacon converted the lowest level into a gym of sorts not long after reaching Thornfall. We covered the center of the floor with practice mats. The outer edge has a makeshift track for running. There are weight benches and hand-me-down exercise equipment spread throughout the space. And in the far corner, my favorite spot, a weapons range, and targets for practice.

Deacon had already been in the concrete-filled training arena for quite some time, judging by the sweat on his brow. "So, you two finally showed up!" he pokes at us with a sarcastic smile, going back to the stationary punching bag. "I've got you beat by an hour, Slackers."

"We better catch up!" I laugh as I punch Linc in the bicep.

Deacon taught us all our lives the secret to hand and foot combat is your bottom half. 'If you don't have balance, you don't have a solid foundation. If you don't have a solid foundation, you're getting knocked on your ass, and then you're at a disadvantage.' His voice echoes through my memories, repeated so many times the words are ingrained. Linc grabs the warm-up pads as I stretch.

"So, you want to talk about it?" Linc grunts as I kick up and out, slamming the side of my foot into the pad on his hand. Staying centered on my other leg, then switched. Kick, Swipe, Switch, Kick.

"Talk about what?"

Jab, Cross, Jab, Cross, Kick, Switch, Kick.

"I think I want to work with knives today," I smirk. Avoiding his question. No, I do not want to talk about being the freak who lights her sheets on fire in her sleep.

"Hilarious, Dork. You know what I mean. What were you dreaming about this time?" His easy smile cuts right through the tension as he swipes his foot beneath me, and I land on my ass, chuckling.

"Oh, you know. Wicked witches and flying monkeys." I reply. Pulling myself up from the ground and rounding on him. Hooking my elbow into his arm and using my weight, I flip him over onto his back. He lands with a thud, knocking the wind out of his lungs.

"Quit screwing around and run some laps." Deacon barks from across the room. It's never a wise idea to land on his shit list while training, so I roll my eyes and head to the track.

"We focus on physical training, weapons training, combat, but I don't have enough magical training to control fire." I voice my concern as we keep pace jogging next to each other.

"We can't do that, Viv. We don't know who might track you through your magic. It isn't safe, you know that." he recycles the same old line.

It's not safe. You can only use Blood magic, no elements outside the Academy wards. Blah, blah, blah. He sounds like a Deacon doppelgänger. Meanwhile, I have magic I can't control, and I want to learn. I love them both, but it gets old having them make my decisions for me.

"What are you two going on about?" Deacon scolds as he strolls to the track to meet us.

"Oh, nothing important." I give Linc a stern glare.

Don't say a word.

"I see you two are conspiring again," Deacon smiles, smacking the back of my head. "Hey, listen. Something came up, and I have to leave for a few days. I trust the two of you and the lovely Marlow can hold down the building without burning it to the ground?"

He's leaving again. Something smells fishy around here and it isn't the harbor. Deacon grabs his towel, gives me a damp hug, and nods at Linc. A silent command I don't understand, but I hate when they do that. It's like I'm not standing right here.

"I don't see you sweating!" his parting words as he pointed back at the track, a not-so-subtle hint to get our butts moving again. We train until our legs are numb and both of us are starving.

After showers and a change of clothes, we head to Enchanted Brew to meet Marlow. Her training comprises something different from ours: magic lessons with her father. I wince at the thought. Faustus Culpepper makes Deacon look like a pixie in comparison.

Waiting for Marlow to arrive this morning is a tad anxiety-inducing. I've spilled the beans to Linc about what's been happening, and now it's time to fill Lowe in on Bridgewater and the sister debacle. Something tells me she will not be as calm and understanding as Linc when I break the news to her. As usual, my intuition is spot on.

"I cannot believe you kept this from me!" Marlow shrieks, trying to keep the volume low but failing. "What were you thinking? The Academy is not a joke. The Elders will come for you. My father will come for you."

"Can you yell at me more quietly?" I hiss. "I think all of Thornfall can hear you."

I would have spilled my guts to her last night if we had the chance before everything went into *Tales of the Dark Side*. I haven't admitted everything, though, not to either of them. But telling them about Killian in the alley or my mind-boggling reactions to his nearness seems like a bad idea.

Linc would find something wrong with him and then tell me all the ways he's not worthy of me; that I should stay away. Like he does with every guy who's ever been near me. None of them are good enough. He's usually right.

Marlow will do the exact opposite. She'll have me shopping for slinky lingerie and sex toys, pulling out Kama Sutra books, and telling me to invite him over before I could even put up a fight.

I don't know which of those things sounds more appealing, and that's fucked up.

No, whatever trouble I'm in with Killian, I want to keep that to myself for now. I'll stick with the sister news, and whatever attacked me at Gravestone and left this nasty mess on my wrist. That's plenty.

Hearing I have a sister, fictional or not, is the ultimate mind fuck. If she's real, then I've been deceived by the people I trust most in this world, and that's not something I'm sure I can handle.

Asking Deacon about it feels like a last resort. He served my mother; he was a dedicated guard. I know he cared for her, but we don't talk about the past. It's too painful for us both. The thing is, I know my mother would have confided in him. If there's a possibility that I have a sibling, he would know.

Both Deacon and Rowena had instructed me as soon as we arrived in Thornfall not to use my title or the name Genevieve in any conversation others could overhear, that my life depended on it. So, when I started school at Underhill, my name was Vivi Graves, and that was final.

I was a kid and had known Deacon and Rowena my whole life, so I never questioned it. They said it was dangerous, and I believed them. I'd always felt it best not to ask questions, but now I have quite a few.

The night creature knew my name last night, said it out loud in a bar full of Thornfall citizens. In front of Killian.

Night creatures don't have a hierarchy. They're minions. They have masters, which means whoever sent him knows my name, and judging by the message delivered, I don't think his master wants to sit down for tea and make friends.

I need to talk to Rowena. She's always been easier to crack than Deacon.

Marlow shakes my arm. She's been brainstorming, and I'm not paying attention. "We will make a trip to Tanglewood and see Willa. There are some older scrolls in the library. I can't believe I'm saying this, but fuck if I know what the mark on your wrists means."

She runs her finger over the shape that had taken root on the underside of my left wrist. The brand is still reddish and raised up off my alabaster skin, but at least I'm in less pain now.

"Ugh, can't we go to the public library? I'd even be willing to break into the Academy archives. Anything but Willa!" I whine with all the enthusiasm of a toddler at naptime.

Linc clears his throat. "I've, uh... there are some things today. That I need to do, I mean. Mind if I duck out and you ladies can fill me in later?"

He's making an excuse, the coward.

"I don't know who you're calling ladies? I don't see any at this table." I joke, trying to lighten the mood. We don't need the inquisition rolling up to Willa's lair, anyway. It would be hard enough with Lowe and me. *Okay, mostly me.*

I toss an apologetic glance in Marlow's direction. It's just that her aunt is top shelf creepy,

mean as a firedrake, too. And Tanglewood?
It's sort of alive. As in, the house itself is a
living entity. Which is fascinating but equally
disturbing. I try to avoid visits when possible.

Our saving grace is that Lowe and her aunt have
a close relationship. Me? Willa hates me. She's
always mumbling about how I'm an evil seed,
corrupt with chaos magic. So, I'm going to start
the apocalypse. Harbinger of death. The usual.

Marlow's father is a warlock, an Elder. As in,
the Elder. Her mother is human. Which makes
Marlow a halfling like I mentioned before, but she
isn't recognized in the Academy's eyes (because
her father is powerful enough to disregard it).
Faustus Culpepper is a monstrous prick who
barely notices his daughter is alive. Unless she's
spending too much time with me.

Willa is his sister, a priestess of the Moonfall
bloodline. They're Dream Riders. Masters of
Illusion. Mind Magic. They also hold our records,
the keepers of many secrets. The Moonfall line
wins the award for the most mysterious bloodline
because they traffic in information and secrets.

"Excuse me for a second. I'll be right
back," I assure Marlow and Linc. Speaking of
information. It's time to talk to Rowena, and this
conversation doesn't need an audience.

Heading towards the kitchen, I wonder if she
could reinforce the amulet? It's never failed me,
not like this. But ever since Killian showed up in
Thornfall, it's malfunctioning left and right. Part
of me wonders if he's somehow influencing it, but
that's a whole detective novel for later. I'm up to
my ass in mysteries right now, as it is.

I find Rowena rummaging through her stock room, pulling random jars of herbs and petals down from the shelves. "Sweet Girl, you look as if you've spotted a ghost." My eyes welled up. One sympathetic word from Rowena, and I'm just a scared little girl without a mother, in a heap of trouble I can't fix. I wipe my eyes.

"Oh, Vivi. Dry your tears. Come, let's go to the office where curious ears cannot follow. You can tell me all about it over some tea."

I nod in agreement. Not trusting myself to speak, I follow down the hallway into her disturbingly pink office. Everything in this room is reminiscent of Pepto Bismol and candy canes. When I was a child, I would play in this office, pretending I was Strawberry Shortcake with my play garden. I take a seat on Rowena's rose-colored couch and grab a neon pink throw pillow, fidgeting with the edges.

She takes a seat in the high-backed chair across from me. "Well, spit it out."

Rowena watches me, waiting for the dam to break. But I can't. If I do, she'll go to Deacon. So, I take a deep breath and calm myself.

"My amulet isn't working." I start with that. "Yesterday, I lost control here in the shop, and then again at Gravestone, when a customer made me angry."

"Let's have a look," she says with too much hesitation in her voice. The uncertainty gives her away, and my heart sinks.

"Rowena? What aren't you telling me?"

She looks away for a fraction of a second before stuttering, "W-w-we couldn't be sure, but there was always a possibility the amulet would fail.

Your fire-wielding gains strength in the presence of... well, another like you. Or something far worse."

"Wait, another like me? What does that mean? Far worse. What are you saying? Are you saying I'm evil?" I stare at her.

"Good and evil. Now that's a divisive topic, isn't it, my dear? Good is something we can choose. Evil is the same." Her answer isn't an answer at all. It's a riddle.

"If I could nullify it all, bind it somehow and render myself human, I would." sadness etches across the lines of my forehead. "I'm so tired of being someone's weapon."

"I suspect that's about to change, dear girl," her eyes filled with regret. "I cannot restore your amulet's protection without cracking it."

"Wait, so you're telling me you can't fix it? Like, that's it?"

"I'm afraid not. When the fates come calling, you know as well as I do - the call must be answered." She hugs me. "Everyone's ticket comes due, my dear girl. There are some things even a wise old faerie like me can't interfere with."

When the fates come calling...

***

Tanglewood Mansion is a sight to behold. A few miles out of Thornfall, close to the ocean, the sprawling gothic beauty is breathtaking, if not a little disturbing. Two enormous Live Oak trees loom over the front of the property, dwarfing the wrought-iron gate that hangs off the hinges. The Mansion reaches several stories into the sky, ending with a tower that pierces the clouds, a sight so imposing that it dances between menacing and magnificent.

At the front, there's a terrace that wraps around, with ornate wooden arches throughout. The side-garden smells of moonflowers and sage. Purple vines curl and climb the trellises, reaching out with their thin stalks like gnarled fingers. We're talking real deal "a witch lives here" type of shit.

Standing at the gates with Marlow, I'm incredibly nervous. I want answers, but the foreboding feeling in the pit of my stomach grows, stretching inside me like a sponge. Call it a premonition, but I suspect I won't be coming out of Tanglewood the same person.

The unsettling thoughts creep back into my mind. My amulet is going to fail. And when it does, what will happen to me? Will I go all dark, as in no stars? I mean, yes, I've always gravitated towards chaos; that's a given. On the other hand, I respect the darkness, maybe even a sense of belonging. Nobody can fault me for that. I am what they created me to be.

It doesn't make me evil, though. Does it? Rowena's words burrow deep. Do I have a choice? Am I destined to be wicked? And the scariest thought of them all is whether the amulet is the only thing standing between me and the monster living under my skin.

Stop it, Vivi, you're not a monster.

"Are you ready to go in?" Lowe takes a deep breath and straightens her shoulders.

"Hell yeah! Let's find out how many foul labels Aunt Willa can create for me today!" I smile, eyes full of mischief. When things get tense, I get sarcastic. The best defense is a good offense, right?

We march up the main stairs to the stained-glass double doors. They open the moment Lowe lifts her hand to knock. They always do, but it gets no less intimidating. As we step through the threshold, Willa materializes in a dusty armchair. Iris, her partner, strolls through the flowery doorway from the kitchen area with a delighted grin on her aging face. "The house told me we would receive company today! I made raspberry lemonade. Come. Sit!"

She's more pleasant than her other half.

"Look at what the demons dragged in." Willa points at me. "Come to siphon my blood, have you?"

Goddess, no, I wouldn't want her blood if someone paid me. It's probably made of battery acid.

"My dear niece, still running around with the likes of this one, I see." her milky eyes settle on Marlow now.

Willa is blind, but only in the most literal sense. Her eyes may not work, but she sees everything.

Suddenly, we are sitting in two mustard-tinted chairs that appear next to us in the lounge that we didn't walk into. An unnerving silence envelops the room. Willa's disdain is making the wallpaper change colors. We watch in fascination as shadow vines wrap around the roses on the walls; their blooms die, petals shrinking to dust before our eyes. Iris glances at the walls and 'tsks' out loud, an unhappy sound aimed at her wife. Her face curls in disappointment, and Willa somehow senses she's made Iris upset. A tension-filled moment passes as they have a wordless conversation. Iris claps her hands in excitement, gliding herself into the kitchen to bring us refreshments.

"Keep your Sight to yourself, abomination. You understand?" Willa speaks like the words taste foul inside her mouth.

Why does this crazy old witch hate me so much?

"Of course, Priestess Willa. I wouldn't dream of offending." I reply, this isn't the time or place for my uncontrollable mouth and witty comebacks.

Willa gets up from her chair and places her fragile looking hand on Marlow's shoulder. She is anything but fragile; the electrical surge of magic coming off this woman could fuel a power plant. A tight line forms on her lips as she starts towards the second-floor stairway. Willa knows that if Marlow is here access to the library is what she's after. We climb the dusty wooden stairs, creaking behind us all the way up.

The Culpepper library is a remarkable sight. Stained glass windows loom from floor to ceiling throughout the entire space. Intricate scenes of realms I can only imagine in my dreams stretch across the cut-glass.

There were vivid greens and fresh yellows of the Fae Cities, rich indigos and mauves of the Moon people, and crimson streaks representing the Netherworld's shadows. They call to me like far-away daydreams. Too bad the priestesses sealed the portals during the war; I would have liked to travel these distant worlds. Rows and rows of mahogany shelves fill the space in a way that causes some concern about the laws of construction inside this house, gravity too.

Standing on the creaky floor, I can see up as far as the sky and find curving ledges and balconies winding for what seems like miles. The room is so vast it carries a museum effect. Magic pulses through every nook and cranny.

Marlow goes straight to work, climbing the sliding ladders attached to the shelves. Pulling manuscripts and carrying them all down, arranging them into strategic piles on one of the many elaborate tables spread around the space. She pauses for a moment at a wall filled with yellow parchments, locked away behind crystal cabinets.

They appear delicate, and I wonder if we unroll them, will they turn to dust?

Iris appears next to me with her inviting smile, and I jerk in surprise. I didn't hear her use the stairs or creaky footsteps on the wooden floor. It blows my mind every time. How does she do that?

"I'll leave these here for you girls." She sets down a decanter and two goblets filled with light burgundy liquid. "Holler, if you would like some sandwiches!" She ventures down the stairs as quickly as she appears. I wonder what type of witch she is. Nobody ever talks about it, but I suspect the ability to walk through walls and disappear at will is a rare talent. Willa still stands at the entrance, watching us. Her milky eyes are vacant and cold.

Goddess, she gives me the creeps.

"Before you leave us, Auntie. I'm looking for the Bloodgood family scrolls. Where are they?" I love the subtle hint she snuck in there... before you leave. Yes, please! As swiftly as possible.

"Mistress Bridgewater's assistant, Markham, collected them a few days ago," she gives us one last creepy glance and turns to go down the stairs.

When we were confident Willa was gone, Marlow drew her eyebrows together. "Something tells me that isn't positive news."

We spend hours grabbing this book and that, piling them up on two tables. Lowe inspected every page she came across while I flipped through some old texts on ancient faery spells, looking for the symbol.

"I think I found something!" Marlow jumped up. "This resembles what you have on your wrist. It says here The Spiral is a symbol of the Triple Goddess. It represents internal feminine power rising."

Okay, that doesn't sound so bad.

Marlow moves over to another book laid out on the table. "This passage goes further into the history; the spiral symbolizes the cycle of life, death, and rebirth. Maiden, Mother, Crone." she points to the text.

"Like the First Goddess?"

"I think so. But what I don't understand is how that translates to being marked by something of the Netherworld?" Marlow lifts a finger to the corner of her mouth, working through a puzzle in her mind. "Tell me what he said to you again, Vivi. Exact words."

"He said. Run, Little Princess. Run if you can. He will flay the skin from your bones. He will drain the essence from your soul, and your powers will be his once more." I tattooed those words into a part of my brain I would never forget.

Marlow climbs the ladder with determination and fills her arms with more tomes from the shelves. Piling them on the tables, separating them into categories. Finally, one book caught my eye. It's beautiful, matte black with metallic gold inlay. The spine is decorated in yew branches, with embossed berries in blood red. I'm drawn to it, and before I can think, I've opened the pages. Looking down, a perfect spiral stares me back in the face. It was the mark, the one I now had branded into my skin.

The first page reveals a beautiful woman holding torches in her mighty hands; naked breasted beasts with large black wings surround her. Marlow and I both read the words aloud "The Dark Goddess is capable of great righteousness and evil alike. Along with nurturing mother/child relationships and being a symbol of immense feminine power, we associate her with death, vengeance, creatures of the night, and necromancy."

Wait. What? Creatures of the night and necromancy? Like, playing with bodies and bringing zombies back to life? Ew.

I grabbed the hardcover, not able to believe what I had just read. I studied the picture staring back at me. Her dark eyes burrowed into mine as I heard sultry whispers, beckoning me closer. The spicy aroma of cinnamon warms my nose as the brand pulses once, twice. Sweat drips down my forehead, and I strain to understand the voices. As the room tilts, my arm heats, churning, swirling, and then glows the deepest red. My body made of molten flame. Stars flicker in the corner of my eyesight, and everything fades to nothingness.

CHAPTER FOUR

CULPEPPER LIBRARY

ALICE FELL DOWN THE rabbit hole once. I always imagined it resembled something like this. A starry night, a majestic white horse, twisted faces, and shadow birds. I drift through the midnight sky as gray clouds morph into red and blue flames. Suddenly, the white horse is no longer a horse but a beast. Hairy and ferocious, with gnarled horns and teeth like daggers. The beast bellows his rage, opening jaws wide as a man appears, flowing from its massive jowls.

His features are blurred, unrecognizable now, but I feel him. Compelled to go to him, I stretch my hands to caress his monstrous face. Drawn by the sadness in this beast's eyes. I want him. Before I can reach my hands to his skin, the darkness comes for me.

In the complete absence of light, my fingers drift across something soft, wispy, like a delicate spider web. A veil. The thin material brushes my skin and clings to the curve of my jaw. I should be afraid, but the emotions never surface. So instead, I roll into the lace and let it cocoon me.

"Genevieve. Hear me, child." An otherworldly voice pierces my cocoon.

"What is this place?" I question the darkness.

Am I dying? Morbid curiosity sets in. What did my mother feel? Where did she go... after? All the souls I'd damned. The screams of terror. The damage, the carnage that stains my hands. Dark thoughts fill my mind. Is this my penance? Doomed to the darkness forever? It's more than I deserve.

"You must focus."

"So, the darkness speaks again..." I reply with a snort. I've lost my marbles now. Deacon would be so proud, talking to nothing in the middle of nowhere. Or wherever this is. Maybe it's the void.

"You're in danger, Daughter of Oracles. Soon, you will wake. You must trust him; use your senses, child. Open your elements. Use the Sight."

But my magic hurts them. And trust who? The soothing female voice sounds like a figment of my imagination on an acid trip, but I want to dance and sway at the sound of it.

Perhaps this really is the rabbit hole.

"You will find him. You will defeat him. You must trust ..." the voice grows weaker, like an echo over miles of water.

"VIVI!" A DESPERATE SCREAM rips through the darkness. "DAMMIT, WAKE THE FUCK UP!"

My eyes flutter, and I blink the darkness away. Something painful presses against the small of my back; I groan and attempt to move away from it, failing when pain lances through my skull. I'm hurt, and I don't know where I am.

Think. What would Deacon say? Observe my surroundings. Assess the situation. What can I smell? What do I hear? I'm in full recon mode when a pair of powerful arms hold me in place.

"Hey, Warrior Princess, we should stop meeting like this." Linc. I'm safe, but he's upset.

I feel the tension in his fingers clutching me too forcefully. He's fighting the shift. The roughness of his voice makes me shiver. Tingles of fear and lust settle in the lady bits, and my body warms ... *No, wait. What am I talking about? This is Linc.* I clear my throat and try to lift my head; confusion muddles my senses.

My temples are throbbing, but I try to formulate words, "Um, hi?"

"Hi? That's all you're going to say right now. Un-fucking-believable!" Deacon growls, steam bursting from his ears. Deacon is here. Why is he here? What's the last thing I remember? The library. I was in Willa's library looking for answers about the brand. Marlow opened a book; I couldn't stop staring at The Dark Goddess - and then I heard the voice.

"You passed out." Marlow comes into view, "Your wrist was glowing, and your eyes did the Lite Brite thing. I shook you, but you wouldn't wake up. Iris helped; she pulled out her healing herbs and candles, but Willa ordered me to get you out of the house. Threw us right out on the porch, the crazy bat! I called Linc."

Linc stood to the side of Lowe, his face twisting in a reaction I don't understand. He reeks of guilt; it rims his eyes with redness.

"What's wrong?" I try to lift myself. "Linc?" I raise my voice and regret it. Pain rips through my head again, so intense I might vomit. Talk about a migraine on miracle grow. Ouch.

I lay my head back down on the icy surface, smelling the pine-clean scent. The bar, I'm lying on top of the bar. I'm at The Gravestone.

"I'm so sorry, Viv, I didn't know what to do! You're going to hate me. Don't be mad. Please! I did this for you." Linc is manic and beside himself. He paces back and forth like a beast in a cage; he's throwing off waves of guilt and stinks of violence. Finally, he punches the wall beside him and rushes away. A door slams. Hard.

"What's wrong with him? Is he shifting? Will someone go tell him I'm fine, a little bump on the head? Nothing to freak out about."

"Don't worry about that now," Rowena interjects.

"Water?" I ask, throat dry as the desert. My limbs are made of marshmallows and ache. Marlow hovers beside me, lifting a glass to my lips.

The room is silent. Deacon sits on a stool across from me, a murderous glare on his face. Beyond anger, he's crossed over into panic and rage. And then I understand.

Why is he here and not out of town? Because there were no plans this morning. Linc wasn't making excuses to avoid Willa's. He went to Deacon behind my back! The look they were giving each other in the training arena comes to mind. Has he been babysitting me? Following me around for Deacon and reporting back?

Holy fuck. Linc betrayed me, and I'm going to kill him!

"I can't talk about this right now," I announced to the room. Well, mainly to Deacon. My brain

is spinning, everything hurts, I feel like someone
sucked all the juice out of me, and I can't do it. I
can't face the hurricane of wrath right now.

Deacon inspects me with his perceptive eyes,
looking for chinks in my armor, assessing
weakness. He gets up from his stool and comes to
me, running his finger down my cheek. He nods
and then heads toward the back hallway into his
office.

After finding my bearings and walking on my
own, I flee with Marlow to my apartment. I'll face
Deacon, but it won't be now. So instead, I fake
sleep while Lowe watches over me. Calypso curls
near my chest in house cat form, using her purrs
to heal my body. Linc camps outside, begging
to talk. I can hear him through the door. But
I can't do it. I can't even look at his face. The
bastard. How could he?

And then he says, "I did it for you."

That's bullshit. What a cop-out! Cowardly and
an absolute shithead thing to say. He didn't do it
for me. He did it for himself. He did it because of
some inherent loyalty to our guardian. He did it
because he thinks I'm weak, that I can't take care
of my own problems, and I need a big bad warrior
like Deacon to come and save me from myself.

I can't decide what hurts worse: the betrayal or
the fact he can't trust me enough to give me time
to figure it out on my own. He knew I was trying to
gather information; he knew I was handling it and
knew I hadn't spoken to Deacon about it. That
should've been enough; he should've respected
my wishes. I should've suspected because they
both do this. They make my decisions for me and
then tell me it's for my own good.

Aggressive knocks on the door assault my ears. "If you open that door, Marlow, I will never speak to you again,"

Of course, that's a lie, but I'm livid and having a hard time containing my wrath. Her face twists in disappointment, and I back off. This isn't her fault. Here she is, taking care of me, and I'm treating her like shit in Lincoln's place.

Goddess, I am a terrible friend, and I don't even know how to apologize for it right now. So, my stupid ass stares at her, then at the blank space, and finally I roll back over into my blankets, pulling Calypso closer.

"Vivi, we need to go downstairs and talk to Deacon. He won't let you sit up here in hiding forever. It's been hours. I'm surprised he hasn't busted down your door already," Marlow warns.

"I know. But can we wait a little longer? I'm tired." I roll back toward her, defeat written in my eyes. She gives me a sympathetic nod. She'll buy me a little more time, but judging by the firmness on her face, it's about to come at a price.

"What happened? One minute we were looking through a book, the next, you were on the floor burning up. I thought you were dying! You left something out of the story this morning. I know you did. I should've called you out. No more secrets. Tell me everything." She taps her fingers on my blanket. My thoughts tailspin. How can I explain something I don't understand myself?

"Ever since Killian showed up in Thornfall ..."

"Killian?" she frowns and puckers her lips.

"Yeah, that's one thing I should tell you. TDD is Killian." Marlow's eyes widened. "And the reason I know what his name is that he was in the alley last night after I left Gravestone. Calypso was all cuddle-buddy with him. It was disgusting, but also wasn't. Every time he comes near me, my underpants melt to the floor, but not on purpose, and it's confusing. So anyway, he told me they sent him to watch me." I'm babbling now.

"Who's they?" Marlow interrupts, protectiveness filling her dark eyes.

"That's a brilliant question! I asked, and he evaded giving me an answer, and then he left."

The disappointment on her face is too much to bear. So, I break down and tell her everything after that. I tell her about the amulet, the flames growing in strength, about Rowena hiding something, and Deacon too. I tell her what I saw when I was unconscious: the darkness. About the dreams, my sheets on fire, the voice that calls out to me and the woman. And I eventually tell her the thing I hadn't been able to admit to anyone... I'm afraid I killed my mother. And I'm afraid that Deacon covered it up.

He would do that for me, and he would keep it a secret to save me from the guilt. It makes sense - why we traveled so far from our home at Bloodgood Manor, why my identity had to be hidden, and why the Academy used me as an instrument of death and destruction. He wouldn't have a choice; I understand that. The Elders are the absolute power in Thornfall and even beyond. But my soul is tainted, and when my amulet fails, I shudder to think what I'll become.

"Knock it off. You are not a monster, Genevieve. You have no proof you did anything to your mother. My father is an extremist. So are the rest of the Elders. The worst kind, too. The kind with power and influence. They're so focused on whose blood is more valuable, whose life is more valuable that they forget they bleed like the rest of us." determination sets in Marlow's jaw. Hatred burns in her eyes before she calms herself. "There's one more thing before you go down there to face the music."

"Okay?" I give her a skeptical eye roll.

"You need to talk to Linc. You can't leave it like this. You're angry, and I don't blame you for that. He shouldn't have lied to you, to us. He shouldn't have called Deacon home. And I know that he's with a different woman every week, and he runs off telling no one where he's going, but you can't tell me you don't see the way he looks at you. The way he's always looked at you. You are one delusional bitch if you can't see he's in love with you!" Her voice shakes. "Hop on and ride, Vivi. Or set him free." She says.

This is the moment I hoped I would never have to face. Linc is terrific, minus the whole backstabbing asshole thing he's sporting today. But I've known him practically my entire life, and he has always been the one you can rely on. My constant. Linc is the type of man you put on a white dress for and pop-out a bunch of green-eyed babies with. He's someone's happily ever after.

Me? I'm a walking disaster, a murderer, a suitcase overflowing with issues. So, what can I offer someone like him other than heartbreak? Of course, I've thought about it. Who wouldn't? He's perfect, but every time he's brushed my hand during training or looked at me a little too long, our friendship fills my mind. I can't lose that.

"Can't I just punch him in the face and call it even?" I shrug my shoulders at Marlow like it's a viable option.

There's an awkward silence before she cracks the slightest grin. "Fine. You can break his nose a little, but then? Talk to him." she pauses, "You push people away whenever someone gets too close to your heart, you find reasons to cut them out. You lost your mother; you've been mistreated and used at every turn. You're always waiting for the other shoe to drop because it usually does. You feel alone and abandoned; I get that. But you're not. You have a family right here if you'd open your eyes."

Another knock at the door makes us both jump.

"Speaking of facing the music," she turns past my dresser, touching the picture she drew for me when we were fifteen years old. A fantastic rendition of her and me, laughing in the sun. Our cheeks touched. It's us in the future, free from the chains. Living somewhere bright and peaceful. She continues past it, down the hall to answer the door. And I want to crawl into my blankets and find the entrance to another dimension.

Linc stands in the doorway. No trace of the light-hearted comedian we all love so much. He has on a pair of ripped jeans, a white button-down, and his black Chucks. The intensity in his eyes makes me nervous. Marlow chooses this moment to duck out past him, waving as she rushes down my stairs. The traitor! He closes the door, and his eyes meet mine. The emotion threatening to spill over through them is overwhelming.

"How are you feeling?" he whispers.

"Well, my eyebrows don't hurt, so that's a positive."

"Viv, I... I don't know what to say." he stumbles on his words, looking down at the floor. "I know what I did was wrong, and I should've talked to you first. You're so good at getting yourself in trouble, and this time it seems like more than you can handle. I panicked. I'm a dumbass. That sounded like an excuse, but there is no excuse. I'm sorry. On a scale of one to ten, how bad do you want to kill me right now?"

"A solid eleven," I glare.

The uncomfortable silence stretches on for minutes. Eventually, I give in and pat the spot next to me. Inviting him to come to sit. Yeah, I'm still crazy pissed; how can I ever trust him after this? But the waves of grief coming off him knock me on my ass.

"Can you just fuck off already?"

"How did that feel?" he asks, a lopsided grin forming on his lips.

"Honestly? That was pretty helpful." I try not to smile; I wasn't expecting a charming response, which lowers my defenses. I know we should talk, but I can't find the balls to say any of the things out loud that hang between us.

He's looking at me like I'm a bowl of ice cream he wants to lick clean. But, dang, why haven't I ever noticed the sexy alpha wolf vibes before? My body must be on the fritz, full of unresolved tension. This is my friend I'm talking about right now.

His eyes dilate as he breathes in a lungful of air. Weird wolf stuff, I guess? Omg, I hope he didn't smell my, you know... curiosity.

He moves towards me. Oh shit. Is this happening? Linc leans in carefully, like a hunter trying not to spook his prey, which freaks me out, but I can smell the familiar apple woody scent wafting from his skin, and that calms me. He brushes the hair from my face and tucks it behind my ear.

I know what he's about to do, and I know I should tell him to stop. But a part of me always longed for something simple, straightforward. This could work, right? I won't know if I don't try. We've never crossed this line before. We shouldn't cross it now, but I don't move away as his legs brush up against mine, and he lays his hand on my face, dragging it to his gaze.

Holy hellfire, there's no mistaking what's swirling around those forest-green eyes. Maybe the whole 'Vivi got hurt' thing is messing with his head?

"Don't punch me for this," he whispers, eyelids hooded.

His lips are smoother than I imagined, soft like a cloud, like cotton candy. A toe-curling rumble vibrates his chest as he deepens the kiss. Slowly. Calloused fingers trail the curve of my hip and wander higher, grazing the bottom of my breast, and my breath hitches. Heat unfurls in my stomach, and an aroused moan escapes my lips. Linc's eyes darken as he pulls me onto his lap. Gripping my thighs, pushing me down into his hardness. His kiss becomes more frantic as he raises up, grinding himself into me. I wrap my legs around his waist, pressing my breasts against his chest. His mouth moves to my neck and I unravel. It's been so long since anyone touched me like this. I crave it. His hands curl into my hair, and he pulls my head back, exposing my neck. Making me vulnerable to him, his wolf peers from the dark forests in his eyes, challenging me.

I close my eyes, soaking in every touch, every place his soft lips graze my skin. Then, I let my mind go free, riding the waves of pleasure as stormy turquoise and dark lashes flash behind my eyelids. Something deep within me awakens at the thoughts of a particular dark-haired, tattooed, sexy asshole. My mind wanders to Killian as I moan and buck against my friend...

Wait. No! Goddess below, what am I doing?

I pull away, searching his eyes for a signal that he understands how off-base this is, but he doesn't. He's all in. Ready to go as far as I will take him. I panic, jumping up off his lap and scrambling to the other side of the bed, my heart beating out of my chest.

"Linc, I ... I can't do this." Tears threaten to spill down my cheeks.

"Do you love me, Genevieve?" He stares into my soul.

What have I done? Stupid. Stupid girl!

"You know I do." I cast my eyes to the floor.

"But?"

"But I can't give you what you need. I can't be what you want me to be." It comes out in a strangled whisper.

He flinches like I've slapped him. "So now you get to decide what I need? That's just perfect. I've watched you be unappreciated for years, Viv, YEARS! Used, abused, lied to, robbed, cheated on. I have watched men who didn't understand the first thing about you being allowed to have pieces of your heart, and what did they do with it? They threw it away. Tossed you aside like trash, not knowing they had pure gold. You are enough for me! Exactly the way you are. Why can't you see that?" he shouts.

I'm not. He's blinded by our history, by our bond. I'm damaged. I'm in darkness. There is something wrong inside me, something unnatural. This is wrong. I shake my head as a tear breaks away from the corner of my eye. This was a mistake.

Fuck Killian and the stupid things he does to my body. Fuck him and his sexy lips that keep me up at night and make me dream stuff I don't want to dream. I didn't want to be touched before he showed up and cursed me, spelled me, or whatever the fuck he did to make me so stupid. And now... now? Look where I am. Look what I've done.

"I'll wait for you. I'll wait as long as you need me to." Linc plunges another dagger into my gut. I am a terrible person. How could I be thinking of someone else at a time like this? What is wrong with me?

"Don't," I whisper and look away. Staring at my sheer curtains, past them into the mountain peaks in the background, the wall of the building that blocks my view to the south, at anything but Linc. Agonizing silence fills the room as I wait for the blow-up. The anger. The hateful words I deserve, but they never come.

"We better get downstairs. Deacon is waiting," Linc says in a soft, steady voice.

He stands up, fixing his shirt, and shoots me one of his famous quirky smiles as he rubs his fingers across my cheek. And then he leaves, giving me some space.

I climb into my tub, letting the water wash over me. My thoughts consume me, and I allow the tears to flow in the privacy of my tiny moon décor bathroom. Why do I ruin everything? Marlow was right. I push everyone away; but they don't understand. Everything I love turns to shit. Everyone who loves me pays for it with their lives. Deacon gave up his life as a warrior. Rowena isn't with her family. Marlow's parents barely speak to her because of me. I fucked up with Linc. And let's not forget where it all started, my mother. Did she hurt me or did I hurt her? I don't know. But I am a walking-talking curse in heels.

The water soothes me as I shake with too much emotion. Steam rolls off my naked skin, filling the bathroom. The aroma of earthy smoke tingles through my nostrils. Damn this fire! I don't want it. I wish I had thirty amulets that could push it away forever; all it stands for is destruction. I climb out of the tub and wrap myself in a towel. Lowering to my knees, I lay on the floor of my bathroom and sob, letting it all out.

It feels like hours I wrestle with my ugly truths and pretty lies. Calypso stands guard in the doorway until I'm ready to get back up.

DRESSED IN BLACK LEATHER pants, a black bralette, and a white tank - my Moonstone dagger attached to the holster on my wrist in plain sight. I lace up my heeled boots and steel myself. All the hurt, all the pain, the self-loathing. I transform it all into the only emotion I'm comfortable with. Anger.

Deacon may be furious with me, but I'm not too happy with him, either. He wants to play hard-headed? I can be hard-headed too. He taught me everything I know, after all. I'm done tiptoeing, afraid of asking questions, and being even more terrified of the answers.

I withheld information from him these last few days, yes. But Deacon has a lot more skeletons, and for a lot longer. Rowena, too.

Let's do this, bitches.

CHAPTER FIVE

THE GRAVESTONE

I WALK THROUGH THE door to Deacon's office with my head held high and plop myself down on his worn-out leather chair, surrounded by motorcycle pictures, concert posters, and signed equipment from the bands that have passed through. Marlow is on the matching leather couch with Rowena. Deacon is sitting behind his industrial-style desk. Linc is standing near the door, fidgeting like he wants to bolt, but he's stuck in place by the magnetic force of everything Deacon. Linc glances at me like he doesn't want to but can't help himself.

Yep, I fucked up. I fucked up a perfectly good friendship. What an absolute idiot I am. If I didn't need to be a total badass right now, I would facepalm myself so hard. But I'll have to deal with the repercussions of my stupidity later. What's the saying? Bigger fish to fry? Yeah, I've got that.

"Well, I'm here." I stare at Deacon first, placing my elbows on my thighs and leaning forward with my hands clasped together between my knees. I glanced at Rowena with the same defiance. "Go ahead, rip me a new one."

They glance at each other cautiously. I can't
deny the small satisfaction I get from making
them uncomfortable, for once.

"Why didn't you tell me? I gave you more than
a few chances to tell me you were in trouble,
Genevieve. I asked you!" Deacon spoke first.

"It's one thing to go a little crazy on the tequila
and find yourself in a street brawl. That you
can handle, but a night creature attacked you,
Genevieve! You were threatened. You've started
your bed on fire. You have a brand on your gods
damned wrist. You knew a Netherworld warrior
was tracking you, and you said nothing. Shall I go
on?"

*Netherworld? Killian is from the fucking
Netherworld?*

"Yeah, you're right. I said nothing. But let me
ask you a question, DAD." I spit the word out like
poison.

It was a low blow, and I regret it immediately. I
used to call him that when I was a child. I stopped
when I hit my teens, but he is my dad in all the
ways that matter and I know that cut him deep.
Although he'll never show it.

"Oh, now you think you're the one asking
questions around here, Genevieve?" Deacon
stares at me.

"Did you know about my sister?"

Rowena gasps and clamps her hand over her
mouth. Shocked speechless, I guess. Does that
mean that it's true?

"Where did you hear that? Who told you that?"
Deacon roars. His face is red as magma now.

Okay, so Linc hadn't told him everything. He
gets a brownie point.

"I wasn't sure if it was true, but I'm sure now. Your reaction says it all. What were you saying about hiding things from each other?" I place the knuckles of one hand up to my chin, rolling my eyes and scratching my temple.

"Vivi, I'm sorry you're hurt. But there's so much you don't know. Don't judge him so harshly." Rowena tries to chime in, but I whip my neck in her direction and flash her a wicked smile.

"What was your role in this? You spelled my amulet. What was in the spell? Is it truly to mask my fire element? Is that all it's for? I somehow doubt it," I hiss. I'm shaking now, my hands itching with raw power.

Sensing things are about to become heated. Marlow leaves the opposite couch and climbs into the massive chair with me, wrapping her arms around my shoulders. "Easy, Vivi. We're all family here."

Linc also moved to comfort me but stopped, looking at Deacon with an unsure scowl on his handsome face. What the hell was that? So, it's a loyalty thing for him. And obviously, Deacon wins.

I should have punched Linc straight in the face like I originally planned.

"Start. Talking." I stare pointedly at both Deacon and Rowena. "And when I'm satisfied with your answers, we can discuss my current predicament, which I'm assuming could have been avoided if either of you could TELL THE TRUTH!" A sparking fireball flies from my waving hand. Flames swell on the carpet, and Linc jumps into action, stomping them out.

Marlow hugs me closer, pressing calming thoughts into my head. Damn. Moonfall and their mind manipulations. She's only trying to help, but it's too late. I'm so sick of being used and lied to. I can't contain it. Blazing fire erupts in my palms.

"Genevieve, there are things at play here I can't share with you. Be angry if that's what you need, but I can do without the dramatics. If you can calm yourself, I will tell you what little I can." Deacon asserts in a nonchalant tone as he observes the flames swaying in my palms, not terribly disturbed by them.

"I'm listening." I raise my voice, flames shooting higher. Marlow rubs my shoulder, reminding me to take some deep breaths.

"The prophecy has been around for a long time. Longer than any of us have been alive. A child of darkness and a child of light." Deacon sighs, wiping his hand across his forehead.

"I've heard it. Everyone has. It's an old witch-wives' tale, Deacon," I counter. I'm not going to be taken in by a lie or even a partial lie. An old witch-wives' tale isn't likely to be about me. I will not be distracted.

One made of darkness, and One made of light. Air burns to Ash, Shadows take flight. When light pierces night. A new dawn will rise.

Nobody knows what that ridiculous riddle means. Some Oracle, hundreds of years ago, wrote it on a scroll, and it's been passed down like the telephone game ever since. I doubt it's even the original prophecy at this point. There are more theories about that riddle than fish in

Thorn Harbor. It's an urban legend—bedtime stories for naughty little children... right?

"'When the world falls to evil, the Princesses merge, coming back to destroy the world, or maybe to restore the balance.' That part is a little unclear, but it's a bunch of nonsense, right?" I flick my gaze between them, waiting for an explanation.

"When Evanora became pregnant, her power waned. The further along she got, the more power she lost. We suspected you were not only the child of a Bloodgood Witch, but something more." Deacon let me digest what he was saying. Then he continued, "Back then, rumors circulated of great evil in our midst."

Wait, are they saying what I think they're saying?

One of Darkness and One of Light...

"And then you were born, my dear girl. With raven hair and those lavender eyes, the perfect likeness to your beautiful mother. You were a wonderful child. You were *good*. We searched for the truth of who fathered you out of concern for the safety and well-being of our High Priestess. But your mother wouldn't budge. She said even speaking his name would put you in danger." Rowena adds.

"Evanora asked us to partake in a blood oath, swearing to protect you, and if the time ever came, to keep you hid." Deacon chimed in.

I gawked at Marlow. Does she hear this too? I struggled to judge her reaction by her eyes, but she wasn't giving me a thing. Linc had taken up counting the ceiling tiles, avoiding eye contact altogether.

"We were under orders to preserve and protect the future of the Bloodgood line. We were bound. We did as commanded. We still do as was commanded." Deacon's arms hung limply at his side.

"Did you see my mother die?" Hope and anger bloom in my chest simultaneously. "Did you *watch* her die?"

"Bloodgood Manor fell. Nobody made it out. Deacon has contacts throughout the realms. We kept our feelers out for years. No word ever surfaced about High Priestess Evanora. If she'd made it out, she would have contacted us." A teary-eyed Rowena pleaded.

But they didn't *see* her die.

"So, you spelled me. You hid my *forbidden* magic. To keep me away from my sister? My father? Am I getting that right? Which is it? Oh wait, and then you whisked me off to attend Underhill Academy, where I was used as an executioner. Faustus made me into a fucking murderer!" I shouted at them both, eyes glossy.

"You didn't have a choice, Vivi." Marlow gently interrupts. "That's not your fault."

"Underhill has wards stronger than what Rowena could put in your amulet. The Academy offered you the protection we couldn't." Deacon reminded me.

Protection? I was thrown to the wolves. Was he oblivious to the trauma I endured for years? Is duty the only thing that matters to him? I've suffered all this time because of some stupid oath?! My world crumbles in on itself, the air becoming so heavy I feel the stirrings of genuine panic.

"How long were you going to keep this from me? When the fire manifested right through your shitty protection spells. You didn't think *that* was a good time to let the pixie shit out of the bag?" I was lashing out again, but I couldn't stop.

"What do you know about her?" I deadpanned. Deacon growls in frustration, hands moving through his salt and pepper hair. Indecision etched in his forehead creases. "Tell me!!!" I shout in anger and frustration. I move to stand up, and Marlow stands with me. If he would not give me something to work with, I was going to walk out the door and find it myself.

"Sit down, Genevieve!" Deacon barked. A look of resignation swept across his features before he continued. "My contact found some information in the Netherworld."

Marlow's eyes widened as large as hula hoops with that revelation. So, my sister is in the Netherworld? A desolate wasteland of darkness and depravity. Sealed off from the rest of the realms to keep the abominations on their own side of the portals. Cool. What could go wrong with that scenario? This is where my sister was raised? Is being raised? I don't know if she is older or younger. She could be just a child or a full-fledged adult. Wait, if the portals are sealed, how did Deacon get information? Unless they aren't really sealed...

One of Darkness and One of light.

There's not a place on Earth Realm (or any other realm) where I would be considered "light." Couple that with the psycho fire and my talent for finding the worst likely scenarios. What if my sister is a pure soul stuck in literal Hell? And I'm up here all *mistress of darkness*, mucking it up all over the place, sending people to their deaths.

Was she safe? Is she with our father? Who is he, and how the hell is anyone getting through the portals? This story has gigantic holes in it. Massive ones. They're both smoking fae flowers if they think I'm going to take it at face value. My life just turned into the most fucked up fairytale retelling there ever was. And plot twist... *I'm* the villain?

In my overthinking, emotionally whiplashed, what the fuck is happening right now brain. I forgot there are still people in the room. And when I search the faces of the most significant people in my life, they all look at me like I am about to grow horns and a tail.

"Did you hear anything I said?" Deacon taps his foot in irritation.

"Well, excuse me if I need a minute. It's kind of lot you're throwing at me, ya know?" I snap back.

He continues, "It concerns me that the Elders at The Academy had knowledge of your sister's whereabouts, and now they don't. And it coincides with an attack on you from a night creature ... I see that look in your eye. The one that's reserved for when you're going to do something stupid. Remember your training Genevieve, you don't know if she means you harm."

I didn't dignify him with a response because he wasn't wrong. The night creature, the voice in the darkness, the prophecy (if it wasn't total bullshit). This stupid brand on my wrist. My sister. Killian. It had to be connected somehow.

After some intense conversation, a healthy dose of brooding, and far too many debates. We settle on a makeshift plan. I'm not the type to run from anything, but when Rowena and Deacon suggest I get out of town for a while, I can't logically disagree. It's not like I didn't know this moment was a possibility. I've been preparing for it all my life. But something deep inside of me feels like it is collapsing. Breathe, Vivi. Breathe.

Giving in to what makes sense, I look at the logistics. It will take a few days to set up a new identity, pack up my belongings, and find a place to hide out for a few months; I can gather more information this way. It will give me more time. Deacon and Rowena are in a flurry of activity, calling in their favors, making detailed plans about cabins and supplies.

Linc volunteers to go (of course he did) to protect me and get messages back and forth from Deacon and Rowena. Marlow is not budging; she's determined to leave with me as well. Her father will never let that happen. I know in my heart he will pick this moment to give a shit where she is, and he will find her. And find me. So, I let them make their plans. But it isn't any of their lives that bore the burden; it's mine. I'm a danger to them. They can't see it. And now I know my sister is real. She is out there somewhere. I will move The Earth Realm, The Netherworld, and any other world that stands in my way to find her.

After the shit show of a night I've had, I tell them all to screw off and let me have some room to breathe. I leave the Gravestone to find Calypso waiting by the back door. "Let's go home, Lippy." I scratched behind her ear as she winds herself between my legs in figure eights, rubbing against my leather pants as we make our way down the alley.

I wave at Frank on my way up rickety stairs. He is sitting next to the dumpster in his usual spot, flickering in and out of view. Keeping the shadows in check, I would have to sit down with him and get his story one of these days.

Stepping into my apartment squeezes on my heart. Sure, the heater doesn't work like it's supposed to and every day is a gamble between 'middle of a volcano or tundra.' The handle on the toilet doesn't work without some jiggles, and sometimes the freezer door doesn't stay shut, so I have to use magical means. My apartment is as chaotic as I am. It's not much, but it's all I have.

I strip down to panties and a t-shirt and climb into bed, ready to have an uneventful night in front of the television. Looking forward to catching up on the newest episode of a supernatural dating reality show. It's getting to the juicy part when my phone chimes. I grabbed it out of habit, not because I'm interested in talking to anyone, even by text.

Marlow: *I know you're knee deep in a tub of cookie dough ice cream by now, but remember, you're a badass. We got this. See you in the morning?*

Vivi: *It's chocolate cherry, Smartass. And Stephan is about to confess he's gay. He's going to hook up with Mercutio, and I'm so here for it... it's a big night!*

Marlow: *No way. He's got a boner for that Pegasus shifter girl, even though she's a total Rainbow Bitch. Who has that much glitter and still makes everyone around her so miserable? I don't know what he sees in her.*

Vivi: *He's so not into her. I'm right, you'll see. And no shit, btw. We always got this. 11 a.m. and don't be late or you're buying! Nite, Lowe - xo.*

Marlow: *Nite, you beautiful bitch. -xoxo*

I smile as I set my phone back down beside me, shifting my fuzzy blankets to cover my feet and settling back into someone else's drama for the night. I'm happy to be free of my own train wreck for a while. Calypso purrs next to me, and I slide closer, making her my little spoon. I am about to drift off when my phone chimes in again.

It must be Marlow ready to tell me I'm an asshole and stop using the Sight to prove her wrong, which I wasn't! I snicker as I pick up the phone again, prepared to give my acceptance speech for the most brilliant friend alive, but when I peek at the screen, my heart thunders, and my breath hitches...

Prince Charming: *Miss me, Kitten?*

Oh shit, oh un-holy shit! I cover my face with my hands in total embarrassment. This can't be happening right now. I'm in my underwear, for star's sake! I slam the phone face down into my lap as if he can see me through a text. What the fuck, Universe? *And Prince Charming? Really? Gross.* Goddess, he is so self-absorbed it's impressive. How does he have my phone number, anyway? Better yet - how did he program his information into mine without me catching him? The sneaky bastard.

I stare at the text for a few seconds. Reading it again, trying to produce a reply that doesn't reflect the shock I'm experiencing. He gets one point for catching me off guard; I'll give him that.

Vivi: *You wish. I see your stalking skills have improved.*

Prince Charming: *I'm resourceful. How's my feline friend doing this evening?*

Does he mean... my cat? Or...? Omg. I can envision his aggravating smirk lifting the corner of his lip right now. Thinking he's so clever. Pushing my buttons to see which ones light up. A shiver races through my nerve endings, but I'm not taking the bait. Not today, Satan.

Vivi: *Is there a reason you're gracing my phone with your presence? Or is this my nightly check-in? Are you my glorified babysitter now?*

Vivi: *And how did you get this number?*

Prince Charming: *Now, now. Is this how we treat our friends? Although being a nanny for such a naughty girl sounds like a magnificent time, it's my understanding that naughty girls receive spankings.*

Spankings? Whoa, wait a minute.

My mind travels to a dark room with the most giant bed I've ever seen, red sheets curled between my fingers as I'm bent over the edge, shaking with pleasure. Killian's hand caresses my ass, moving slowly. Creating a storm in the core of my being, I lift my hips, inviting him closer, wanting more. A resounding 'smack' echoes through the air as the sting pulls a breathy moan from my lips...

The vision disappears as fast as it came on. Umm. I'm going to pretend like he hadn't said that. And this, whatever this is, never happened. Yeah, that's the plan. My legs tremble, and I try to catch my breath...

Vivi: *I don't remember offering my friendship to you.*

Prince Charming: *I like a challenge.*

Vivi: *Goodnight, Killian.*
Prince Charming: *Sweet dreams, Kitten.*
Vivi: *Please stop calling me that.*

Like a hormonal teenager, I sit and watched the screen waiting for a response, but it never comes.

It's a little warm in here, so I crawl out of bed to get bottled water and then curl back into my blankets, thoughts spinning. Talking to him is a bad idea. No, strike that; it's a monumentally stupid idea. I might be in over my head on this one, but when I drift off into a fitful sleep, stormy turquoise eyes that eddy into swirling galaxies fill my dreams. The softest hands I've ever felt roam over me, touching every part of my soul. And he finishes what he started.

CHAPTER SIX

THE FESTIVAL OF LIGHT

THE FESTIVAL OF LIGHT is upon us, which is a blessing. Most of Underhill will be preoccupied this weekend. It's the perfect cover to get the hell out of here. After the last few days, everything I've seen and all the bombshells sitting in my lap... well, I know what I have to do, but there are some things I need to tie up first.

Sipping a morning latte in the quirky coffee shop I love so much, emotions swell in my chest as I soak in my surroundings. Brom and Baela dart through the air on their batlike wings, knocking into the displays along the walls. Looking for an opportunity to sow chaos, no doubt since that's what sprites feed on.

The bitterness of freshly picked herbs mixed with an array of fragrant flowers drying from the rafters waft on the gentle breeze. They will be the last of the season. The cold months will press in on Thornfall soon. It gives me a sense of familiar comfort. I guess you could say I grew up here in this hidden gem. My childhood scribbles still decorate the old wood underneath the tables. It's odd how I spent over a decade hating Thornfall so much all I ever thought about was leaving, and now there's hesitation. How do I walk away from the worst memories when all the good ones I've ever had are intertwined?

I'm relieved to see Marlow walk through that sticky front door holding a stack of brochures and a notebook. I was spiraling down the pity tunnel and in desperate need of a distraction. She had devised a plan. Not the best strategy. But since we had no way of knowing where spies may lurk, we have to be crafty. So, we are going to plan a trip in full view of the public. As far as the gossiping throng would know, it was a graduation present. Delayed by quite a few years, but that's easily explained away by the demands of The Gravestone.

"Where's Linc?" I ask. He hadn't shown up to spar with me this morning.

"I'm not sure, but he knows to meet us. Let's start without him. He'll stumble his hungover self in at some point. He was in a tizzy last night, which I assume has a lot to do with you. I will not ask. I don't want to know. But I think he went to blow off some steam after we all left Deacon's office. That boy likes to disappear. If he wasn't a shifter, I'd swear he was a professional magician. Don't sweat it." Marlow brushed it off.

But I was sweating it. Marlow had no idea what had happened between Linc and me in my apartment. Part of me feels embarrassed to explain it to her. Another part of me is terrified to tell her I may have ruined our friendship forever. I don't know what her reaction would be in either scenario, and she said she doesn't want to know. So, I'll save that conversation for later.

She was right, though; Linc was spectacular at disappearing tricks. He was probably running through the forest near the estate the Academy was on. Hunting bunnies or girls. Either option was viable.

Marlow and I spend a while talking noisily and excitedly over road trip destinations. Discussing what kind of swimming suits we are going to get for the occasion and the places we will eat. Customers file in and out of the shop as we make a production of it. They hear everything we are saying. It won't take long for the rumor mill to do its job. All of Thornfall will know by the end of the day. After talking it to death and going over all the details twice, we both conclude that Linc isn't coming. I kind of tore his heart out, so I can understand if he needs some time before he can look at my face again. My chest squeezes at that thought. Ugh, I am a terrible person.

"You want to get out of here, then?" I asked Marlow as she finishes her third latte. "I know this sounds silly, but since ... you know." I hinted without saying it out loud. "I thought maybe we could check out the festival? For old times' sake."

Marlow understood what I was trying to say and nodded.

One last time...

Calypso meets us on the steps outside Enchanted Brew. We stand on the sidewalk as we watched the parade roll by; the gaudy floats in golden hues creep past us—brightly colored currents of magic prance in the air. The Academy's best and brightest students show off their elemental abilities while onlookers cheer.

"Ooh's and ahh's" float through the air as a young witchling student calls up the rushing wind, carrying fall leaves through the streets. Crunchy leaves spin in figure eights through our legs and up to our arms. Branches circle a woman's hair in the shape of a crown. Another student sends a stream of water over our heads, like the deep-sea doing ballet before our eyes. The water doubles back and boomerangs itself to its master. It's all nostalgic to watch, but not without a twinge of pain.

A memory of a parade Marlow and I were in so long ago resurfaced.

Marlow was on a float of clouds and stars, whispering beautiful lyrics into the atmosphere, directing them into the onlooker's ears. You could tell when they saw their wildest dreams come alive in front of them. It was the ultimate illusion. Joy swept across their faces as the Dream Riders worked their craft.

My float was a stark opposite. I must've been ten or eleven years old at the time - I stood tall and imposing in a midnight robe with golden threaded embroidery. They had instructed me to keep my face neutral before we boarded. I am something to be feared and respected. I am the symbol of what happens when you step out of line.

We came down the major thoroughfare, and the crowd went silent. No cheers, no excitement. Instead, The Academy's Blood Seer inspired dread in the citizens of Thornfall. They thought I could reach into their brains and pull out every secret, every word uttered in privacy, every lie. They feared me. I was the last thing they saw before the Council dragged them to the part of the sprawling estate that wasn't a school...

The Halls of Repentance, also known as the dungeons. Where the Rune Force did their most disgraceful work. Those who went in rarely came back out; the atrocities committed in the dungeons are only whispers in the darkest corners of this city. I suppress a shudder at the intrusive thought.

Marlow and I stroll a little farther down to check out some street merchants. There are gifts and wares, food and drink, spells, and concoctions. The smells of funnel cake combined with sweat and earth, make a strange but pleasant mixture in our noses.

The atmosphere was electric. A twist formed in my chest; the sights, smells, and sparkles in our gloomy town are a refreshing change. As much as I criticize anything in the city, at this moment I appreciate that I'm going to miss it. I would never miss The Academy or its Elders or the blood they placed on my hands. The stain left on my soul. Still, the decent memories of Thornfall had made an impact as well. This community had become somewhat like home over the years, even for an outcast like me.

Marlow wants to check out some of the food vendors, so we start up the street towards the square, taking it all in. We stop at an open-air tent to sample artisan cheeses paired with exotic wines from across the sea. Another merchant waves silky scarves and wraps as we near, beckoning us to feel the airy fabrics on our skin.

I'm drawn to a wine-colored tent, covered as though it is part of a traveling circus. So, we head down the lane towards it. Crossing the threshold between the heavy folds of a woven curtain, we find a bewildering array of gemstones and crystals. They lay on display in rows and rows of shimmering brilliance. Sparkling amethyst points as big as my hand, aura quartz shimmering iridescent rainbows, and chakra cleansing selenite buzzing with energy. There are so many varieties and shades it's overwhelming in the most satisfying way. My Witchling blood sings in harmony with the crystals.

Marlow stops to grab black tourmaline on our way through. Not a bad idea, I'd be able to charge them with my Sight sometime this evening; it would transform them not only into fierce protection stones but also spyglass that would alert us to intruders.

As we're browsing, a gleam in the distance draws my attention. A table further down, nestled into a darker corner of the tent, is calling to me. My feet move of their own accord as though I was being guided by an invisible force.

Resting on a raised velvet display is a moonstone dagger, so reminiscent of the one I had inherited from my mother that I let out a tiny breath. It is mesmerizing. I reach for it, hovering my palm above. Imagining my fingers roving across the smooth raw material, feeling the strength living within. The expertly made weapon entrances me.

When I lift my eyes, a peculiar woman appears next to me. Where did she come from? The exotic woman wears a lengthy ceremonial robe that hugs her ample curves. A slit up one side revealed her seductive legs and bare feet. Midnight hair hangs in shiny waves down past the veil of black lace that obscures her face. The shadows play tricks with the dim light. Dark lashes and crimson lips are the only features that flicker through. Everything about her is captivating.

"A blade fit for a Princess." She speaks in a husky voice, eyeing Calypso with interest. Although her accent is vaguely foreign, something about her feels familiar. I want this dagger badly, but to betray it on my face to a street merchant would be tantamount to asking to pay full price. She would ask for the price to be doubled. *Act cool, Vivi. Nonchalant.*

"The blade chooses a worthy master or mistress," she answered the questions in my head like I'd spoken them out loud, but offered no other explanation.

An overwhelming desire to hold it in my hands passes through me. I sense it on such a profound level, my fingers moved for the hilt. A gritty, sandpaper lick from Calypso on the back of my leg jars me from stupidity. I'm not known for being well mannered, but even I know better than to touch an object of power without permission.

"May I touch it?" I ask the enigmatic merchant.

"You may." She nods.

The realms slow to a crawl. Everything around me is in sluggish movement as I pick up the dagger. Soft indigo light flows up my arms, tingling at every nerve ending. A sigh escapes my lips. 'Home,' it whispers deep in my veins.

"She has chosen." The veiled woman spoke in a low, sultry voice. "Use her well, Genevieve."

Genevieve? My ears must play tricks. She doesn't know my name. The cloying scent of pomegranate and honey clings to the makeshift walls; a hazy memory struggles to resurface in my mind...

A fearsome goddess dressed in black leather stands on the top of a cliff, her eerie beauty menacing and formidable. It hurts to look at her. Black dogs below her circling a crossroads - some were tearing through soft flesh, gnawing on bones. The crunching sound echoes through the tunnel next to them. The vision fades. Large ornate gates stand in front of me. I'm in a ballroom; everyone is wearing masks. Foxes, Antelope, Wolves, Bones. There's dancing and whirling; they're moving around me in circles, making me lightheaded. Someone grabs my arms and yanks me against them. A simple black mask covers his features; I melt into his defined arms, rubbing my hands over them as his lips press into mine. My mate. The vision fades, and it all falls away.

"What did you see?" Marlow asks.

"Nothing ... nothing... I don't know." I try to catch my breath, my pulse pounding in more ways than one.

"Your eyes went glow worm. You can't bullshit me."

"No, for real, Lowe. I do not know what the fuck I saw."

Calypso sprawls on the ground next to my feet, grooming herself. She doesn't appear to have a care in the world, although I know she felt it too. My heart is still beating out of my chest. I glance up to ask the mystery merchant if she knows the dagger's origins? But she's gone, along with the tent and all the gemstones. Marlow, Calypso, and I are standing in a vacant lot with the sounds of the festival in the distance. The blade rests in the palm of my hand, pulsing with the beat of my heart.

"That was top shelf strange, Vivi. Even for witches." Marlow speaks shakily as she looks around us in confusion.

I can't disagree.

I STAND BEHIND THE bar wearing a flowing black skirt and a tight t-shirt that said, "More Issues Than Vogue." This top always sparks humorous conversations with the regulars, who were more than willing to poke fun at my laundry list of issues, knowing this was the only time they could get away with it.

I had fashioned a second holster from some leather straps I'd taken off an old pair of boots (not the most professional setup, but I worked with what I had). I now carried two moonstone daggers, almost identical to each other. Hugging my thigh underneath my skirt.

"Hey Viv ... Genevieve ... er, Vivi? I'm sorry, I don't know what to call you." Bronwyn stammered.

"Vivi is fine. How are you doing tonight?" I cringe.

Why did I say that?

"Well, that was awkward, wasn't it? I'm sorry, I hate small talk. Can we start over?" I bit my lip; I don't know what the hell is wrong with me today.

Bronwyn smiled, genuine amusement on her face. "You look like you could use a drink."

"Or an exorcism," I suggested. "You can call me Vivi, by the way."

She giggled; the sound was like tinkling bells in a forest of fireflies (note to self - she's most definitely fae). We settle into a comfortable rapport. She was new to town, so we chatted about the story of Thornfall. This city is now the wealthiest in all of Earth Realm, built upon sea trade and the hurt of the past. Many witches benefitted from the bloodline war, not that you could tell by looking at it. Most of the wealth had a strange way of isolating itself to a particular castle estate turned den of elite vipers.

We talked a little about the trade and shipping docks seaside. Fishing was big business around here. Among other not-so-legal things, if you dock late enough at night. Bronwyn was especially interested in the trade routes - she must be the intellectual type.

"Hey Bronwyn, we meet in the mornings for coffee at Enchanted Brew. Maybe tomorrow you could swing by?" I don't know why I said that either. The last thing I need right now is a new friend, given the circumstances and what I planned to do soon. But our conversation was so effortless that it felt like talking with an old friend. And Marlow would be okay with it; maybe she could connect with Bronwyn as I have. She always had a fascination with the fae. They will get along, I suspect. Linc might even save some room for a new friend in his life.

"I'm so grateful for the invitation! But I won't be able to make it in the morning. You know how it goes, responsibilities." She shifted uncomfortably, and I wondered to myself what that might be about. Maybe she wasn't permitted to fraternize with witches? Some magical orders have specific rules about that kind of thing. Since I didn't know which order of fae she belonged to, it was a definite possibility. I ask her some more general questions about her life, not trying to pry. Her answers were friendly but short, like the first time she had worked a shift with me.

Her family was spread about the realms. They had separated some from each other when the portals were sealed. She doesn't have any siblings. A slight blush crept over her delicate face when I asked about boyfriends, so that told me that there was someone in her life, whether they knew it I couldn't be sure.

Bronwyn has a haunted look about her. Not something that comes and goes, but a permanent sadness under the surface. I recognize that look because I've seen it in the mirror every day of my life. I would bet my prized bow and quiver that her background was much more similar to mine than she was letting on. When you've had a life of trauma, there are indications. Not wanting to discuss it with anyone is one of them. Those who don't share their lives with others always have their reasons. It made me want to know more.

As we work, she asks a bit about me. Odd questions, not the typical 'getting to know each other' subjects like where I was born and how I grew up. Although she asks about any boys or girls in my life (I guess some things are universal no matter what order you belong to, like girl talk). She asks about my preferred foods and what kind of music I like, my favorite flower. The fae-folk have strange customs, so I go with it.

Our night is plugging along uneventfully, which is unheard of during the Festival of

Light. The tables are all served, nobody needed refills, customers gather in small groups having conversations at an average volume. My tip jar is full. This could be the definition of a perfect night. Maybe the long-forgotten gods had looked at the madness they'd dragged me through and found a moment of sympathy? But peace isn't a relaxing feeling for someone like me; too much time to let my mind run wild.

The text messages from Killian still had me rattled. I can't figure him out. It doesn't help that I hadn't seen him at the coffee shop since that first day; he hasn't stalked me at my job since the night creature attacked me. He has been suspiciously quiet. If he's been ordered to watch me, then where is he? Kind of a shitty babysitter, if you ask me.

But every time I'd seen him, I had assaulted him and then asked him to leave (whoops), so what did I expect? Maybe he got the hint. He almost certainly thought long and hard about what he signed up for and then went straight back to his employer and quit. Isn't that what I wanted? He is the most infuriating man I've ever had the displeasure of meeting, after all. So why do I feel an uncomfortable dip in my stomach every time someone comes through the door and it isn't him? Followed by pangs of guilt, of course. Because if I could recreate that feeling when I see Linc, I could make it work.

It's just like me to have an unhealthy interest in something that will end in disaster. Call me the chaos magnet. I really should buy a cape and some spandex.

All the what-ifs are messing with my head; I still haven't processed that Deacon and Rowena deceived me. That was a box of problems I'm not ready to open yet. I have a sexy stalker who may not be my stalker anymore, and I don't know how I feel about it. My best friend put his tongue in my mouth. I lost my marbles and took it a step further - and I hadn't hated it. At least half of what I know about my childhood is a dirty lie. I have forbidden magic that could easily put me where I had damned too many souls to count; poetic justice comes to mind on that one. My dream of leaving Thornfall and having total freedom from the Elders is coming true, but it doesn't feel like I thought I would. There's no joy in what comes next. And I have a sister who may have been raised with the beasties in the Netherworld?

It's fine, nothing to see here.

A loud crash and gods awful shrieking broke my train of thought. Someone was screaming for help outside. My Sight picked up on the intensity of her panic, and it shocked me into motion. I bolted for the front door with Marlow on my heels. We smelled the blood before either of us saw what was coming.

CHAPTER SEVEN

VIVI

LINC WAS BENT AT an unnatural angle on the sidewalk, blood pooling underneath him. Too much blood for me to put back in, even with my blood magic.

A woman screamed and screamed, staring at his unmoving body in horror. I didn't have time to think before I launched myself at him, throwing my ear to his chest and using the Sight to find his aura.

Ignoring the puddle of lifeblood that I kneeled in, cold liquid soaking into my clothing and filling my shoes. I dove deep into my inner self, straight to the core of my power, searching ... searching ... not sure what I was searching for? I've never gone this far, and I have no idea what I'm doing, but he can't die. A singular purpose drove me. I will not let Linc die.

The stars cannot have him.

It's right there, faint but not gone. A thread of auburn light, moving further and further away from me. I don't know where the knowledge to search for it came from; I operate on pure instinct. I have no time to question it, so I take a deep breath and pour my magic into him, reaching for that thread with everything I have in my heart and soul. When I have it firmly in my magical grasp, I yank. Hard.

The sights and sounds on the street came blaring back to life. Persistent screaming filled my ears. I whipped my head at the blonde-haired, blue-eyed, long-legged shrieking banshee of a woman next to me and screamed, "Stop it!" She looks at me wide-eyed and she wails some more. "I said stop it, NOW!" I growl, putting some power behind it. She stops howling, but her mouth hangs open like a fish gasping for air.

With the noise no longer distracting me, I felt along the thread until I find a rhythm. Linc's soul calls to me like a song. A melody of running rivers and singing birds in the forest branches. I dance myself up and down the thread, matching the tempo, chanting with his spirit, luring it back to me. And then he opens his eyes wide, grasping at the air.

He coughs up blood as he tries to speak. "Ni... Ni... night creature Vivi!" his ruined voice laced with sheer terror as he struggles to get the words out. The terror not for himself, but for me. *Goddess, please don't take him from me. I'm sorry. I'm so fucking sorry!*

Calypso leaps from the terrace, landing on all fours, and takes off down the street, warning growls reverberating through her chest. Whatever hurt Linc didn't stand a chance with Lippy on its heels.

"Shh, don't worry, Calypso will find it. You're safe. I'm safe. This is going to hurt like a bitch, though. And I'm sorry, but we need to move." I snare his feral eyes and stare apologetically.

Then, I hoist him up to my shoulder and stumble through the Gravestone entrance.

Deacon is already heading toward the commotion and intercepts me as I struggled to haul Linc into the building. He lifts Linc from my arms, and I take off at a frantic run toward the office, wiping everything off the desk and onto the floor with a wild fling of my arm. Glass crashes, pens scatter, papers fly. I rush to the door and prop it open for more room. Deacon places Linc on the desk, and I grab his hand. Holding on to his fingers for dear life. His superficial wounds had already healed, but I sobbed anyway.

Bronwyn rushes through the door, looking at me with a determined shout, "I'm a healer!" she waits a fraction of a second, probably to gauge my reaction and if I would let her touch him. Then goes straight to work on the wounds that are still oozing his blood onto the desk and carpet. There's so much, way too much. I'm not sure even a shifter can survive being fully drained. They're tough to kill, but something has to keep the heart beating, like any other supernatural (besides vampires and incubi).

Bronwyn tries not to sound bossy as she calls out for towels, thyme, and crushed garlic. Marlow rushes to the kitchen for the supplies she needs. The annoying woman from the sidewalk sits crumpled on the couch, sniffling. Anger surges in my veins at why she may be here. A pang in my heart tears me up inside. Had he tried to find comfort elsewhere after I rejected him? It looked that way. Something feral stirs within me. I slide closer to Linc with a grip on his hand. The King of The Underworld himself wouldn't be able to break.

"You're going to be okay," I murmur through tear-soaked eyes. "I'm sorry, this is my fault, oh Goddess, I'm so sorry!" Linc did his best to give me a reassuring smile before he lost consciousness. Hopelessness consumes me, and I turn my wrath to the unidentified woman on the couch. "Get the fuck out!" I snarl at the Malibu Barbie Linc had been with all day. I realized I was damn near crouching over him now, like a wild animal protecting their prize. The darkness inside me whispering violent things. I will rip the veins from her body if she steps any closer. I will tear her throat out and spit it into her face. I shake with the need to make someone pay, consumed with it.

Marlow watches with concern twisting on the bridge of her nose. "Vivi, you need to chill the fuck out. Okay? He's right there. He's breathing. He needs you. Focus on Linc, look at Linc."

So, I do. I watch him with the ferocity of a she-wolf. Jerking violently at anyone who comes near.

Once Bronwyn and Deacon have Linc bandaged and stable, they handle the worst of it. They lift his head as he groans and opens an eye. Bronwyn gives him a swig of hot liquid for the pain, and Deacon helps to move him to the worn leather couch. I climb underneath his blankets and hold him, pressing my body heat into his. Calling to his wolf, begging the alpha within him to fight. To stay.

The unknown woman has removed herself from the couch, but she lingers near the doorway for a few minutes, looking as if she wishes to speak but is too afraid to attempt it. Bronwyn takes her by the shoulder and guides her towards the hallway exit. With a second and then a third glance, she turns to leave.

Not wanting to discuss night creatures, escape plans, or anything else. I give Deacon a glaring challenge. *Speak, and I'll burn the world down-*. Eventually, he walks out too. After having ushered the Barbie out, Bronwyn gives me a sympathetic nod and follows Deacon. When the room is empty, I lay my head on his broken body. Feeling the slow rise and fall of his chest. My emotions threaten to consume me; I can't imagine a realm in any part of the Universe where I could survive if Linc's heart stopped beating. Anger, fear, sadness, rage, love, guilt. They swirl in a frenzy through every inch of me, churning and suffocating, begging to break free and unleash something frightening under my skin.

Dark thoughts consume me. All day. Linc had been missing all fucking day, and I never looked for him. I had been too wrapped up in my head to stop and notice the surrounding details. I knew better. Deacon trained me for this.

Lincoln said he would be at Enchanted Brew. Why didn't I look for him when he didn't show? He would have never neglected a chance to explore the sights and sounds of the festival. I hadn't even noticed when he wasn't at work tonight. Remorse takes hold of my throat and squeezes; I struggle to get enough air. Linc could have died. He could have died! And I was too worried about what he thought of me, about my pride, to pay attention.

The night creatures are in Thornfall because of me, and I ignored the warning. The orders to send them after me in the Earth Realm had to come from someone high ranking on the wicked scale. Someone with considerable influence. Now that my skin has been marked, there wasn't anywhere in any realm they wouldn't find me. Not even the furthest ocean could conceal me now. They will track me, they will hunt me for the rest of my days, and the ones I love will pay the price.

This is all my fault, and I can't hide from this. I can't run from what I know. I have to stand and face it this time. I don't know why any of us thought it would work, but nobody else will get hurt because of me. Marlow stands in the doorway, giving me an intense look as she searches my face with her keen eyes. Trying to gauge how close I am to losing my shit, but she has no idea how insane I've become.

After several hours of wrapping myself around Linc's resting body, refusing to move, Deacon takes a seat in the matching leather chair next to us. "You should get cleaned up. You're covered in blood and you stink. I'll stay with him."

My clothes are stuck to me, dried blood flakes from my hands, and I can feel it congealing on my face like a macabre jelly. As I peel myself from the couch, Bronwyn comes back into the room, wiping her hands on a towel. Overwhelmed with emotion, I throw my arms around her neck. "Thank you so much. You saved him, Bronwyn. I can never repay you for what you've done."

"There's no need to thank me, Vivi. It's an honor to be blessed with the healing hand," she whispers. Tears form as I hug her again, leaning back and looking her in the eyes, hoping she understands. We could have been the best of friends if given a chance.

Calypso and I stagger to the apartment; her soft rumble purrs calming my soul. Thank the Goddess it's late, because if someone came upon us right now, I can't imagine what they would think. I look like an extra in a slasher flick; my gore-crusted clothes are stiff and cracking with every move I make. Lippy's maw is covered in a foul liquid stench. We look like a pair of apocalyptic cosplayers gone wrong.

Once inside our home, I shower. Scrubbing my skin until it glows red with irritation. The blood-soaked memory of Linc crumbled on the ground replays in my head. Who would it be next time? Marlow impaled on a blade? Deacon with his insides ripped out on the floor of the Gravestone? My imagination gets the best of me as I play out every tragic scenario I can think of. The thought of them getting hurt cleaves my heart in two; fresh tears trickle down my cheeks as I wash Calypso with a cloth and soapy water. We sit on the floor of my moon-themed bathroom, getting every bit of sinew and putrid blood off her coat. I work through my thoughts as I caress her silky fur.

My faithful friend, my protector. I crumple to the floor at the thought of having to let her go, but that's what I must do. I have to let them all go, because I can't survive another minute knowing I've put them in danger. I'm about to do either the dumbest or the most self-sacrificing thing I've ever done in my life.

I'm going to The Academy, whatever the cost.

Once my mind is made up, I hurry. I grab my backpack and search the apartment for anything I might need. Candles, in case I need to conjure a spell. My mother's ring. My daggers, a few tops, some shorts, and underthings.

Then I crawl under my bed and knock on the wooden planks. My hand searches the space under the floor for the loose board; when my fingers skim a ledge, I dig my nails in and pull up a plank in between the floor joists; I hid something there a long time ago. When my hands find what I was looking for, I pull it out and into my lap. This tiny box had been under there as long as I've been in Thornfall. I take a deep, shuddering breath as I touched the intricate carvings...

My mother sits in her study, writing letters with her quill. I stand in the doorframe's corner, half in the room, half out. Admiring her long silky blue-black hair, the soft material of her elegant sapphire dress flowing around the legs of her chair.

"Come in," she smiles as she turns her head to look at me; with a knowing look twinkling in her eyes, she says, "I summoned you today because I have a job for you, Genevieve. But first, I need to know, can you keep a secret?"

I nod. "Yes, Mother."

"Good. This box belonged to your great ancestor. I need you to put it somewhere safe. Never lose it, Genevieve; it must never leave you. Do you understand?" I nod again, standing proud. I feel like a trusted advisor to the Priestess.

"Don't break the seal unless your life is in danger, Genevieve." she waves her hand across my vision, and I suddenly can't remember why I've been summoned. But I know what is in my hands is precious, and I have to guard it.

As the memory fades, I'm stunned at the spell that activates when I touch the box. I know it is vital and has to be hidden, but I marvel because it has never triggered any visions when I have touched it before. Not until tonight. I am filled with a torrent of both sadness and profound understanding. My mother was the greatest Seer of her time. If she spelled the box to trigger a vision at this exact moment, then I have to trust it.

I pull Calypso into my lap, petting her head and rubbing her soft black fur. Tears stream freely down my face as I explain to her what I am about to do. Leaving her feels like cutting off a limb, removing a piece of my soul. It destroys me just thinking of going anywhere without her, but it's the only way. If things go sideways with the Elders, they won't get their grimy hands on my familiar. I'd rather die a thousand deaths than allow them to hurt her. No, I won't give them anything to use against me.

Calypso bays a mournful cry, and I break into a million jagged pieces. I don't know how long I sit on the rug with her and sob, but my eyes feel sandpapered and bruised. I have felt pain; I've known grief. But this? This is unbearable. I sniffle as I try to crack a smile while giving her reassurance that this is what the Universe has charted for us, and we will see it through.

SO HERE IT IS, the moment of truth. I take one more look at my meager apartment, my big fancy bed, and the memories of the life I built here. My chest hurts as I lay a note on the counter for Deacon; he's going to fight this. But I need him to understand why I have to go. Without answers, we're all in danger.

The night creatures want me, only me. They want me so badly they're willing to hurt the people I love if I don't heed their warnings. I need to know why, and the path to answers starts with my sister. I can't explain how I know. The Sight doesn't always map out detailed directions; sometimes, it's just an understanding. A gut feeling that becomes a fact. Something that has always been and always will be. Even though those motherfuckers are the dirtiest backstabbing lot of filth ever spawned, Bridgewater was telling me the truth. I suspect she may have risked herself doing it. They had my sister at one point, which means the Elders know who she is. And if they know who she is, then there's no telling what else they might know, but it's time to find out.

I have every plan to someday make it back to this sleepy seaside town and everyone I love, but for now, the best thing I can do is leave and hope I make it out of the Academy alive. If I do, I'll go far across the realms and draw the night creatures away from Thornfall. And if I don't? Well, then I guess they will have to come in after me. And if I'm fortunate, they'll take the entire council down in a bloodbath on their way through.

CHAPTER EIGHT

KILLIAN

RESTLESS ANTICIPATION STIRS THROUGH my kingdom with whispers of a powerful Blood Seer living in Thornfall. My Netherlings mutter the words in secrecy, but voices carry through my realm. All whispers make their way to my ears. Rumors of her beauty and wild darkness interest me. The Oracle had confirmed her death, but the hag fled my father's Dark Court soon after. Over a decade has passed and yet there are still questions. I despise questions.

The Shadowfax forces grow bolder. Without an official transfer of power and coronation of a Dark King, they've infiltrated our outer borders. Recruiting the most gruesome and bloodthirsty of our kind. I'll see the traitors' heads removed before they can cross back through our wards, but the insult to my throne isn't as easily remedied.

The true ruler of the Netherworld, my father, rests beneath our caverns. Cursed to eternal slumber by the Enchantress who put him there. The Enchantress who then died by my hand. It was vengeance, but my actions left the Netherworld Princes alone to sort out the chaos. We've been ruling in his stead for a decade.

Between us, we have immense influence, but our realm is fading. If it fails, I can no longer control the portals and destruction will set upon the entire world, releasing horrors even the Shadowfax Warlock himself couldn't dream of.

My mission is to free my father from the clutches of his underground tomb by any means necessary, but as the years pass, the hope of finding an enchantress with enough power to reverse his curse is nonexistent. As the eldest and son to the true queen, I am the rightful heir; I am responsible for the future of this realm. I keep my people safe and in line. In order to keep peace and stability in our kingdom, I share responsibilities with my half-brothers and our half-sister, born from my father's concubines. This allows me the ability to continue to look for someone to release my father from his slumber.

I tap my fingers on my imposing onyx throne in contemplation. As the official acting ruler, I wear the weight of the realm on my shoulders. My people, our survival, the future of our realm. It all hinges on me. A responsibility I never asked for. One I resent more often than I embrace but, the fates don't care what we prefer. So, I play the part I've been handed: Dark Prince, The Cold One, and Death's Henchman. And I play it well.

I circle back to the whispers. If the Lost Princess is alive, then I need her.

"You look like you're about to do something sketchy, bro." Jagger strides into the throne room wearing training leathers and drenched in sweat.

"There are rumors..."

"About the hot female in Thornfall? She can do some crazy wild shit, I heard. My horde won't shut up about it." Jagger rolls his eyes, not taking it seriously.

"But you've heard her description, Brother?" I ask, and he shakes his head in rebuttal. "Raven hair, lavender eyes. She's a Blood Witch. Sound familiar?"

"You think she's the Lost Princess." *Not a question.*

I offer him a slight nod.

"Hot damn! Are we going on a field trip topside?" Interest creeps into Jagger's voice. It had been many years since we left our realm.

"I've already dispatched a darkling ahead to scout. She will report to me soon. Gather Dante & Bane from wherever they're holed up. Might I suggest checking the Den of Sorrows," I say, smirking at my brother, my second in line, and the commander of our forces.

"You got it." Jagger bounced on his heels as he spoke. "What do you want to do with Anise while we investigate?"

"Have our sister summoned to the throne room. She can preside over petty squabbles for the evening. And Jagger, pick one of your best men to keep watch over her; they are to report back if she unravels."

"Let's do some Earth Realm recon, Brother, and who knows? Maybe I'll find a willing earthling to pass some time." his eyes glow with desire.

My thoughts drift as I wait for my siblings to enter the chamber room. If this mysterious woman is indeed the Lost Princess, then she is valuable beyond measure. The Shadowfax Warlock will give an army for her. And more.

THE EARTH REALM IS livelier than the last time I visited. Back then, earthlings traveled by horse and used outdoor plumbing. As my brothers and I walk through the portal and make our way down the cobbled streets of Thornfall, the sights, sounds, and smells are intoxicating. I'd forgotten the scent - a mixture of aromatic foods paired with the faint undertone of lust and pollution.

I'm envious of this society, the creativity and freedoms they possess. It's something I don't have the luxury of entertaining as heir of the Netherworld. Sorcerers and dignitaries dictate my nights with their endless demands. Keeping my citizens safe and alive is a full-time job, and even if I weren't entrapped by the confines of our traditions, my fate is sealed by another type of curse set upon my father's line. One I can't escape.

My darkling scout mentioned a location by the name of Gravestone connected to this mystery woman. How fitting, seeing as that's where she'll likely end up. It's none of my concern. She's a means to an end, but the closer we get to this Gravestone the greater the uneasiness grows.

As we enter, a striking dark-skinned woman stands tending the bar. Jagger lets out an audible groan, "Why don't they make 'em like *that* in the Netherworld? Great Horned Beasts, she is sinfully beautiful."

"Don't even think about it. You know what we're here to do," I warn. If the Lost Princess is in this dwelling, she'll become the most valuable bargaining chip our kingdom could ask for.

Dante and Bane have nothing to add to the conversation. As usual, they sit mute, staring at patrons with serpentine eyes. The twins prefer telepathy and only with each other unless ordered otherwise. I debated asking them both to patrol outside to help us keep a low profile and not alarm patrons with their "otherness," but decided against it. If we're walking into a trap, I need them close.

"Grab us some water," I tell Jagger.

"Water? Come on, man! We're in the Earth Realm. The liquor here is fantastic!" Jagger complains.

"We are not on vacation," I reply. Jagger looks as though he might challenge me, but thinks better of it.

"Fine, but if I get the chance to grab her number, I'm shooting my shot." His gaze observes the woman again, but he's halted mid-sentence by the same thing I am.

Another woman turns the corner, coming from the back of the building. Raven hair and lavender eyes, with an aura so heady it rolls from her in waves. I hold back, keeping my reaction internal. This dangerous creature is striking, devastating. The atmosphere heats with my moment of unchecked lust as the patrons roam each other, gyrating and exploring.

"Turn the volume down, bro. Unless you're into full-on bar orgies? I'm not opposed to it, but I doubt that's your intention." Jagger urges.

"Of course not." I snap, taming the intensity of my power, but my thoughts couldn't be tamed and against my better judgment, I stare, taking her in. The defiant smirk on her red lips. The way she moves as though the floor beneath her exists to hold up her feet. But it's her eyes that draw me in. The sadness under her bravado speaks of deep anguish. My instincts roar to destroy whoever, whatever, put it there.

As I tear my eyes from her, I notice my brothers watching. Tracking her movements, preparing for the thrill of a hunt. A torrent of power rockets to the surface, overwhelming me with the urge to beat each of them into submission. Possessive insanity courses through my veins.

We should go, but I can't stop myself from glancing back in her direction, only this time, she's staring right back. Our eyes lock, and I'm mystified by the lust I see burning in hers. Time stills as electricity builds between us. My instincts flare to life and the need to touch her overwhelms me. My cold dead heart stumbles and for the first time in centuries - it beats.

Rage fills me; this is sorcery, the little witch has spelled me. She will not play me for a fool. I meet her eyes with a ferocious gleam that promises violence. I will destroy her, this creature who dares to toy with the Heir of the Netherworld. Her eyes widen a fraction before she drops the bottle in her hands. The sound of breaking glass releases the hold she has on me. There is no mistake. I'm face to face with the Lost Princess.

"It's her." Jagger's voice drew from my thoughts.

"We'll take her now, brother." Dante and Bane spoke in unison.

My stomach clenches at those words. The thought of her at the mercy of my brothers activates something primal within me. *She. Is. Mine.* "No, we won't take her now. Head back to Anise." They nod as we slip out, using the commotion to move unseen.

We meet in the alleyway across the lane. I lift my hand to rip the fabric between our worlds, and Dante and Bane step through the portal without question. Hanging back, Jagger searches my face, forehead creased in concern. "Talk to me."

"There's not enough intel. She's ascended. Her power is more dominant than expected. By the shape of her legs, her stance, the predatory way she moves - she's been trained to fight. Go to Anise, be sure she hasn't fallen into a fit and ordered your guards to remove anyone's skin."

Jagger hikes a thumb up, ever the dutiful brother, but his eyes are full of suspicion. "Summon me if you need me, bro, and be careful." He gives me one more questioning glance.

"Go." I order, and he obeys.

I shift to an interior room of The Gravestone. Tuning my hearing towards the bar, I'll be alert to anyone moving in my direction. I begin my search, inspecting the desk and the papers strewn about. The Princess hid in plain sight, and I intended to find out how. There's a rectangular machine attached to the wall, slats holding cards with names and odd markings. I shuffle through until I find a name, Vivi Graves. So, that's what she's called on Earth Realm. I roll the words through my mind.

As I turn to exit, I come across a picture on the bookshelf. A little girl stares back at me from the lawn of Underhill Academy, beside a face I would recognize anywhere. Deacon Harwell. Evanora's lapdog and a formidable Warrior of Light. "You

clever bitch," I whisper to myself aloud. Evanora
had spirited my betrothed away, out of the reach
of The Netherworld and her agreement.

Gods below, it's true. The Lost Princess lives.

I spend the rest of the evening lurking in the
shadows of Thornfall, listening for whispers of
this 'Vivi Graves.' wanting to learn more about
her. The time for betrothals has long passed, and
without my father to honor it—I'm free from that
responsibility. My chest tightens. The way she
looked at me, she felt something.

Have the fates turned? No, her destiny lies with
the Shadow Warlock now. I'll deliver the Princess
to him as planned, and he'll do with her as he
pleases. The future of my realm depends on it.

BACK IN THE NETHERWORLD. I release my glamour
and enter our formidable caverns, where I'm
greeted by Anise shrieking in a fit of fury, "Kill
them, kill them all! Let me sit upon the throne
and deliver them to the Fields of Agony!"

Jagger has his hands full.

"Anise." I whisper as I enter the throne room, as
if consoling a child, "Why is my beautiful sister
so disappointed?"

"Killian!" a genuine smile appears on her
cherub-like face. "I was on the throne for hours,
and then Jagger demanded I leave. He doesn't
understand! We must punish them all. I've seen
evil, Killian. They took mother, and they ripped
her apart. I saw it, and they must pay!"

There was nobody in the room. Her mother,
Analle, had been dead for centuries, executed

by my father for attempting to drown Anise in the Dread River as an infant. Sirens are prickly, the nature of their power is emotional manipulation. They often go mad under the influence of their own magic, unable to separate reality from fiction, but my sister is in another situation entirely.

"Of course they did. And we will have our revenge. Does that sound nice?" She nods enthusiastically. "But first, we must get some rest. Right, my dear?" I sweep her crimson hair from her forehead. "Because what happens when we don't rest?"

"We aren't sharp of mind." she blushes, looking to the floor.

"And we need to be sharp, don't we, Anise?"

"Yes, Killian." she leans her head into my shoulder.

"Why don't we have some cakes sent to your rooms?" She smiles like a Cheshire cat at the mention of cakes. By the time she eats her favorite pastries, she'll sleep and when she wakes, she won't remember this.

"I don't know how you do it, man," Jagger bows his head to me, half-serious, half banter.

"Our sister grows more unhinged with every year that passes that the madness takes her mind." I frown at uttering the words aloud.

"Come, we can wax poetic about our fragile-minded sister later. Right now, we have much to discuss. The Lost Princess is no longer lost, and we now have the Shadow Warlock's greatest weakness in our grasp." I clap him on his shoulder as we head to the training fields.

CHAPTER NINE

VIVI

CLUTCHING THE TOWER CARD in my hand, I inspect the back and front until I'm satisfied there are no enchantments attached. All is clear, so I slide it into the liner under my bomber jacket. It's time to leave, but I can't resist stopping one more time to glance over my shoulder. I burn a picture into my memory, the culmination of my life. A nice bed, some quirky knick-knacks, piles of clothes, and memories. Because something tells me, this is a crossroads.

Whatever happens next, nothing will ever be the same again. I'm waving goodbye to life as I know it. My heart clenches at the thought of my loved ones finding the note I left; the pain I am about to cause them hurts me to the core. All I can hope for is that Deacon trusts me on this. He has to know I wouldn't do this without a damn good reason. The man created me in his image for the star's sake. He taught me everything I know. And by watching his actions closely, I learned much more than he had intended. And now? I will put every skill he'd ever shown me to good use.

Waltzing back into the Academy is a risk, the biggest one I've ever taken. I know the monsters who hide behind the gates; I've seen the evil glinting in their eyes as they forced my hands to do unspeakable things. The satisfaction plastered all over their auras after they wielded me as a weapon. It was a power rush to them. Ultimate control happens when you have something to fear. And I was their monster.

I could leave the first time because they had nothing to blackmail me with. Manipulation has been the only recourse for the Elders. But now? Checkmate. They have something I can't walk away from. I don't believe for one second all they want are questions answered - I'm smarter than that. They have eyes all over this town. They are aware of my movements. They know I haven't been in contact with my sister. So, I'll be ready for whatever they can throw my way. If I have to use my magic against them, so be it. I will find her, and I have no plans to be held there.

A brush of fur on my leg brings me back to my present reality. Calypso belts a low, drawn-out howl. The saddest sound I've ever heard. It's painful to be apart from our familiars, and I feel her distress like a second skin. *"I'll always find you."* I brush comforting words through our bond, and she purrs against my mental barrier. "But you need to lie low, okay? Go to the mountains and don't come out, no matter what is happening to me." I looked into her golden eyes and held my forehead to hers, holding in a strangled sob. *"I will come for you."*

She growls low, her way of expressing discontent. But she obeys (for the first time in her entire life) splitting off the path headed towards the caves on the mountainside. When she's traveled far enough out of view, I crumple to the ground, sucking tears back up into my face and stifling a silent scream. I cannot falter now; I must see this through.

Slinging the backpack across my shoulders, I start the mile-long trek through the empty streets of Thornfall. Up, up, up the hill we go - to the Temple of Doom, House of Horrors, Nightmare on my Street, Bordello of Bullshit. And yeah, okay, also the place where I failed algebra... twice. But who's counting?

The snaking path propels me further into the tree-lined forest. A chilled breeze lingers over me while I climb the steep incline. My skin stiffens as I catalog every sound, every shadow. During the day, the trees are beautiful, swaying in the breeze. But at night, they take on a foreboding presence. Like claws on a beast, dark limbs reach forward, ready to rip and tear into my flesh. Call me paranoid, but after tonight? I've got reasons. The closer I move toward those imposing gates; the louder the silence grows with my apprehension.

My phone chimes, and I jump, startled half to death. I thought I left it back at the apartment. This doesn't seem like the ideal place to stop for a chat. So, why am I reaching into the pocket of my backpack? Because I'm an emotional masochist.

I turn the light down on the screen and pull up the message.

Prince Charming: *Miss me, Kitten?*

Of all the messages in all the fucking world right now. Why this? I throw my gaze upward at the stars and viciously flip them the finger.

Is it wise to tempt the fates? No. But godsdammit! This man is the equivalent of a supernatural lady Viagra. I don't have time for this.

Vivi: *You tell me. You're the professional stalker.*

Prince Charming: *Only when they have bewitching eyes and vicious mouths like yours.*

Vivi: *They? So, I'm not your one and only then? How disappointing.*

Prince Charming: *Where are you?*

Vivi: *I'm on a date. And he's wicked cute! Why?*

Prince Charming: *Lies don't suit you, Kitten. I know what happened at your place of business.*

Ahh, shit. I don't want to talk about this right now. I know I said I didn't need a fucking Prince Charming in the bar when I was attacked, but when it comes to my friends' safety. Where was he? I type the only words I can say.

Vivi: *Then why didn't you help? Asshole.*

I don't know what I was thinking answering messages. I should throw my phone straight into the ocean or smashing it to pieces on the rocks. We'll just call it temporary insanity, fueled by being a total chickenshit in the eerie woods. Fuck him and his mind games. I don't know why I never learn? The hot ones are always crazy. I turn off the phone and stomp it into the hard ground, satisfied by the crunching sound it makes. I'll get a new one later, but for now—no more distractions.

As I moved to stand back up, an arm snakes around my neck as a soft hand covered my mouth. I positioned my hand to pull my dagger from my boot when a voice whispered. "Vivi, it's me."

"Marlow?"

As I turn, she steps from behind the thicket of bushes I was up against.

"You thought you could run without me? I knew it. I knew you were going to do something stupid. Dammit! Why are you always so primed and ready to rush off headfirst into bullshit and martyr yourself?!" she scream-whispers into my ear, hands around my neck, trying not to bring attention to us in the middle of this forest path. Some sentinels patrol these trails.

I pull away and swat at her arms, motioning for her to let me go, and she squeezes harder. She squeezes until I think I might pass out before she relaxes her muscles and slumps into my back. I turn around in her arms and come face to face with tear-streaked cheeks and dark eyes that looked like they might stab me with my own dagger.

"Marlow," I plead, "You don't understand. They'll track me. They'll keep coming. They almost killed Linc! What if they had succeeded? And what happens next time? Will it be you, Calypso, or Deacon? I can't let that happen. I can't! The Elders want me. The night creatures want me. I'm the common denominator!" I suck in a shaky breath, not able to get enough air into my lungs through the panic climbing my chest.

"So, you run without saying goodbye? You always think you know what's best. What's wrong? Can't be bothered to tell your friends, your family, what you're doing - so we can be left to wonder if you're dead or alive. You don't think we will search for you? That Linc won't go crazy tearing this town to shreds, and Deacon won't comb the entire realm to find you!"

"Saves on group rates?" I stare down at my boots, unable to meet her furious eyes. I have never seen Marlow this angry, and if we weren't in such a messed-up situation, it would impress me. But I don't have time to say another word.

"You're not funny." She takes a deep breath and gears up for ass-chewing round two. "And of course, you didn't, because you can't think past that wall of fury living inside you. One-track mind, you don't think about anyone or anything except vengeance and spite. When are you going to let it go and start living? Your anger makes you selfish, Genevieve." Marlow shoves me hard as she releases her frustration.

I stumble backward, falling over a branch, landing straight on my ass with a thump that reverberates through my tailbone as my hand slips in a mossy substance. The smell of damp soil and rotted leaves on my fingers.

"Did you just hit me?" A laugh bubbles up in my chest. I try to stifle it, but a choked sound squeaks out. We lock eyes, and the tension fizzles into comedic relief. I grab her arm and drag her into the dirt beside me, laughing through streaky tears. Marlow throws her arms around me and we hug until the giggle-tears are all dried up.

"I'm sorry, Lowe. I know I can be a real dickhead, and I don't think before I act. But this time? I promise it's the right thing. I saw this, my mother showed me." I recounted the vision that played in my head when I touched the box. Trying to convince her this time I wasn't being impulsive.

"You're going into the Academy." She states plainly.

"I have to. I don't know why my sister is so important - aside from the obvious, but I know I need to find her. It's all connected."

Marlow releases a shallow breath, searching my face. Her mouth is tight and angry, but I know she can see the truth of it. The first puzzle piece is in that shit hole - and I can't start without it.

"Well, don't be stupid bringing your bag in." She looks around at the treetops swaying with the wind. The smell of ozone hangs in the air.

"Give it to me; I'll put it in our spot." There was a corner of the grounds that had a retaining wall. Back in the sixth grade, we had carved out some stones with our elemental magic. I used earth, and Marlow used air. We created an undetectable pocket to stash the contraband we didn't want to take before entering the gates. And they said I lacked creativity? Pshh. They weren't paying close enough attention.

"Yeah, okay. Good idea."

"Surprise! I have those sometimes, especially when my best friend lets me help her." She couldn't resist the dig, and I deserved it. "I'll stay close to home and monitor my father. If he makes a move, I'll know about it."

We sit in stillness for a few minutes. Neither of us wants to give life to our fears by speaking them out loud. I'm going to pull this off, or I'm in deep shit. Possibly a coffin. It's a toss-up, really.

"Where is Calypso?" Marlow finally asks.

"I sent her to the caves." My eyes well at the thought of it, and she grabs my hand. No words are needed.

"You are positive this is the answer?" Marlow has to ask; it's who she is.

"Lowe, I can't let anyone else get hurt." With determination showing in my eyes, we sit on the jagged rocks and dirt in the dark for an unreasonable amount of time, trying to prolong the inevitable. But eventually, I hand over my backpack, my belongings, and everything important to me.

Before we part ways, she grabs me by the shirt and grasps my chin. "Listen closely. You are a mother fucking badass. I don't care what you have to fight through. You will come back to me, or I'll rain hell down upon every single one of these fuckers until I have you back. That's a promise."

CHAPTER TEN

UNDERHILL ACADEMY

A VAST IRON GATE with enormous metal doors on either side stands in front of Underhill Academy, like imposing armor, protecting its secrets and sins. The thirteen thick, round towers are both defensive and decorative, connected by wide stone walls made of dark limestone. A wooden bridge and gate building is the only passage into the fortress, built upon a mountain surrounded by cliffs and water. Unless you have a boat and some dynamite to break through the portcullis in the underbelly, you aren't getting in. A handful of waterfalls flow into various small channels that lead to the sea; too bad I'm fresh out of boats.

So, the front gate it is! My nerves are absolutely shot; my throat constricts like I've swallowed a handful of razor blades. Standing out of sight for several minutes, second thoughts creep into my psyche. *Am I really going through with this?* The memory of Linc lying bloody on the concrete flashes through my mind. I stand up straight, puff my chest, and hold my head high. *Yes, I am.*

I reach into the inner pocket of my jacket and pull out the card Bridgewater left for me. Striding up to the gate as though I don't have a care in the world, I say, "Hello, Churchill. Long time, no see."

We're very much acquainted already.

"Vivi Graves. What are you doing out in the forest at this time of night? Nothing disorderly, I hope." Churchill roams suspicious eyes over me, noting my lack of... well... everything but a piece of flimsy cardboard.

"I have a golden ticket this time, Churchy!" I smile boldly while waving the tower card in front of him. "Aw, did you miss me?"

"Not particularly." The distaste crinkling his features amuses me. So much for a warm welcome! Churchill nods to the Rune Force Guards, and they pull the iron gates open to let me pass.

Down the rabbit hole we go...

"Thanks a bunch, fellas!" I mutter as several black and red-clad operatives follow me to the archway, faces solemn and cold. They sure are stuffy around here, no sense of humor at all.

One of my personal escorts knocks twice on the heavy wooden door as a small framed, wiry-haired staff member opens and glances at me with shock. "Churchy number two!!" I cry out like I'm seeing an old friend for the first time. Churchill and the other Churchill are brothers. I never learned their names. I only know the difference because one is built like a brick shit house, and the other looks like he's been dug up from a grave site and stuffed into a fancy suit to greet guests.

"Miss Graves," Churchill number two offers me a displeased expression. "Do you have any idea what time it is?"

I glance at my empty wrist. "No, sorry. The watch must be broken. I've always been fantastic at making grand entrances, though, huh?"

"Indeed," he delivers another withering glare before he remembers his impeccable manners. "Please, come in. Proceed to the lounge while I wake our headmistress. I'll have our kitchen staff fetch you some tea."

"Got any tequila?" I waggle my brow at him, pushing my luck as far as I can stretch it. He turns on his heel for me to follow, not bothering to dignify that with a response.

The ornate hallway is shaped like a T. The two extensions branch into separate wings of the Academy. Turn right, and you're headed towards dormitories and classrooms. Turn left, and... well... you're headed for the "other" part of the fortress. The second floor is bigger than the first, which creates a stylish overhang around the entire foyer. This floor has a more distinct style than the floor above.

We come to a stop at the first door to the left, which houses a sitting room. One long table and five high-backed chairs live in the front. Bookshelves and various portraits of long-gone former masters and mistresses cover the walls. A velvet couch rests along the wall closest to the door. "Please have a seat, Miss Graves. The Mistress will be along," Churchill number two announces as he turns on his heel and exits the room.

I exhale a long, shaky breath. This isn't the first or even the twentieth time I've sat on this couch, awaiting instructions from the Elders. Or punishment for my disruptive behavior, depending on the incident. My eyes roam the walls—it hasn't changed a bit. Still sterile and impersonal. I stand up to grab a generic magazine from the coffee table, fully expecting to be here for a while.

When the door opens again, Agnes walks through with a cup and serving platter. Looking as though she hadn't had a good night's sleep in years. "Vivi! What a sight for this old lady's sore eyes. Have some tea, dear. What on earth brings you back to Underhill? And at this hour?" her kind eyes threaten to open up my trap, spilling all the details of what brought me to this moment.

Goddess, I have missed her! I didn't realize how much until now. Agnes is one of the few staff members who showed me kindness. Never judging what I am or what they had forced me to do inside these walls. "Agnes, I've missed...." I'm cut off by several voices as I am about to stand up and give her a hug.

"The Elder's approach," she eyes me. "Watch yourself, girl. Things have changed since the last time I found you in this room." She turns to curtsy at the string of jackasses entering the doorway, glancing back at me with a warning in her eyes.

"So, kind of you to grace us with your presence, Blood Seer." A booming voice fills the space, moving to his seat at the head table in the lavish room. Dark slicked back hair hangs over a lean, menacing face. His narrow eyes follow me like prey—Faustus Culpepper, Marlow's father, Head of the Council, and a genuine piece of shit.

"Like I had a choice," I snort. What a joke.

Behind him, the rest of the Elders file in. Invidia Tamsin, Niam Blake, and

Meredith Bridgewater representatives from each bloodline. A Shadowfax stand-in, a Bloodgood nobody, and the Darkmoor bitchface turned Head Mistress. Niam doesn't belong on the Council - he's not even a true Bloodgood, just a distant relative with a less than a drop of my heritage in his warlock veins. But seeing as I am unfit to take my place, which translates to "won't bend to their bullshit," there he sits, with his mocking sneer and greasy shit brown hair.

Invidia stares me down, twirling long bony fingers in her frizzy red hair. Cold indifference spreads across her gorgeous face. How the gods could make someone so beautiful be so ugly on the inside is a mystery to me.

I observe each of them as well as my surroundings, like Deacon taught me. Watching their mannerisms, the way their eyes move, opening the Sight to search for anything I can exploit. I'm sizing up my competition, finding them all detestable. My eyes move to the empty chair at the table as Faustus observes me.

How did I miss an empty chair? I'm kind of a big deal if we bring in guest appearances, yeah? Guess they think they've caught the big fish. Jokes on them.

"I hope you enjoy our newest representative, Genevieve. They'll be along shortly, but first, let's catch up." The sneer forming on his lips gives me pause. I don't like this vibe at all.

So, I run my mouth. "Aw, you found a new friend for your club, Faustus? How sweet. Did you get friendship bracelets?" I smiled big, blinking my lavender eyes at him as if there was nothing strange about this meeting at all. Inside, my heart is beating out of my chest.

"You will address me as Elder, Miss Graves." Violence flashes in his eyes.

"You wish." I clap back. I'll pay for that later, but I don't care. I hate this motherfucker for so much more than how he treats me, so this isn't the first and won't be the last in my line of insults.

The rest of the Elders sit in uncomfortable silence as they wait for Faustus to begin whatever this "discussion" entails. Niam bounces his feet in anticipation under the table. Whatever they have in store for me is making him pleased. Bridgewater lends me a melancholy gaze. She's the only one who doesn't appear pleased to be in this room right now. If I weren't suspicious of all of them, I would say she wasn't on board with this. *Interesting.*

"Genevieve Graves, we have accused you of using dark magic to release your sister from our care. How do you plead?" Faustus smiles at me.

WHAT!!!

"That's bullshit, and you know it!" I'm searching the faces of the elders in front of me; I do not know what I'm looking for, but I don't find it.

"Is that your formal plea, then?" Niam devours me with his eyes, loving the turn of events taking place.

"My formal plea? You're kidding, right? And how do you think I used dark magic to free someone I knew nothing about until a few days ago?" I blatantly stare them all down. Clenching my fists, willing the flames to stay inside my body.

This is fucked.

"Am I to understand you're entering a plea of not guilty, then?" Faustus asks, brow raised.

"Of course, I'm not fucking guilty, you flaccid ogre! But it doesn't matter, does it? You have me where you want me. Where is she? What did you do with her?" I launch into a rather foul-mouthed tirade, losing every shred of civility I have left.

The door opens before I can continue...

"Ah, our newest comrade has arrived! Welcome." Faustus smiles wickedly, "We were getting to the good part. Please sit."

I turn to see who the next asshat on parade is, and feel like someone has punched me straight in the gut. *What the fuck is he doing here?* No way, this can't be happening! I refuse to believe it. Faustus's voice breaks through my mental stupor. "Genevieve, this is Killian. Our newest emissary. Though I believe you've met?"

"Emissary? Are you working with him?" I ask Killian, betrayal etched into my disbelieving face.

Killian shoots me a passing glance, his gaze judging and calculated. A cool indifference settles on his gorgeous face. I try to force him to look at me, to give me that heat filled flash of turquoise. The irritating smirk. I'd even allow the sexy mojo thing right now. Something, *anything* to let me know he's not really here working with these tyrants. But it's pointless. He won't look at me at all. Did this motherfucker think he can play with me?

The glare I aim in his direction could melt steel. I brush my hands across my face. *What an idiot!* I knew I should have incinerated him the moment he stepped into my life. Turned him to ash! The backstabbing, double-crossing, panty-melting shithead!

Sent to watch over me, my ass. Prince Charming blah blah blah. Mr. Cute text messages and sexy dreams. But what do I expect? I mean, of course, he's a monstrous prick. Those are the only men I attract! I should've known. Stupid. So fucking stupid to care about him at all! My heart trembles; I can feel it cracking in my chest as he opens his mouth to speak...

"Vivi has been quite entertaining." He cocks his head in my direction. No sign of the familiarity he's so boldly displayed in the past. No recognition of what's been burning between us.

Did I imagine it?

No, I just fell for it.

My heart cracks a little more...

I will not shed tears in front of these monsters. I refuse, I won't do it. *Think, Vivi. Pull your head out of your ass and your vagina out of the daydreams about this fucking liar and think!* My blood sings, rising to the surface. No, no, please. But it's too late. My hands erupt in flames, incinerating the couch and curtains next to me.

Well, the secrets are out now. There's no going back. Might as well have a bonfire!

I raise my hands in the air. For the first time in my life, I let my flames free. They barrel towards the council, poised for maximum damage. And then Killian stands before them, hands glowing blue - and a barrier surrounds them, repelling my flames.

Are you kidding me? First, I fall for his bullshit. Then, when my guard is down, he drop-kicks my ass with a plot twist I should've seen coming. *Hot guy is really working for the enemy.*

In hindsight, I walked right into that one.

I throw everything I've got at him, eyes wild with fury and the sting of betrayal. But he does not burn. "You're *protecting* them?" a heartbroken scream tears from my mouth. When he finally makes eye contact, all I see is icy dismissal.

"I will fucking kill you, Killian!" I scream, throat ravaged with unshed tears.

"Seize her," Faustus's booming voice rises above the chaos, and a string of Rune Force guards fill the room. The click of metal resounds behind me, and my flames sputter out as I fall to my knees. *Magic nullifying cuffs.* "Take her to the Halls of Repentance."

"NO! No, you can't do this. You can't put me down there, please!" Panic fills my chest, threatening to suffocate me. "I didn't do this. I didn't set her free. I don't even know who she is!" I plead, but it falls upon deaf ears. I turn to Bridgewater, knowing she saw my reaction to the news of my sister. Hoping she will come to my rescue, my eyes search her face, begging. She knows I am innocent of this, but she turns to me with an apologetic glance and makes no move to intervene.

Fuck. Fuck, fuck, FUCK!

The guards drag me up by my arms as I fight back. Kicking at shins, aiming for balls, using my elbows as pointy weapons between their ribs. Screaming my rage all the way down the hall and to the dungeon, where they toss me into a piss-filled cell and slam the door, locking it behind me. I scramble to the only semi-clean corner and curl in on myself.

"I've been waiting for this day for so long, little Bloodgood." Faustus picks at his fingernails. "It will devastate my daughter. The tragic loss of her dearest friend, of course. Shall we hold an execution? A beheading!" he claps his hands together like a child with a new toy.

I gasp, a strangled sob leaks from my lips, not able to hold it in.

"Oh, don't be so dramatic." he sneers.

"I don't understand," I whisper, lifting my head to meet his smug gaze.

"I expect you don't. You'll keep your pretty little head for now. But we'll have to make it believable, won't we? Can't have your shifter mutt and a meddlesome blood warrior sniffing around. That would put such a damper on our plans for you." His gleeful expression creates bile in my throat. "Remove her cuffs; the cell is warded."

I sit quietly as the guards file into my cell, removing the cuffs. I posed myself to hide my hand, calling fire to me. I was about to light his ass up as he kicked me hard in the stomach. Knocking the air from my lungs. My gasp echoes off the walls surrounding me.

CHAPTER ELEVEN

UNDERHILL ACADEMY

A PAIR OF WORN statues mark the entrance to
this dungeon. Beyond them lies a bare room.
Its dusky stone floor is covered in puddles of
unknown body fluids, rodents, and jagged broken
stones cut into the skin of my legs and feet. A
nauseating stench of rotting flesh burns my eyes
and nostrils, causing my stomach to clench. The
torches lining the halls are the only light offered
in this dank place.

They scarcely allow me to see the outline of
the other cells, but I know this place through
memory. Those memories assault my mind now,
like dreams on repeat. At one point, I was the
scariest monster in these halls. Prisoners shook,
pleaded, and pissed themselves as I took down
my hood and stepped into their cells. Placing my
hands on either side of their head as I sucked
the memories from them with brutal, agonizing
swiftness. If found guilty - I was the judge, I was
the jury, and the executioner. I was young when
it began. Under the thrall of warlocks and witches
more powerful than me, stripped of my free will,
my only option was to obey.

I lay unmoving in the furthest corner of my
cell, replaying every face I had committed to
memory.

*Black, oily hair hangs over a thin, wild face. Round
hazel eyes watch me in terror as I gently touch her
temples. Just a child, she was innocent of the crimes
leveled against her. I sensed it with every fragment
of my being.* "She is innocent." *My small voice echoes
through the hall.*

"Do as you're told!" *Faustus's sinister voice
commands without mercy.*

*I suppress a cry as I push my power into the child's
mind. Blood pours from her eyes first as she screams in
agony, begging for mercy. The man standing behind me
doesn't have to speak. I can feel his satisfaction as I drag
the life from her veins - it pours from every available
surface until she sways and falls to the ground. Her
red-stained eyes lay open, unseeing.*

*Rough fingers press into the underside of my arm as
I'm dragged sobbing from the Halls of Repentance back
into the opulence and exquisite background of the main
floor.*

"Go wash yourself and don't be late for morning
assembly." *I am dismissed.*

The vision fades, and I'm transported back to
myself, cold and starving on the filthy ground. A
pair of boots come into my hazy view as I attempt
to lift my head.

"Pull yourself up, girl. We have an assignment
for you. A cell to visit. I trust you haven't
forgotten your purpose." Faustus and crew are
standing before the iron bars, staring down
at my humiliation. Invidia and Niam position
themselves behind him, exchanging knowing
looks with one another. My gaze travels to

the handsome face next to Faustus. Killian's nostrils flare, tightness showing in his eyes. For a moment, I hoped he wouldn't really let this happen. I hoped whatever was between us was real.

"Fuck you." I hiss, shaking my head at Faustus.

"That's unfortunate, Miss Graves. I hoped you would be more accommodating given your current circumstances." He stares at me, waiting for my change of heart.

When he doesn't receive it, he lifts his hands and mutters an incantation meant to steal my will and replace it with his own. A vein pulses in his jaw, sweat beads on his forehead as he exerts more energy, trying to bend me to his will. But what he doesn't know is, the first magic lesson I requested from Marlow when I freed myself from the clutches of this cesspool was mind barriers. I bolster my defense as he strains to gain control. His body tensed as his teeth grind.

"Not so much fun when your *prodigy* can stand up for herself, is it?" I smile widely, enjoying his reaction. "Punish them yourself."

"Open her cell! You will submit, Genevieve. Or you'll be on the receiving end of my wrath. Get up!" A heavy kick connects with my ribs. Sucking in a painful breath, I wrap my arms protectively around my middle.

"I'll die before I submit to you." My body stiffens in pain, but I roll myself to my side and spit on his boots.

I mean it. I'll let him kill me before I become what I once was. I'll let him murder me twice before he uses me as bait. Did he ever even have my sister here? I'm doubting it. This was a trap. I

let my emotions rule me and walked right into it.
Face first.

His lips curl back, baring teeth. He cracks his
neck from side to side and kicks me violently
in my side, my stomach, my ribs. Uncontrolled
rage surges through him, and all I can do is curl
into a ball to protect my head. He lands blow
after blow until my vision blurs. I glance at Killian
through the haze of agony, hoping for... I don't
know what I am hoping for, but his face remains
expressionless.

Dizziness takes over as the next blow connects
with my face. "Enough!" I think I hear the word
fall from Killian's lips before I lose consciousness.

*Sweet, blissful peace washes over me as I open my
eyes. I'm lying in the softest bed of strange gray
grass, next to a massive tree with multiple stems and
needle-like leaves. Red berries dot throughout the
gnarled branches. It reminds me of Samhain, or maybe
the 'Sleepy Hollow' movie. I reach for one of the berries,
so hungry I can hardly think.*

*"I wouldn't do that if I were you." A pleasant voice
calls out.*

*It's familiar, but I'm unable to place it. As I turn to
investigate, the woman from the festival tent comes into
view. Her black veil covers her creamy skin, red lips
showing through. She sits on a large rock close to where
I lie.*

*"The berries are edible, but the seeds will kill." She lifts
her veil, and my mouth falls open. The Night Queen...*

"You're the... you're her." I stumble over my words.

*She smiles, and it immediately softens her sharp
features. She moves from the rock closer, cupping my
shoulder, offering comfort. "The Goddess of Night? Yes,
child. Among many other things."*

Her sheer red dress moves like she's captivated by the wind as she glides toward the tree and picks berries, piling them in her palm.

"Where am I?"

"You're somewhere between." She states matter-of-factly. "I've been trying to reach you. It seems I've missed an important window," her hands move to her breast bone. "No matter. You're here now, but in a few minutes, you'll be pulled back to your current reality. So, you must listen, Daughter of Oracles. Take these, and when the time is right, use them."

She hands me the berries, dried now, shriveled to mostly seed.

"Why do you keep calling me that? Daughter of Oracles. What does it mean?"

"All in time, sweet one, all in time. But now you must obey. When the time is right, you will put three seeds into your guard's mouth. Do not hesitate."

"Okay?" I don't understand, but my instincts tell me to trust her.

She bends over me, a pained expression in her captivating eyes. A bone-shaking howl cleaves the silence, and she turns to listen intently. "It's time."

Her voice sounds like graceful music, and my eyes grow heavy. I want to stay here forever...

Pain erupts through me like a raging fire. If I had anyone left to pray to, I would pray now. For forgiveness, to wash away the blood on my hands I never wanted. For salvation, maybe. But our gods abandoned us long ago, replaced by greed and false idols. Those with the most power are the gods now.

Searing agony spreads through every part of my body; the smell of death and decay fills my nose as I struggle to open my eyes. Was it a dream? A vision? I'm not entirely sure. But a voice from the cell beside me jerks me back to reality.

"Fight," it whispers.

My fingers brush my side as I assess my injuries. A cracked upper rib juts into my lung as I struggle to breathe. Hot agony radiates from my spine into my side, and I still myself, listening to how my breathing sounds. Nothing is coming from the left side. It's punctured; I feel blood filling my lungs as my breaths become shallower. My head swims with the need to succumb to the damage.

"Tell me your injuries," the voice from the next cell whispers.

"I... umm. My rib is broken, it's punctured my lung." I wheeze, words almost inaudible. "My head, I think it's..." I'm struggling to stay awake. My hand moves to touch my face and slips into something wet, vomit.

"Tell me more," the voice calls out like a beacon, tethering me to it.

"Concussion. I have a concussion." I struggle to get the words out as dizziness overtakes me, and I vomit again. Covered in sweat. "Fever, infection."

"Use your blood magic, whatever you have left. Guide your blood from your lung into your chest cavity and then seal the hole. Get it into your stomach." The whisper is becoming faint now. "Are you still with me?"

"Yes," I croak out through the pain threatening to pull me under.

"Pull it through and seal the hole. Save yourself. Do it now." The voice grows more insistent.

So, I do. I will myself to pull the blood from my chest. Using everything I have within me; I guide it drop by drop to my throat, and then down. When I feel my stomach filling with blood, I choke and sputter. Pink froth dribbles from my mouth to the stones under me. I'm choking on it, there's too much. I struggle with every breath.

I'm going to die here.

An involuntary cough radiates through me. Pain etches every cell as a clot as large as my fist dislodges itself from my throat and spills out of my mouth. This is the most disgusting thing I've ever experienced. *Push it out, push it all out.* Okay, I can do this. I move the blood from my lungs for several agonizing minutes and let it ooze from my nose and mouth, choking me in reverse. The effort takes me back under...

My mind swims with visions of Killian's face, his beautiful face. He slides beside me as his warm hands caress my stomach, moving lower to my thighs. Gentle kisses pepper my neck as I lean back into him. I can't get enough of his heat and the feeling of him against me. My body lights up involuntarily with lust; his hands are everywhere and nowhere at the same time. Sweat beads between my breasts as he leans over me, running his tongue along the edge of my neck. I shiver; a slight sound escapes my throat as he growls. His mouth crushes on mine, and electricity fires through all my nerve endings. I kiss his demanding lips back with matching intensity. He leans back, blue flames dancing in his eyes as he leans down. "Come back to me, Kitten." His husky voice in my ear drives me wild. "Come back to me..."

Come back to him? I can't. I'm dying. This can't be real, right? I must be delusional.

Leaning over in misery, I vomit dark brown dregs of something resembling coffee grounds onto myself. Choking and gasping, more pink froth and jellylike clots exit my mouth and leak from my nose. The taste is putrid, and the smell is even worse.

"That's it. Get it all out so you can breathe." The voice from the next cell is whispering again. "Fight, it won't be long now."

"How long have we been here? How long have I been out?" I choke out through the haze. Slick sweat rolls down my forehead as I watch rats gnaw at the pile of fluids I've left next to my face. Sharp pains dot my legs as I notice them biting my calves and ankles. My lips tremble, and I shake, fear gripping me.

"Three days, maybe four. And you were out for a couple of hours," Urgency fills the space between our cells as the voice pauses. "Close your eyes right now! Do not sleep, but close them and keep them closed until I toss this stone to the empty cell across the way. When you hear it? Move."

Within moments, a thunderous clanking noise echoes as the outer dungeon doors open. Heavy footsteps inch closer. I can smell overpowering cologne as a key lodges into the lock on my cell and the creaking bars open. I take inventory as I lay still, keeping shallow breaths steady. My thumb moves involuntarily, and I realize the seeds from my dream are in my clenched fist.

So, it wasn't a dream? The heavy cologne tells me Faustus isn't here. It's not his scent. The smell becomes more potent as the guard comes closer until he's leaning over me - checking my breathing.

A stone hits the limestone wall across the narrow walkway. It lands in an empty cell. As I crack one eye open, the guard turns his head towards the noise, and I see my moment to strike. *Goddess, I hope I'm not crazy or hallucinating.* It takes every ounce of energy to lift myself, but I manage it. The guard looks back to me, jaw hanging open at the sight of me standing up - staring him in the face. I take the seeds and shove them in his mouth, simultaneously kicking out to his shin; he reacts and swallows. Nearly choking, which gives me the utmost satisfaction.

And then all hell breaks loose.

Flames erupt in the cell next to me, and I watch the metal pooling on the rocks in a neat puddle as a hulking beast burst into my cell. Flames still blazing from his mouth, he roars as he picks me up and slams my cell shut with the guard still inside it.

With another fiery bellow, more flames melt the lock to itself. And then we're moving fast. My eyes roll in my head. My battered body is a writhing mass of agony and suffering. It's too much to bear, so I tuck myself into this creature's chest, inhaling the musky scent on its skin as I lose my battle with consciousness.

CHAPTER TWELVE

VIVI

A BURNING SENSATION RADIATES from my chest down to my toes. I clench my fist, digging my nails into my palm in search of some relief from this torment. My head feels weightless, everything around me seems to spin, and nausea skids up my throat. For a moment, I think about giving in to the hurt, letting it take me. I will not live much longer, anyway. With every passing minute, my body grows weaker. I can feel infection slithering its way through my veins, sweat pooling on my forehead.

I struggle to open my eyes. Dark clouds spin through the sky above me, vicious and angry. Lightning strikes close, making the hairs on my body stand on end. Terrifying monsters reveal their expressions through the blue and purple flashes of light. Blood rains down in tiny particles from the sky. I close my eyes, blocking out my Sight. Willing the nothingness to devour me. *I don't like this vision.*

"She's fading, Bro. Her skin is slick and pale, her lips are blue. She has a fever, man. Infection is setting in. Row faster!" An anxious voice disrupts my imagination.

Again, the discomfort is disorienting, and it's affecting my judgment. It is strange to be aware of when you're not working with all the marbles and helpless to change it. I think I might be hallucinating. But I can't be sure. My body jerks to the side, hitting something solid, and I cry out. Throbbing pain bathes me in misery.

"Don't you die on me." A pair of warm hands cradle my face. The voice attached to those hands whispers softly, so quietly. Delicious warmness overflows inside me, and I feel like I'm floating in a dream world.

"Take the paddles! Her rib is getting knocked around. I need to stabilize her before it punctures her lung again." I like this voice; I want to wrap it around my fingers and rub it all over me.

"I can stabilize her; the shirt needs to come off, it's filthy. And I need to bind her ribs. Row! It was your stupid idea to climb into the sea, you idiot. Now, look at us, caught in a Hell storm in a gods damned paddle boat. There were decent portals we could have taken." The other voice argues.

Goddess, my visions are bizarre.

"We don't know what she is. Therefore, we don't know if she can survive the portals! I already told you that. And you will not *touch* her!" the voice growls, possessive.

"I think it's a little too late for that now, isn't it?" a needling response hurtles back at him.

Another growl erupts. "Take. The. Paddles. NOW."

Why did the voice say I have an infection? I strain to remember... Faustus! That slimy motherfucker put me in a cell. I refused to use my powers. That happened in the dungeon, but someone broke me out. I remember fire. Was it mine? No. It was a different type of flame.

A blood-curdling scream interrupts my thoughts. My body tenses, someone is tearing my skin from my bones, the pulling feeling threatens to tear me in two. The screams are coming from *me*. A sharp bite grips around my middle section as my heart pumps so fast it makes me dizzy. I'm shaking, the edges of my vision blur. I think I hear something tearing. Oh, Goddess, I'm dying, aren't I? An icy sensation settles over me. Tiny blood particles from the sky hit my bare chest. My mind sways, pulling me back under.

A violent jerk pulls me from the darkness. My eyes open as I stare up at a naked chest, large black wings tattooed from shoulder to shoulder. The words 'daemonium rex' wrap around it in scrolling letters. Warm hands drape around me as soft fabric pulls on my ribs. I try to adjust my vision as I sway back and forth. I... I think this is real. My thoughts are muddy. I try harder to focus, fighting against the fatigue.

"Hey, Little Monster. You're awake." The other voice calls out from the opposite side of the boat, grabbing my attention.

The man from Gravestone. The tall one with the amber eyes... he had jokes, the one who came with Killian. "You're a dragon."

"A dragon and a God, why else would I be so good-looking? Don't think I didn't notice you peeking." he grins at me, a mixture of mischief and teasing. The wind whips his dark hair into his glowing eyes as the rain pelts his angled face.

"That is enough, Jagger." Killian bristles.

Jagger, I like that name. It fits him. I'm doing
my best to focus, but my body is numb now. I'm
cold, soaking wet. Glancing down at my chest,
I find an unfamiliar shirt wrapped around me
like a tube top. It smells heavenly, it smells like
peace. There's no blood. Wasn't it raining blood
particles on me before? I can still sense the
sickness darkening my veins, poisoning me from
the inside. But this is real. Isn't it?

I'm in a boat, in a storm. I'm with Killian.

I'm with Killian? Realization blooms in my
befuddled mind as I strain to look into the face
next to me. A fresh wave of anger and adrenaline
courses through my veins as I recognize him.
Why is he holding me?

"You took my clothes off? Did he see my tits?!"
I motion to the dragon boy, who's watching our
conversation.

"Where are you taking me? Why were you in
the Academy? You let them hurt me. You lied to
me." I hurl accusations at Killian, but he doesn't
respond.

A fresh wave of excruciating pain blossoms at
my side. I lean over and dry heave over the
side of the boat. Pink foam pools on top of the
angry water surrounding us. Strong hands hold
me steady. My head swims, I'm out of breath.

"Stop shrieking. Would you prefer I kept these
plastered to your body?" Killian lifts a clump of
gore-filled fabric into the air, letting it fall back to
the bottom of the boat with a soggy plop. I look
away, disgusted.

"You didn't help me," I murmur under my
breath, the words barely audible.

I don't want to let on how much my heart is breaking. I won't give him the satisfaction of knowing it mattered to me. Soft hands brush my shoulder, lingering, warming me from the inside out. I hate how he makes me feel safe. I hate how I don't want him to stop.

This is a crime show documentary waiting to happen. One where the dumb girl gets murdered by the deceptively charming guy who says he's someone he isn't. *'The Dumbest Women No Longer Alive - Witches Edition.'*

I close my eyes and open them again, hoping he's not real, that somehow this is a vivid fever dream. But there he is, still staring down at me, all bare-chested and godlike. His warm hands are still brushing my face. I'm gravely injured, feeling more than a little vulnerable laying here spread out on my ass completely defenseless. A torrent of rage swells inside me.

"Fuck you. Don't touch me." I strangle out the words before another wave of nothingness threatens to take me under, and this time, I welcome it.

"Even half-dead, she wants to murder you. I like her!" Jagger smirks and keeps rowing.

———————◄○►————————

SOFT SWAYING EASES ME awake. All is quiet now, peaceful. Muted colors dance in the sky as I observe the breathtaking horizon- ash gray with a subtle hint of plum and tangerine, just enough to announce the coming sunset. I must've been asleep for hours; twilight is settling upon us now. Staying silent, not ready to inform my captors

of my alertness, I take it all in. Watching the
sky, I imagine this is what the other side of the
veil looks like. Beautiful, ethereal, magical. As
we move in silence, a pillar of rugged gray rock
comes into view. The closer we drift, the more
details reveal themselves.

We're coming up on the edge of a massive cliff.
It sits imposingly on a bed of dark sand, looking
menacing against the backdrop of that gorgeous
sunset. I don't see vegetation, no buildings—only
rocks and sand and sea. Suspicion overtakes me;
I don't know this place. Where are they bringing
me? I'm still a little confused, concussed, but I
need to stay awake.

Letting my training kick in, I exercise my brain.
Asking myself questions to keep alert. What does
Killian want with Faustus? Why screw him over
and take his prisoner? Does he need a Blood Seer?
Is he going to make me work for him? How did he
know about my fire? He's been watching me. He
said that much, but how is he watching? It must
be by magical means. Who is he working for? I
found nothing out about my sister. I don't think
the Elders ever had her. It was an ambush, but
why?

The momentary reprieve from the world of
pain I've been drowning in ends as the boat
slides across a bed of beady pebbles, sliding to
a complete stop. Despite my trying to remain
overlooked, a whimper escapes my lips.

"Welcome to the gates of the Netherworld,
Little Monster." Jagger leans over me, holding out
a hand to help me sit up. It pulls at my muscles in
a deeply uncomfortable way, but I'm too curious
to complain. My eyes rake over the surroundings,

confused. This is the Netherworld? It looks like a rock filled beach.

"It's the back door. The actual gates are way cooler, by the way." Jagger grins.

There's something about Jagger that I don't hate. I remember him talking to me in those cells; he kept me alive. Could he be a bastard too? I'd be willing to take bets. He is. It's not the most brilliant idea, but I reach for his outstretched hand. An animalistic snarl vibrates behind me, and suddenly my battered body raises into the air. I'm weightless before being tucked against a warm, solid chest.

I already know who the chest belongs to, and I sigh in frustration. Yep, he's an alpha-hole, alright... "Put me down, Killian."

"You can't walk on your own." He replies, all bristly and broody. Of course, he's right. I can scarcely keep my head upright with the fever still taking its course. My legs are shaky. Searing pain rips through me as he steps over the edge of the boat. I throw my hands around his neck. "We still have a trek before we're safe. Get comfortable Kitten. And try to keep from squirming. I wouldn't want to get distracted."

"Give me to Jagger. Let him carry me. I don't want you to touch me."

"No." an angry snarl in response.

'Animals mask their pain; it protects them from predators.' Deacon's voice echoes in my mind as we make our way towards the cliff. A quote from one of our many training sessions that's feeling helpful right about now: I can't run. I can't fight. And forget swimming. I can't even walk. So, what are my best alternatives for survival?

Rest. Recuperate. Reconnaissance. As much as it bothers me, I'm going to act tame for now.

I reluctantly lean into Kilian's chest. It's that or stare at his stupidly sexy face. And right now, I'd rather wear a hot pink tutu and a tiara for a month, in public.

I'll play along until I'm healed, and then I'll find a way out of this mess. I will myself to stay awake, alert, and taking mental pictures of everything around me. I'm about to enter the Netherworld through a secret entrance. That's got to be valuable information.

Near the bottom of the cliff, Killian stops and waves his hand left to right and utters the word 'patentibus'- the air ripples as a small opening appears between the rocks. Jagger motions for Killian to step in first as he follows behind, closing the portal?

So, they can manipulate portals, but I thought they were all sealed. What kind of creatures are they?

Jagger is a dragon and a GOD (if you ask him), but in all seriousness- he's more than a dragon. Is Killian also a dragon? No. He can't be. He's something else, but they *are* brothers.

We descend the rocky steps, downward and downward some more. The steps seem carved from the rock itself. Oil lanterns come and go at regular intervals. We venture lower and lower into the cliff. I always wondered if the Netherworld was really under the Earth Realm? Or if it was parallel, on the other side of a portal. It appears I was wrong on one account, at least. The Netherworld is on the other side of a doorway, and we're under something. But it's not the Earth Realm.

The repetitive motion and erratic thumps in Killian's chest lull me into a false calmness. His heartbeat is strange. It's slow. Sometimes I can't hear it at all, almost like it's not there. The war is still raging inside my body as I close my eyes, but I'm so tired. Just going to close my eyes for a few minutes...

When I open them again, we're stopped in front of the most darkly magnificent gate I've ever seen. Thick black iron hangs upon sleek hinges, with flourishes of silver gracing the edges. The filigree is intricate and mesmerizing. I can't tear my eyes away until a breeze caresses my cheek, breaking the spell. As I turn my head to discern where fresh air is flowing from, I realize we're standing in an open circle, like a courtyard made of stone. Several ornate tunnels lead to... I'm not sure where. But the real marvel is above me. This entrance is open to the night sky. Nothing but velvety midnight as far as the eye can see, dotted with multicolored lights. I marvel at the deadly beauty. Starstruck, I hadn't paid attention to the conversation happening between Killian and Jagger.

Listening now, they're talking about the intricate locking mechanism on the massive gate. '*Shit, I probably missed something important,*' I'm thinking to myself when I hear a scratching sound somewhere near the arching tunnel opening to my left. Or possibly the one on the right? The acoustics in this cylinder made of stone throw off the senses. I can't be sure. But Killian hears it at the same time as I do and goes still. Jagger stops too, tensing up. Green-tinged humanoid-looking creatures flow through all the arches.

"Ghouls!" Killian roars. There had to be fifty of them, maybe more.

Jagger springs into motion, skin ripping free of his beast as his top half morphs into a crimson and gold scaled dragon's head. Fire erupts from him as he incinerates a group of them. Their mouths unhinge and reveal rows of jagged teeth, screeching and writhing, they fall to the ground, digging their dagger-like claws into the stone beneath them.

I remember learning about Ghouls when I was in school. They were once men before they fell into darkness. The hunger and greed ate their humanity until there was no more, and they were dragged into the Netherworld. Now, they're cannibals. Perversions of what they once were. But Ghouls hunt in packs, which means...

"Watch out!!"

I barely uttered the words from my mouth when about ten snarling ghouls who had broken off from the fold came up behind us. Bellowing and gnashing their bloodied teeth. One leaps for us and knocks Killian to the ground, as I go flying out of his arms, landing with a hard thump on the cold rocks. My head smacks the stones and my vision blurs.

Killian whirls to stand over me, throwing dark bursts of power from his palms. When it hits the rabid creature, he falls to the ground, convulsing. One after another, Killian hits them with whatever kind of magic that is, I'm not even sure? But we're getting overpowered.

Jagger shifts into full dragon form and takes to the air, screaming in fury and laying waste to as many as he can hunt down. An inferno engulfs another group as he doubles back and flies over us and dips down, picking a ghoul up in his jaws and flinging it.

Body parts fly in every direction. For a moment, I'm stunned. A fucking dragon! I've never seen one in real life before; he takes my breath away. Like, I'm struggling to breathe. Seconds pass before I realize although a dragon *is* breathtaking, my rib has punctured through my skin this time. It must've happened when I fell. And not only is my lung collapsed (again) by the jagged rib inside of me, but there's a hole in the side of my chest where part of a bone is jutting out as well. I'm seeping crimson fluid onto the stones, a puddle growing around me.

"I need warriors!" Killian screams to Jagger, struggling with his arm in the mouth of a ghoul, rows of sharp teeth shredding his skin.

He is trying to stop them from reaching me. Looking around, I try to assess the situation. It is impossible for Killian to cover every angle. This puts him at a disadvantage. Panic sets in as I lift myself off the stones and start dragging my crumpled frame toward the wall. As I pull myself to a better vantage point, my bare legs leave a bloody streak on the rock floor. *If only I could get back against the wall.* My mind slows down. Breathing becomes more difficult the more I move. My chest is filling again, and I am losing too much blood. As my heart rate rises and shock settles in.

Making it to the wall, I prop my back against it, my vision blurring, consciousness slipping.

I grab a jagged stone from the ground and smash my hand, crushing my finger bones, jolting myself with adrenaline. Insane? Yeah, for sure. But I've bought myself some time. Not much, though. All around me, bodies lie scattered, some piles of ash and bone, some still jerking on the ground, missing limbs—total carnage.

I got separated from Killian in the chaos, and now he's surrounded. As the ghouls lunge at him, their teeth rip away at his flesh. Waves of indigo magic surround him. But his eyes are glued to my every move, staring through them. He stares at me. There is something affectionate and possessive about them that makes me feel warm all over.

An ear-piercing cry wails from above. The ghouls have scaled the walls, and there's one on Jagger's back, slashing and slicing. Aiming to penetrate his scales. Rage boils up from the deep well where my magic lives and something snaps loose within me.

I will not die here.

Before I even understand what's happening, violent flames burst from both palms. One blue, one red. Mixing to make a deep purple. I throw everything I have at the throng surrounding Killian. My screams are feral, inhuman, as they fall away one by one as they disintegrate into a fine dusting of powdery ash.

I recognize the sound of a gate moving. An army of creatures wearing black on black with wicked looking spiky armor pour into the courtyard of stone. Half of them scream a vicious battle cry, cutting down the remaining ghouls with fierce brutality. The other half surrounds Killian as he closes the distance between us and swoops me up in his arms.

"We need a healer NOW!" He orders.

Two soldiers? I don't know what they are, so that's what I'm calling them - they take off at lightning speed back into the fortress. Killian is running now. We rush past a blur of shiny black and red furniture.

Jagger runs in step beside us. "How did she do that? What are you, Little Monster?"

I wish I knew.

CHAPTER THIRTEEN

THE NETHERWORLD

THIS MUST BE HOW it feels to wake up after being run over by one of the Titans. As my dreams linger, I rise to the sound of pleasant humming. A cheerful woman with shimmery blonde hair, bright green eyes, and an ethereal face stares back at me. I'm still in the Netherworld, right? Because she looks like an angel.

I was always taught the Netherlings were grotesque, bloodthirsty, and demonic. And although the ones I encountered last night fit the bill, this one smells like clary sage and reminds me of a sunbeam. "You're a lucky one, pretty girl." She addresses me in a sing-song voice. "You almost landed yourself in the Immortal Fields. A nasty place, that is, nobody comes out the same. I'm Selene. May I inspect the hole in your chest?"

The hole in my chest? That's graphic. Obviously, bedside manners mean very little in the Netherworld. What a strange healer. But I feel alright, so I guess she's done an excellent job of keeping me... not dead.

"Sure," I tell this mystifying goddess in front of me, "Um, can I ask where I am?"

"I don't see why not," she says. Pulling on some veiny leaves pasted to my chest. I'm guessing she put them there while I was passed out.

I wait for her to expand upon that and answer my question, but she continues to hum as she cleans my side. Mixing herbs that smell like something between dirty feet and roses. Maybe she's a little eccentric, so I try again, "Umm, okay, so where am I?"

"You're in your rooms, of course." Selene croons. "Drink this."

Before I can accept or reject the concoction, the cup is on my lips, and a sweet liquid is gliding down my throat. Bright side - at least it tastes better than it smells. This is one of the most bizarre situations I think I've ever encountered. I want to tell her I think she's mistaken, because these rooms look like they were furnished for royalty. This bed is insane. Four posters, all black, with ornate woodwork on the remaining wood between the posts. Deep red walls and the softest bedding I've ever felt on my skin. A massive closet is situated off to the side of the room, a large fancy dresser with a bouquet of my favorite flowers -deep purple larkspur. Weird.

There's another door that looks to be locked, but I'm assuming it's for cleaning supplies. And a bathroom to the other side with the most oversized marble tub I've ever seen. No, this room is nothing like my rundown apartment. This room is a gothic paradise. I want to ask her more questions, but this conversation is making me dizzy.

"Would you like to take a bath?" she interrupts my awestruck stupor, and I nod my head in excitement as a smile spreads across my face.

"Well, then I'll leave you to it. Your wounds are closed, and the bruising is minimal. I'll summon someone to glamor the ones on your face before dinner, pretty girl."

"Thank you." My chest swells with emotion. I don't want the glamor, but the kindness she's shown is overwhelming after everything I've recently been through. "My name is Vivi."

She nods and smiles, gliding across the polished natural stone and slipping out the door.

I cannot wait to climb into the tub, so I pull my blankets aside to head into the bathroom, which is when I notice I'm wearing a damn near see-through nightgown. Embarrassment heats my face. Goddess, please tell me it was Selene who removed my clothes and saw me buck naked. I gingerly step over into the bathing room and fill the tub with hot water and herbal scented bubble bath, every muscle aching. How does running water work inside a cliff, I wonder? And electricity. My brain can't dissect that mystery now, so I drop the nightgown to the floor, step over the ledge and sink into the heavenly bubbles.

Everything has been such a blur these last few days. Or weeks? I don't even know anymore. I haven't had a moment to breathe and process the shit show my life has become. I grab a cloth and the bar of freshly scented soap, rubbing it across my chest and lathering my blood-crusted hair, deep in thought.

Tears spring to my eyes, imagining Calypso's face. I miss her so fiercely it hurts my soul. I hope she's warm and safe. Maybe Marlow went up the mountain to check on her. Oh, Marlow, what I wouldn't give to hear one of your filthy jokes right about now. She would have a lot to say, I'm sure. And Linc, did he lose his shit and wolf out when Marlow shared the news? Did Deacon help, or did he lose it too? I never got to hug Rowena. Are they trying to find me? A hundred questions invade in my mind.

Then there's Killian. What can I even say about him? I thought maybe something was budding between us. I saw goodness in him, and the texts were flirty. Weren't they? But he had a seat at the council. He let them throw me in the cells. Watching Faustus beat me within an inch of my life doesn't seem like future boyfriend material to me. His expression was cold and heartless. My rib cage hitches at the memory of how hollow his eyes were, devoid of any emotion at all.

I remember him touching my face and gazing into my eyes. He asked me not to leave him. The fever made my recollection muddled, but I know what he said and the way he held me like I was precious, and now I'm here in this fancy room with all these elegant things. He looked like he would rip the world apart to save me when we were attacked, and against my brighter instincts, I saved his ass. I'm so conflicted about this man. I can't trust him, or maybe it's myself I can't trust. There's something between us. I can't deny it when he's close to me. I don't know what I feel, but it's not hatred, not entirely. His actions don't convey the same sentiments, but his eyes. They say he feels something too.

Killian is a walking contradiction.

I grab a towel. Exiting the bath, I towel dry my hair and then wrap it around myself as I head to the counter and check the drawers. Sweet! A brush, some lotion, and toothpaste. I grab the brush, running it through my hair as I walk back into the bedroom refreshed, inspecting the closet. Which is full...

Holy pixie shit! There are dresses of every shade. Elegant dresses; expensive dresses. And shoes to match. Everything looks my size, but this is a little too much for me. Those stories Marlow reads about stolen girls locked in gilded cages with pretty things and dark lovers come to mind.

I am not one of those girls.

Closing the enormous closet, I walk over to the dresser. Sending a silent prayer to the sky. Please let there be regular clothes in these drawers. I can't be 'Vivi the badass' in sparkly ball gowns and jewel-encrusted shoes. As I slide open the top drawer, my mouth drops open in surprise. My moonstone daggers lay on a velvet pillow with a handwritten note scrawled next to them. It reads:

I believe you've misplaced these. Do try harder to keep them in your possession, and preferably away from my throat - Prince Charming.

I change my mind. I hate him. Killian has my backpack, which means he was stalking me, and he watched Marlow stash it in the bricks. That asshole must've watched me walk into the Academy.

Texting me *where are you,* like he didn't already know.

Ugh, infuriating! Smoke drifts from my hands, freaking me right out as I try to hide it. When I realize, I don't have to hide it. Relief blooms in my chest, along with shame. My forbidden power makes me something wrong, something dark.

I can't deal with this right now. I want some clothes on my naked ass, and some food would be excellent too.

I open the next drawer and sigh. Thank the goddess for normal clothes. Whoever picked these knows what I like, and I think I know who that someone might be. He's the only stalker I've had that I know of. I frown, still not sure what to think.

I grab a pair of ripped leggings, a t-shirt, and lacy underthings. Then I sit down on the bed. I am seconds from dropping the towel when Jagger bursts through the door munching on an apple.

"Do you knock?" I pull the soft terry cloth closer to my chest and death glare at him.

"Not usually," he grins, casually strolling past the dresser. "Nakedness isn't a big deal. You spend too much time around humans."

"Well, it is to me! And yeah, maybe I do, but..." Jagger plops down on the edge of the bed. "Umm, excuse me!!"

He chuckles. "I wanted to say thank you. You know, for what you did to help us. How did you do that, by the way? What are you?"

"I don't know." I hang my head. I don't know why I feel ashamed of that. I never have before. But at this moment, I really wish I could give him an answer. "I'm a Blood Witch, and a Seer. I know nothing about my father. I don't know where the fire comes from. That's the truth."

"I see, so you really are a mystery girl." He smiles conspiratorially. "I'm probably not supposed to tell you this, but things have been strained around here. You've got my main man in a hell of a tailspin. He doesn't know what the hell to do about you, but we've got some factions rebelling and you need to keep close to your rooms."

"Why?"

"Uh, yeah. I can't tell you that. Sorry, babe." He curls his lip and fumbles with his hands. He wants to tell me, but something is stopping him.

"Jagger, am I a prisoner here?" I hate the vulnerability that bleeds through my words. My walls are thick for a reason, but something about him puts me at ease.

"Not exactly." He runs his fingers through his dark hair, and I notice the resemblance between him and Killian even more now. "You have freedom. You can go where you want if you stay within the gates, but you'll need to be escorted."

He pauses, choosing his words wisely. "You aren't a prisoner, you're a guest."

This is so fucked up. I want to blow my fuse and incinerate this entire room. Not that I could figure out how to do it because I do not know how I did it in the stone courtyard. But my temper got me into this mess. Constantly reacting before thinking, running face-first into danger because I can't keep my anger in check, or my mouth shut.

Deacon spent years warning me that one day my actions would have serious consequences. I wish I'd listened. This time, I need to be clever. Observant. Docile. I must play along while trying to find my way out of this mess. I have a feeling my life depends on it.

"If you're going to listen from the other side of the door, just come in, bro." Jagger nods towards the door I thought was a cleaning closet, shaking his head. "You might be right about all the 'stalker' business, Little Monster."

"What's on the other side of that door?" I ask suspiciously.

"It's not a what, it's a who. Who do you think is on the other side of that door?"

"Oh." my cheeks redden as we hear muffled footsteps walking away.

Killian gave me the room attached to his.

I'm not sure which personality to file that under? His fourth... fifth? I can't keep track. Warmth grows in the pit of my stomach, imagining what his side of the suite looks like. Does he read? Does he play chess? I don't see any television here. For a second, I wondered what his bed might be like. Sue me. I can hate him and still be curious.

A knock on my door brings me back to reality. My nerves fizzle as I look at Jagger. Unsure if I'm ready to meet anyone in my current state of undress, and really hoping it isn't Killian on the other side.

"It's almost dinner time. The girly shit cavalry's here to primp and fluff you, or whatever it is you ladies do behind the scenes. I'm outta here." Jagger responds as he rushes to open the door.

I stifle a giggle as two stunning women step into the room, and I remember I'm in a towel with my hair looking a mess. Great. One more reason to feel like an unkempt goblin. Before being abducted, I thought Netherlings had extra limbs and lumps. Instead, I'm surrounded by runway models.

This is not what we learned at the Academy.

"Um... hi? That wasn't what it looked like. With Jagger, I mean. I just... I was going to wear these?" I hold up the ripped leggings and t-shirt. A little humiliated.

The copper haired supermodel clicks her tongue at me, running her hand through her wild spiral curls, brushing them past her shoulder. Rolling her eyes toward the brunette supermodel in mocking disgust. Awesome. I guess it's good to know that mean girls in designer dresses are universal.

Miss Redhead strides over to the closet and throws the doors open, digging through dresses like they've insulted her personally. She grabs a sparkly sea-green number with an empire waist and tosses it at me. I reach to catch it before it hits the floor and my towel drops. *Kill. Me. Now.* This tops every 'naked in front of the class' nightmare I've ever had.

"Samara, you're going to have your work cut out for you. Best get started on the glamor. She's not fit to sit at the table with our Prince looking like a drowned gargoyle. She's not fit to be in his presence at all, but I'm sure she'll ruin that herself."

"Yes, Lilia. Right away." Samara damn near bows and starts pulling at my hair.

Keep your cool, Vivi. We're on shaky ground around here. This isn't like Thornfall, where I can kick her ass up and down this fancy room. Meditation breaths.

"You're all sickly bones. I hope we don't have to take these dresses in," Lilia finally addresses me directly.

"That kind of happens when you're in a dungeon beaten half to death and then kidnapped and thrown in a boat." It's the best I can do for cordial when all my instincts are screaming for me to smash her face into the side of this bedpost.

"Just put the dress on and be quick about it. We're late." She dismisses me as her minion quietly paints up my face and glamours my hair into wavy midnight curls. At least Samara is trying to be decent. I think. A few minutes pass, and my door glides open.

"Are we almost finished, ladies? Our Dark Prince is waiting." Selene's sing-song voice is a breath of fresh air. Although, the mention of this *Dark Prince* makes me nervous.

"Oh yes, mistress Selene! Doesn't she look beautiful?" Lilia plasters the fakest smile I've ever seen on her face, beaming at the sunshine goddess.

Gag me, but now that Lilia has shown her hand, I've got her number. Stuck up assholes like her were a dime a dozen in the Academy, and I've got a PhD in dealing with fake bitches.

CHAPTER FOURTEEN

THE NETHERWORLD

IRON BRAZIERS LINE THE hallways, shrouding them in soft orange light that reflects off the polished stone walls. I'm wondering if everything in this cavernous palace is stone, too?

As we continue down the hall, I'm mesmerized by the detailed murals. The one closest to my room depicts a beautiful maiden in a flowing burgundy dress. She's walking through a field of poppies, and the further I move down the hall, the scene changes. Now the maiden is bent down, picking the flowers. As I take a few more steps, she stands back up.

How cool is this? It must be magic. Are there witches here?

The fantastic view through the corridors almost makes me forget the she-demon staring a hole into the back of my head, but I can hear her footsteps and sense her energy. What's this girl's deal, anyway? I'm not much for drama unless you count fists flying and asses being kicked. The catty stuff isn't my thing. She's a thousand times more attractive than me, anyway, so why the hostility?

Selene walks in front of us, guiding me to whoever this Dark Prince character is. I find it odd someone so dazzling lives in the Netherworld. Not that I hate it here, which is hard to admit. It's just that I pick up a real gothic vibe about the place. Dracula's Lair type of shit, which is my style. But Selene? She appears out of place in such a macabre setting.

We turn a corner, and the corridors open into a Great Hall. Paintings of dark landscapes and fiery skies adorn the walls. I peer above our heads as we step into the domed room, and it registers that the starry night isn't part of the paintings. I'm looking at the Netherworld sky through a glass dome, and it's breathtaking.

There's an onyx throne to the right, with stone beasts on each side like effigies watching over their domain. The floor shines like black nail polish. Lavish balconies wrap around the entire second story, looking down onto the extravagant flooring. The enormous room is empty now. I wonder if they have grand balls here. Executions? Does this Dark Prince preside over a court?

We proceed to the left, and a massive dining table comes into view. The walls match the entrance of the Great Hall. Everything does. But instead of thrones and gargoyles, there's a blackened table with thirteen wine colored velvet chairs, five of which are occupied.

My gaze gravitates to Killian, dressed in a black pinstripe suit, wearing a dark red tie. I can't deny my reaction to him as my heart rate picks up and my cheeks flush. As he takes me in, heat flashes in his eyes. Then the mask is back. Cold.

"Princess Genevieve," Selene announces as the other four sets of eyes settle on me. *Well, that's uncomfortable.* I hate being the center of attention, a throwback to when all eyes on me meant I was being put on display as a monster.

Jagger pulls back his chair and stands as I walk toward my seat, along with the silver-haired twins from the night at the Gravestone and a stunning woman with fire engine crimson hair and a cherub-like face. Is everyone here blessed with unreasonably good looks? I smile at her as I'm guided to my chair across from Killian. He doesn't stand.

"Uh, hello. No need for all the Princess stuff, though. I'm sorry. I don't know how I'm supposed to be acting right now." I stammer, fumbling to my seat next to the crimson haired woman.

Lilia, with her perfect copper ringlets, suppresses a snicker at my expense and slips into the chair next to Killian. I'm tempted to mock her, but I decide to quit while I'm ahead. *Just sit down and shut up, Vivi.* It kills me a little inside to play nice with assholes, but this dinner is awkward enough.

"You're beautiful! What sort of creature are you?" the fire engine woman reaches out to twirl a lock of my hair around her finger. What is it with these people and personal space? She's an odd one, almost childlike. My Sight tells me she might not be all there, so I'm extra tender with her despite the breach of my personal bubble.

"Thank you. I'm a Blood Witch, and... well, I'm not sure what else. You're lovely!" I smile, letting my dimples show. "What's your name?"

"Anise!" she bounces in her chair, smiling wide, revealing a row of startling razor-sharp teeth. "Do you want to be my friend?"

I nod my head and grin from ear to ear.

A choked sound echoes from across the table. As I turn to investigate, Killian gapes at me. Jagger coughs, dribbling wine on himself, eyes wide and disbelieving. I search the other faces in the room. Every one of them has a stupefied expression plastered on their face- even the silver twins. Samara is smiling a little, but when Lilia glares at her, she puts the bitchy mask back in place. Yeah, she's a minion, a follower, not a threat.

"Have I done something wrong?" I ask the collective group, wondering if I'm not supposed to be speaking. I'm still going for the submissive thing; I hope I haven't made a mistake.

"Anise doesn't make friends." Jagger throws me a lopsided grin, glancing at Killian with questioning eyes.

"Oh! Well, then I'm honored." I glance back to Anise; she's still excitedly bouncing. Maybe they should lie off the caffeine with this one.

She places her delicate hand on my shoulder and says, "Do you like cakes?"

"Let's eat," Killian grumbles before I can answer her.

I think Anise is a gem. I'm not sure why he's so unhappy right now, but to be honest, I don't care. I'm hungry and still pissy about what went down at the Academy. If he thinks he's getting away without a fight. He's wrong, but I need to be smart about it.

As soon as Killian gives the okay, the table is a flood of activity. Everyone digs in and starts talking amongst themselves. I spy a plate of fruit and pick off a few pieces, inspecting them with my Sight to be sure they're safe to eat. I know that's a Fae thing, but nothing about the Netherworld is what I've expected so far, and I'm not taking any chances.

"It's not poison." One of the silver twins says. The other nods.

"Oh, I didn't think...." I whisper, a bit intimidated.

"You did." Silver twin number two speaks this time, as twin one nods. Do they always mirror each other? Note to future self, at least one of them reads minds. I'm guessing both.

"Okay, yeah. I did." I chuckle, and they go back to eating in unison.

The vibe is a little lighter now, minus Lilia and her sour face. I pile my plate with pieces of bread, fruits, and cheeses. There's meat also, but I'm not so sure about what types of creatures they considered food in the Netherworld? So, I'll pass on that.

Using my recon skills, I eavesdrop as I dig into my plate. Nobody is talking about anything of interest, so I relax a bit. It feels like forever since I've sat down to an actual meal, and although I'm not in the safest place right now, I'm safe for the moment. Might as well take advantage. We eat in companionable peace, and then I overhear Lilia whispering to Killian...

"Are you ready to feed tonight, my Prince?" she grazes his arm with her ample breast as she leans into him suggestively, trailing her fingers down his arm. making a show of it.

My Prince?

I keep my eyes lowered, straining to appear disinterested. Killian is the Dark Prince? What a lying liar pants! I saw the empty seat at the end of the table and assumed we were waiting for him to show up. Killian said he was a warrior, not the fucking Prince of the Netherworld!

Shit, I'm trying to recall everything I've learned about this realm in school, but not remembering much beyond what I've already mentioned. We learned it's a brutal place filled with Night Creatures, Soulless Beasts, the Wicked, and the Damned. A cesspool riddled with debauchery and madness. Was it the King who was dreadful or was it the prince? I should have paid better attention to Mrs. Wainwright's *History of the Realms* class. Karma arrives at my ass once again.

While I'm still doing my best to appear unfazed, I detect movement out of the corner of my vision. When I glance up, Lilia is plastered all over Killian's lap. Undulating, nuzzling his neck, running her hands over his abs and making a lude spectacle of herself. She gazes in my direction, a cunning sneer forming on her lips.

Ah, this is a show for me. Someone's staking her territory.

I clench my teeth, muscles tight. An odd bristling sensation spreads through my chest and settles into my stomach, and a slight growl passes through my lips. Did I just *growl* at another woman? What is my malfunction? I'm not even sure why I'm having such a visceral reaction to this. I don't have any claim on him. Half of the time I've been plotting his demise. Still, I grip my fork, imagining it lodged in Lilia's bimbo throat. I can't look away; it's like watching an awful movie. When Lilia slips her hand under the table, I nearly fly out of my chair! I've seen enough.

I have no earthly clue why tears are forming in the corner of my eyes, but I refuse to let them fall. Killian must've forgotten who he's fucking with. Prince or not, he doesn't get to see me rattled. So, I stare, challenging him. He meets my angry stare and reacts with a surprising amount of heat in his gaze. Who the hell is this guy?

He waves Lilia off his lap. Dismissing her as if she were a used napkin. I almost feel sorry for her... *almost*. But I can't bring myself to make it genuine. As for Mr. Smooth Talker? I've been here before, and I should've known better. When someone shows you who they are, listen.

Batting my lashes, I turn to Jagger and strike up a conversation, "So Jagger, I was wondering about those cells in the Halls of Repentance. You know, when you saved my life. Anyway, they're warded. I can't believe you melted through them! How did you do that?"

"Dragon flame can melt just about anything, Little Monster. I told you I was a god. it's not my fault if you didn't believe me." A flirty smirk slides across his lips. It's harmless, but I know he's on to me. So, I take it a step further.

"I have never seen an actual dragon before; I didn't even know you still existed. You're beautiful... or majestic? Beautiful sounds weird,

doesn't it? Do you want to know something kind
of embarrassing? I've always wanted to be a
shifter with wings. How does it feel to fly?"

Jagger winks at me, those amber eyes shining
with utter amusement. And then he doesn't skip
a beat. "I guess I'll have to take you for a ride
sometime..."

I grab my cloth napkin and pretend to wipe
my face, concealing my shit-eating grin. Killian
grows still, indigo flames dancing in his eyes. His
jaw clenches, muscles twitching. Jagger laughs in
response and shrugs his shoulders. In case you're
wondering, I don't feel any remorse. That's what
you get for trying to embarrass me in public,
asshole.

Killian grabs his goblet and takes a sip of wine,
waving his hand in the air. A Brownie emerges
from somewhere I hadn't noticed and refills it.
What a dick. Who just waves a hand and has
someone at their beck and call? Pretentious fucks,
that's who!

Brownies are household elves who love to do
things for others. Their love language is acts of
service, but if you cross them or mistreat them
in any way, they'll leave, and maybe even add
itching powder to your underthings before they
go. Despite that, how ridiculous is it to wave to
get one to serve you? It eats at me until I can't
help myself. In my defense, sarcasm *is* my second
language.

"So, Killian. If dragon boy is a god, then what
are you?" I ask, arching my brow as I take a sip of
my wine.

He thought I was going to behave like these other girls, throwing myself at his feet? I think not.

"I'm your worst nightmare, Kitten." He replies, using the nickname I hate.

"I don't doubt that, but you didn't answer my question." I fire back.

"Is that right?" he lifts his goblet to his lips, sexy mojo in full effect. A vicious smile spreads across his mouth as he stares me down.

Anise claps her hands together. Loving the conflict, I suspect she's a Siren. If the vibrant, unnaturally red hair didn't give it away, her reaction to chaos does. Sirens are a lot like Sprites in that way. They feed off emotions. The crazier the better.

Killian shoots me a scrutinizing gaze, like he can't quite figure me out. Good luck! He isn't the first and won't be the last man to think he can pull one over on me, only to find out I can play petty games, too.

Voices echo from the corridor as a black-clad warrior enters the opulent dining room. Ice gray eyes and lavender hair stare back at me in silence. I'd know that face anywhere. Bronwyn.

My stomach drops. My new friend has been working for Killian all along. She's a gods damned spy? Of course she is. It all makes sense now, the odd questions, the interest in our trade routes, the timing. He can't even stalk me on his own? That's just plain lazy. I sense my temper taking the driver's seat...

"Are you fucking kidding me?" I slam my hands on the table, forcing Killian to look at my face.

"Am I a joke to you? I won't be your play toy, Killian. I bite back."

His expression is apathetic, and he can shove it right up his ass.

"Nothing to say, huh? I'm not surprised. You've been a fraud this whole time, and to think I thought I saw something good in you. I thought we might... You know what? Never mind. I was mistaken." I spit the words at him.

"He is your Prince! And you will respect him!" Lilia screeches, her puckered face red as the curtains.

"He may be *your* Prince, but he isn't mine." I reply, dismissing her.

She stands and lifts her arm to strike me from across the table.

"Sit down, Lia!" Killian bellows, and her mouth drops open in disbelief. But it's Anise that acts out, throwing her dinner knife with deadly precision as it lodges into Lilia's shoulder. She cries out in pain, dark liquid soaking through her dress.

Whoa. That was awesome.

"You will not touch my friend, or I'll skin you alive!" Anise warns in a menacing tone, jagged teeth bared.

Her fiery hair lifting into the air of its own accord, flowing in terrifying waves as if she were underwater. Power surges through her arms down to her fingers as they light up from the inside. I wonder what kind of magic *that* is. It doesn't look mild, that's for sure. I don't want Lilia dead for the goddess's sake.

"I think I'd like to go to my rooms now." I interrupt before things become more heated, casting my eyes downward. Docile. Obedient. Tame. I remind myself.

Killian looks disturbed by the last few minutes. He opens his mouth to speak but closes it, the coward. Of course, he can't face me. Another one of his many shortcomings. His stormy eyes burn into mine, searching for something. But I've had enough.

"Vivi, I..." Bronwyn pleads.

"No." my voice shakes as I stop her from whatever she's going to say next.

Tears threaten to spill from my wounded eyes. Douchebag shitheads acting like douchebags, that I can handle. But the betrayal of someone you thought was your friend? That's different.

"Please take me to my rooms, Selene." She glances at Killian, and he nods. Selene stands in her golden dress, touching my shoulder, guiding me out of the room. As soon as I'm around the corner and out of sight, a silent sob breaks through my defenses.

"Come now, Pretty Girl. Let's get you into a warm bed, and you can rest." Recognizing that I now have a nickname, I follow her down the hall, away from Killian. We wind through the corridors until we reach my rooms.

I look into her kind eyes, devastation written all over my face. "Thank you."

It's all I can say as I enter my gilded cage, closing the door behind me. When I'm sure I'm alone, I climb into the fancy bed, placing my face in the decorative pillow, and scream. Sobbing until I have nothing left, I curl myself into the fetal position, wishing for Marlow, Calypso, Linc. I've never felt so alone and discarded as I do right now.

I don't know how much time has passed, so I stare at the door that divides me from Killian's rooms. I wonder if Lilia is in there now. Touching him the way I envisioned us. A soft feminine giggle flows from under the door, and I have my answer.

CHAPTER FIFTEEN

VIVI

I AWAKEN TO THE sound of shuffling feet and doors moving. Half asleep and still feeling groggy, I take a minute to remember where I was. Oh, right? I'm trapped in the Netherworld version of Dracula's wet dream! My head is coming back to me like a blurry night terror, except unlucky me. It's all too real. My skull aches, and my eyes are bruised. *Probably because you're a dehydrated dumbass.* It's what I get for laying here like some basic bitch, crying over a dickhead who might as well have made out with another girl right in front of me.

I've tried not to care but have failed. The thing that keeps eating at me is that I knew better! They're all the same, and I'm too dense to stop giving a shit. I'd like to go back to sleep and wake up someone else.

My muscles stiffen, and a tingling sensation spreads across the back of my neck. And I can't explain how I know, but I know that I'm being watched. I look around and find myself completely alone. Goosebumps roll down my arms. Great, the Addams family mansion is haunted, too. How many references do I even have left for this weird ass fortress? Ghosts. Really?

On second thought... no, it's *him*. But how? I let loose a long sigh and roll to the side of the four-poster bed. I don't know how he's doing it, but he's watching me like the creeper he is. "Come out and face me, or am I too scary for you?"

Silence.

Touching my feet to the cold stones, I realize the room is slightly brighter than yesterday. The dark corners are no longer dark corners. Inspecting my daytime surroundings, I'm surprised. I have art depicting a woman bent over a pool of starlight. It reminds me of something hidden deep in my memory, something I can't access.

Oh well, probably déjà vu. It really is a beautiful room. And I have windows! Thick crimson curtains are drawn across them, but I can see through the crack. Is that a balcony? I hop the rest of the way out of bed to check it out. Curious about what I'll find when I have my first look at the Netherworld.

Standing on my balcony overlooking the Netherworld, I take it all in. Instead of a blood-red sky and flaming mountains, I'm pleasantly surprised to find a blue sky and strange leafy flower petals floating on the wind while the sounds of unseen beings mill about their morning. Five concrete towers seem to be both defense and decoration. The elegant outer walls are connected by heavy dark stone.

So, we're not inside a cliff? As I look further, understanding dawns on me. We are inside a cliff!

At least partially. Suddenly Jagger's comment about the 'back door' makes sense. This castle is built onto the side of a rock face. One side is the ocean, and the other is a picturesque landscape. Nothing at all like what we've seen in our textbooks. No fiery pits at all. Below me, the land is lush and green, dotted with pops of color from various flowers and trees. A river flows down and through it, the surface glittering like diamonds.

Serrated mountains materialize in the far distance, fog obscured and vaguely threatening. That must be a different territory. Huh, that's kind of crazy. Who would have ever thought the Netherworld would be so pretty?

My stomach rumbles as I smell fresh-baked croissants and coffee. Omg, there's coffee here? Maybe the Goddess loves me after all.

———————◆———————

HOW DID I NOT notice the tray on my dresser when I got up the first time? Honeydew, gummy bears, and a fresh bundle of larkspur. I'm sensing a pattern here, one that makes a lot more sense after last night. Bronwyn asked some bizarre questions at Gravestone. I don't think it's a coincidence that I'm now looking at some of my favorite things.

Another handwritten note reads:

They're beautiful and deadly, like you. My poison princess. - Prince Charming

Clever! The larkspur, ingesting it causes paralysis, respiratory failure and often results in death. Yeah, my favorite flower is literally poison.

So what? I crack a slight grin at his gesture. It's not enough for forgiveness or trust, but we've already established I'm attracted to emotionally damaging men.

The swimming pool... err, I mean... bathtub calls to me. I'm not dirty or anything, but I can't resist the extravagance of having a tub where I can stretch myself out and relax. Back at my apartment, my baths comprised folding myself in half and shivering. The top of my knees are cold from being outside the water or marked up from trying to cram them in sideways. Not all claw footed tubs are the same. I turn the handle, and steam fills the room, opening my pores and rejuvenating my face. There's a minty rose soap and an impossibly soft cloth waiting on the ledge as I dip myself in, lathering my body, and sighing in relief.

This tub is the only place I've found to think clearly, so far, and I need to do some thinking... Killian was at the Academy. It's clear now that he hadn't planned on staying. So, he must have been looking for something, but what was it? I wonder if he overheard the plans for me, and that's how he intervened. I doubt he'd answer me if I asked, but maybe I could find out some other way. Jagger comes to mind. It wouldn't kill me to have some allies here. Selene and Anise are viable possibilities. And Bronwyn? I don't know about her yet.

I need to find out more about my sister. It's not lost on me that if Deacon's informant is telling the truth, then I'm one step closer to her. We're in the same realm now. It wasn't exactly how I'd planned to go about finding her, but beggars can't be choosers; or insert whatever platitude fits, I guess.

As I'm lathering and washing my arms and chest, a different heat swells underneath my skin. An electric one, a powerful wave of lust wash over me - and that's when I know he's watching again. I let my Sight wander without looking in his direction. I can see him in my mind's eye now, standing in the doorway between rooms. A sensual grin creeps across my lips.

I think it's his turn for a bit of punishment.

I lift my bare leg above the water. Deliberately running the cloth along the curve of my ankle, down to the bend of my calf, and I pause at my inner thigh, making slow circles with my hand before submerging the cloth lower. A heady, intoxicating heat drifts from his eyes to my hands. I can sense his need through my magic, his lust. He's hanging on by a thread. Good! Dark satisfaction rippled through me at the thought of driving him mad. The asshole.

I pull the cloth from the apex of my thighs and glide it up to my stomach. Allowing him to visualize what might happen was barely out of his sight. Teasing, taunting. I hear him groan in frustration at the thought of me touching myself. I close my eyes and throw my head backward, seeing him in my mind's eye, refusing to look at him. He's gripping the door frame so tightly he may rip it out of the stone. *Perfect.* But I'm not done yet. He humiliated me last night, and made me feel things against my will. Things I don't want to feel. It's only fair he gets the same treatment.

My fingers stroll across the skin of my abdomen, winding in lazy circles as I move them

higher, a centimeter at a time. It's blistering hot in
here now. I'm visibly sweating - but I continue the
erotic torture. Bringing the cloth back out of the
water, I run it across my breast, sitting up higher
until I know it's visible. I do the same on the
other side, purposefully driving him to the edge
of insanity. And then I stand, letting the warm
water and bubbles glide down my skin as I turn
and meet his heated eyes, smirking.

He moves so fast all I see is a blur, and then
he's standing in front of me. His turquoise eyes
a raging storm. I didn't think he'd actually do it!
That he would leave the doorway. I'm thrown off
guard by his nearness, but I don't let it show. With
another grin, I grab the towel and step out of the
tub, inches from him, and he's not moving out of
the way. A delicious throbbing swirls through my
core. I know I shouldn't want to touch this man,
but Goddess... I do. I'm losing the upper hand
with impressive speed.

The tables turn when he leans in and runs his
knuckle across my cheek, unfurling his fingers
and grabbing my jaw. Easy enough to not hurt,
but forceful enough to melt my insides and make
his presence known. It's carnal, possessive. He
pulls my face to his and runs his tongue along my
bottom lip. His smoky jasmine scent envelops me
as he crushes his mouth to mine.

Killian doesn't just kiss me; he owns me with
his mouth. Leaving scorching trails of slick heat
between my legs, I tremble at the intensity of it.
Forgetting that I am standing in front of him,
wet and completely naked under this towel, I
press my body to his, whimpering into his mouth.
He reaches under the towel and grips my ass,

pressing himself into my stomach and tugging me back toward my room. I'm made entirely of flames as his mouth moves down my neck, licking a trail of lava to my breasts. He stops abruptly, and I whimper at the loss of heat.

"You'll be my undoing," he sighs in defeat as he pushes me onto the bed. He's fully dressed, but the imprint of his massive erection is pressed against the front of his pants. I bite my lip at the sight of him standing above me. I admit, I feel powerful knowing that throbbing in his cock is because of me and nobody else right now. He lowers himself onto my body, pressing himself into my abdomen, and our mouths are intertwined again. I might burst into flames as the need for him inside me grows into a raging inferno. We're at the edge of a different cliff now, and damn my stupid heart, I want to fall. "Oh, gods." I cry into his ear. Galaxies dance in his eyes as my ragged breaths come out in breathless gasps.

"Whoa, nice tits, Little Monster!" Jagger's voice interrupts as things are about to become seriously X-rated up in here. I squeal in surprise and pull my hands down to cover my bare breasts ... "We have a situation on the west wall. And as much as I'd love to grab a seat for *this*, you're needed, Bro."

"Jagger! Shit, get out of here." Killian growls out, looking at me with apologetic eyes. "I've got to go. I'll send Anise. She's been talking about you all morning."

Unable to speak, I nod. He tucks his shirt back in as he rushes through the door with his brother. I lay there for several moments trying to catch my breath, and apparently find my brain while I'm at it. What the fuck was that? I only meant to give him a taste of his own medicine. I wanted him to feel helpless and laid bare like he'd done to me. I didn't mean for it to go that far. Anger and humiliation burn in my upper body. He was with *her* last night. I heard Lilia in his room. What am I thinking? When did I become so weak and pathetic? Fuck. I swore I would never again allow a man to play me, and here I am, moaning into the mouth of my abductor like I've contracted Stockholm Syndrome.

That will never happen again. I slap my hand to my forehead in frustration. Something about this place makes me... not myself. Why does my body react so strongly to this asshole? My mind hates him so much, but when he looks at me? I'm toast.

No, no more, Vivi.

Switching up from one embarrassing thought to the next, I cover my face with my hands and shake my head. Jagger most definitely saw my tits for the second time, I think. I don't even want to entertain another thought about what else he may have seen.

I need to get dressed and stay that way this time.

———◆———

SERIOUSLY, I KNOW I'VE done some dreadful things in my life. Undeniably catastrophic bad things. But do I really deserve Lilia as my personal attendant? I think this qualifies as cruel and unusual punishment. Maybe the Netherworld really is Hell, or Purgatory at the very least. I can dress myself, so her only purpose here is to get punched in the mouth.

She sashays around my rooms, opening drawers, scrunching up her nose at everything, and smirking like a villain in a cartoon. One of the red headed ones, with the pinched face like she's permanently smelling something foul. Samara brushes and braids my hair into a wispy up-do. Apparently, I need to be dressed for tea. Have you ever heard of something so ridiculous? Now I have tea outfits to go along with dinner outfits. What's next? Is she going to come in and dress me for late evening lingerie hour? Fuck, this is annoying. I want pants, dammit! But I'm compliant Genevieve right now, unthreatening... and hopefully underestimated.

Lilia is droning on and on while she rifles through the closet. I'm sure she's insulting me, but I don't have the brainpower to pay attention. Speaking of headaches, Lilia comes over with today's frilly bullshit in her hands and orders me to strip out of the leggings I'd tried to get away with. I don't know why there are regular clothes in my drawers if I can't wear them. Maybe it's psychological torture? But whatever, the strappy red sun dress looks decent with my black hair, so I'll put it on. Whatever gets her out of here faster.

She runs her fingers across the tray Killian left for me this morning, and she picks up the note. Rage burns in her eyes for a moment before she puts it back down on the dresser and smiles at me, "Aw, that's cute... charity case. You think you're special? You know he'll never love you, right? You're just a pawn, *Princess*. He'll be rid of you soon enough."

"What makes you think I want him to love me?"

Hurt pierces my chest, but I mean it. I'm not a prize to be won. I'm not a place holder, and I have no room in my fucked-up life for something as absurd as love. It's better to put some ice on this fire we've started, anyway. Killian and I are a natural disaster. It can only be destruction from here.

Anise wanders into the room. "Get lost, demon bitch."

That was most definitely directed at Lilia. At least I'm not the only one who feels strongly about her. She lowers her head and bows. Is she not even going to put up a fight? Weird. Instead, she exits as quickly as he can. Samara is hot on her heels like a stray puppy. *Excellent work, Anise!*

"Killian says we can go to the gardens today! Do you have any scales? I have scales here..." she lifts her dress into the air, exposing her stomach and underthings. I'm slightly terrified, but also charmed. Something about this fascinating woman-child makes me want to be freer. I bet they call her crazy. I bet they whisper behind her back that her mind is broken. But you know what I see? I see someone unafraid to be authentically flawed. Perfectly imperfect, and unapologetic for it. Anise is a breath of fresh air.

"I always hoped to learn I was part mermaid, but no such luck. Got no scales." I grin at her, waving my arms and legs awkwardly.

Anise giggles, "Why would you wish to be a mermaid? They're weaklings, useless in a fight. What good does it do to be beautiful if you can't use it as a weapon? Boring. If you want to be a badass, then hope to be a Siren instead."

I'm not sure how to respond to that, so I change the topic "I didn't know you had gardens in the Netherworld."

"Oh, we have the best gardens! Better than those mundane Earthling gardens. Your plants don't even bite. They lie around like rocks, useless. Come on!" She pulls my arm, and we're headed down the hallway to a different wing of the fortress.

◆

WE PASS THROUGH TWO stone archways before we encounter anyone. As we come upon the third massive arch, I spy supernaturals of all shapes, sizes, and factions. They're everywhere! Brownies, Pixies, Trolls, a Minotaur, and is that a real Hellhound?

"Grim! Come here, boy, come on, Grim!" Anise calls to the hellhound, and the next thing I know, I'm flat on my ass with something that resembles a wiggly volcano licking my face.

"Princess Genevieve, this is Grim. He's not allowed at the dinner table. That's why you haven't met him yet." She smiles and starts skipping towards the gardens, motioning for me to follow.

It's a hell of a sight to watch an enormous shadowy glowing beast galloping about, wagging a flaming tail, following a Siren through a botanical garden. I'll put that on my *I saw some impossible shit* list.

Several supernaturals bow and call me Princess on our way down the smooth stone paths. Their greetings make me mildly uncomfortable.

I correct them, requesting they call me Vivi, and the response I got ranged from amused to disgusted. What is the deal with all the *Princess* shit, anyway? Some of them watch me, hope in their eyes.

A hope that I don't understand.

Speaking of gardens, I've never seen one quite like this before. Anise and I find a bench and sit. Grim lays at our feet. There's a sizable flowering bush next to us, and as much as I'd love to reach out and touch the bright blue and yellow petals, I watch one grab an insect from the air and jab tiny fangs into its abdomen. I'd like to keep my fingers, so I think this plant, in particular, is an admire-only type.

I feel awful doing this, but this morning before everything got accidentally pornographic, I made plans to learn more about my surroundings. I like Anise, but I also need information. Now seems like a good time to find out what I can.

"So, how do you know Killian... er, The Dark Prince I mean?" I ask. Guilt creeps into my chest. I'm not using her. Am I?

"He's my brother, silly! They all are." She pulls two smashed cakes from her dress pockets and hands me one. She must be talking about Jagger, and I'm assuming the twins? "You were too busy making out to ask questions?" A wicked smile forms on her face as she looks at me.

"You heard about that, huh?" I blush, not knowing what else to say.

"There once was a lonely Prince, who loved to paint and write and travel. But they took his paint, and they broke his pencils, and gave him a sword for battle. There once was a broken Princess in a faraway land, her disappearance severed his hand. But the Prince found her laying in jagged pieces. And then the realms burned, burned, burned." She sings to herself as she shoves smashed cake crumbs into her mouth.

No idea what that means, but alright. Let's try a different subject.

"My mother died when I was young. Does the lonely Prince have a mother?" I spoke in riddles back to her, hoping that may unlock her secret language.

"Oh, she's around here somewhere. They killed mine, you know." She scowls at the rest of her cake, setting it on the bench.

What? They killed her mother!? Just when I think I may be catching up, she hits me with that. She's off on a new topic, so there's no time to get more information, but I catalogue that in my mind for later.

CHAPTER SIXTEEN

TWO WEEKS IN THE NETHERWORLD

KILLIAN HAS REVERTED TO pretending I don't exist. I see him at dinner, and his reception is cold, detached. But I feel him watching me when he thinks I'm not paying attention. Maybe he's more of a voyeur than the conversation type. I don't know and I don't care. I've decided I don't have the mental capacity to unpack his issues for him.

Meanwhile, Lilia comes in the mornings to dress and primp me for... well, not much. But she finds every opportunity to insult me whenever she's able. From my hair to my body, to the lack of decorum I possess. She's made her point abundantly clear; I am no *princess* in her mind. I'm very much unworthy, unwanted, and unwelcome. She makes it a special point to mention the noises I hear from the adjoining room at night that make me nauseous, just to hammer it home.

She's a nightmare.

I don't get to venture too far besides tea with Selene or visits with Anise. But despite the unpleasant parts, my previous sentiments about the Netherworld are fading. For as long as I can remember, I've been taught that this realm is where the wicked were thrown to rot and fester, a purgatory of sorts. Netherlings and Shadow Creatures were too monstrous to exist along with the rest of us, so we locked them behind a portal. The council had convinced me they were lesser than the witches in every way. More beastly than sophisticated. That they have no culture, no values, no souls. Everything about the Netherworld is evil. But the more time I spend in this realm, a sense of belonging settles over me. Either everything they have taught me is bullshit, or I fit in better with the evil things.

Anise and I have spent loads of time together in my rooms, but that's okay. Jagger and I now have a companionable understanding of each other. I don't know if I'd call it friendship, but I don't hate him. And even though Bronwyn and I haven't spoken. I'm no longer staring daggers at her during our 'awkward family dinners.' I've got some serious resentment for this whole princess-locked-in-a-tower bit, but I have daily walks through the corridors, always guarded, of course. And I'm sure they post someone outside my door in the evenings. They have given me books and drawing pencils to pass my time. I may be a prisoner in this fancy cage, but at least I'm not being abused.

In the Earth Realm, I never really fit in. Like a puzzle piece shoved in the wrong compartment. I've always had to hide who I am on the inside. So careful about showing my true self. Maybe I am a monster? Maybe not. But the 'monsters' here wear their forms on the outside. No shame

or punishment for being what and who they are.
And that's comforting, oddly.

They're at war. I've picked up that much. I'm
interested in why and with whom, but I don't
have answers to that yet. The people I see in the
gardens and continue to come across on my daily
walks are happy, safe, and taken care of. Is that
Killian's doing? It must be. I don't see any other
Rulers of the Netherworld running around here.

I can't trust him, though. That's just smart, but
the more time I spend here, the more I want
to know. I see something in him, something
honorable and kind behind whatever this evil
overlord persona is about. Like the way he cares
for his sister and the easy friendship with his
brothers. He's still a mystery, so guarded, so many
walls. I know nothing about him, but my senses
tell me there's more than anyone understands. I
think he wants to let me in. The attraction is there
- but our bathtub/bedroom encounter changed
the dynamic. The only glimpses I get now are
the handwritten notes that come with my daily
breakfast platters.

Guilt eats at me. My chosen family is in The
Earth Realm, and they're always in the back of
my mind. The pain of being separated from my
familiar is ever-present. My soul isn't complete,
and I worry about her so much. I wonder what
Marlow is dealing with. Did Faustus tell her I was
dead? And Linc, we left things in a weird place.
I hope he knows how much I care for him. And
Deacon, Rowena. Am I an outlaw now? I imagine I
am. The minute they saw my flames, my fate was
sealed. If I go back, I imagine I'll be executed.

I have to find my sister.

Soft footsteps and the scent of coconuts and sunshine pull me from my thoughts and back into my current reality. "Merry evening, my Pretty Girl." Selene's soothing voice greets me.

"Hi," I smile. "Is it time for dinner?"

"I dismissed your attendants this evening. I thought I might help you get dressed, and perhaps we could talk?" she smiles, kindness shining in her bright cerulean eyes.

"I'd like that very much."

I mean, who wouldn't love a break from the super-bitch and her sidekick? I'm not in the headspace for whatever the mean girl supreme has in store for me. Her cruel words still ring through my mind *'You're a pawn; he'll never love you.'*

"You seem gloomy." Selene picks up on my sudden change of mood as she sits down on the bed next to me. She pats the mattress, asking me to move closer. "I imagine this has been quite the change for you. I, too, was thrust into a new world many years ago."

"You were? Are you not from the Netherworld?" I gathered that much when we first met. Her gold hair, bright aura, and the gentleness that exudes from every part of her doesn't scream Netherworld.

"I fell in love, against the wishes of my family. Who would choose to go to the Netherworld willingly?They questioned. Who would love a monster? But it was never a decision, it was a calling. A magnetism. And so, I left my home and followed my heart." An unshed tear formed in the corner of my eye. Selene could never go home either. I wonder what she sacrificed to be here, what she left behind? She stands up and moves toward the closet, picking through the dresses.

"Is your love still here with you?" I don't know why I asked such a personal question. It comes out without thinking.

"In a way, he is." She pauses. "There was a darkness in him, as with all who dwell in this realm. His rule was absolute, but he cared for me. I wasn't his only lover, as I'm sure you have gathered. There were others. It was just the way of things, handed down to him by his father and the father before." She speaks, still surveying the closet full of dresses. "Ah, here it is!"

She pulls a magnificent gown from the closet, holding it up for me to see brightness shining in her eyes. The dress is magical, a floor-length deep V neck of the darkest blue, and yet when she moves it to the dressing area, it changes in the dim lighting. Iridescent, subtly sparkling, it reminds me of a swirling universe or a cosmic star. There's a slit along the leg to the thigh, and there's nothing in the back but open air for bare skin to the dip of backside. I lift my arms to allow Selene to pull the masterpiece over my head, and as it cascades down my body, it's feminine yet powerful. I feel dangerous in this dress, and I can't stop myself from running my fingers down the sides, relishing the softness on my skin.

"This is beautiful! No... it's more than beautiful. I don't think there's a suitable word to describe this." I'm stumbling on my words, and my face reddens.

"I wore this dress long ago." Selene grins sadly and glances towards the closet again. "It fits you beautifully."

She picks up a brush and encourages me to sit in the chair near my mirrored dresser, removing the braids from earlier. As she unwinds my long dark hair from the braids, it falls in waves down my back. As she's brushing my hair, humming quietly, my mind spins. There's something happening, something she's not saying out loud, but she's trying to give me clues in her own way. A puzzle to put together...

"Are... are you, his mother?"

She smiles, laying the brush down on the dresser, opening a drawer, and pulling out some cosmetics. She's facing me now, applying a light coat of coal to line my lashes. And then I can see it. It's her eyes. *Killian has his mother's eyes, not the color, but the essence.* Maybe she is a goddess? She adds a little blush to the apples of my cheeks and a shimmery powder on the contour line, and then she beckons me to stand, turning me sideways. I look like a fairy princess from a dark fantasy.

She leans down and whispers into my ear, *"You'll drive him crazy in this tonight."*

As WE WALK THROUGH the corridors, I'm drawn to the walls again. There's a story playing out here in the moving paintings. As if she's read my mind, Selene narrates as we walk.

"Ancient family history. Many decades have passed, but these walls remember."

"So, this is a story? On the walls." I'm captivated.

"There was a beautiful maiden who loved to be among the flowers. She spent her days roaming the fields, always in search of new and exotic petals. This other woman you see here, that's her mother. Always watching. Some say she was obsessed with her daughter. Her beauty drew many suitors, as you can see here." She points to men lining the trees. I hadn't noticed them before. "None were worthy in her mother's eyes, but the maiden longed for more. One afternoon, a new man caught her eye, a mysterious and powerful male. After that, he came every day to watch her picking flowers. Her mother forbade her from the fields. The maiden grew cold, resentful. So, one night, she slipped from their home and sought the Dread Sorceress. Do you see her here?" I did. She was shrouded in shadow and terrifying.

We walk a little further, and Selene continues, "The maiden asked the Sorceress to free her from her mother's cruelty, and the Sorceress obliged, but there was a price to be paid. The maiden was young and foolishly agreed without inquiring what that price was. She was free to walk the fields again, free to go to her ill-omened man. And so she did. She went to his kingdom of darkness and shadow. And then one day, in a guilt-ridden state, she tried to visit her mother. She wanted forgiveness, but they trapped her. That was part of her price."

We were nearing the end of the hall now, but I was fascinated by Selene's story. I didn't want it to end. "So, she stayed in the dark kingdom?"

"Yes, she did. And she was happy for a time. She turned the darkness into something beautiful. The gardens and forests you see now. That was her doing. The fates smiled upon the maiden, blessed her with the ability to change the land, to chase away the darkness. But the worst price was yet to come." She stopped as we were about to turn the corner into the Dining Room of Disaster...

"The Sorceress was a woman scorned by love. Not at all who she proclaimed to be. She wanted the powerful man for herself, and when she could not have him, she threw a curse. Any children that came from their union would be damned, and every generation after too."

I gasp, surprised. "So... is Killian cursed?"

Selene looked at me with encouraging eyes. "Haven't you ever read a fairytale, Genevieve? Curses are made to be broken."

And with that, she wrapped her arm around mine and guided me into the dining room, where everyone was already seated. With a proud beam, she announced, "Princess Genevieve."

We waited in the archway, and one by one, they raised their heads, and then they stood. Killian sat with his back to me, as well as Lilia and Bronwyn. But as they all turned to investigate the commotion - we locked eyes, and Killian stood too. He took me in like we had all the time in the world. His gaze traveled over every inch of my body and delicious heat trailed across my skin everywhere his eyes moved.

Selene nudged me forward, and Killian rushed to my side, walking me the rest of the way to my chair. He pulled it out for me, waiting for me to be seated before he guided it gently back toward the table.

What the hell is going on right now?

Jagger whistles, loud and shrill. "Damn, Little Monster! That dress should be illegal. Are you trying to start a riot?"

I giggle at his inappropriate comment, realizing he reminds me a lot of Marlow. Maybe that's why I like him so much. Goddess, I miss her.

When everyone is seated, I thought it would be a little less awkward... but I was wrong. From each end of the table, the silver twins both stare at me with lust in their eyes. Umm, no. They really freak me the fuck out. Anise has the biggest grin plastered on her face I've ever seen, her row of sharp jagged teeth on proud display. Bronwyn glows. A stunning shade of sky blue, as she beams at me. I'd taken significant steps to ignore her in my short time here.

What can I say? I hold a grudge, but the sparkle in her eyes at this moment softens me a little.

Lilia is enraged. I can see the veins popping out of her forehead, which makes my night a little brighter. And Killian? The way he's looking at me melts something deep into my soul. Something I didn't know was frozen. This man scares the shit out of me in a totally different way.

With all these eyes focused on me, a bit of panic boils up in my chest, and my heart beats too fast. I can feel the fight-or-flight setting in. I never did like being the center of attention. Every time I'd been a spectacle back home, it was because I was an outcast, something evil and murderous, someone to fear. I was a freak on a leash...

"Stop staring at her. She hates it!" Anise screeches like a wild thing, lifting her fork, threatening to use it as a weapon.

Jagger burst into thunderous laughter, throwing his hands in the air, "Okay, okay. Chill, sis."

His shoulders shake with leftover chuckles. "Seems you have yourself a protector, Vivi. She's a vicious little thing, too."

Jagger called me Vivi, not Little Monster.

"Are your accommodations to your liking, Kitten?" Killian pins me with his eyes while asking.

Oh, so the Dark Prince *speaks*. I thought maybe acknowledging me in front of people was forbidden, and that's why he sneaks around my rooms when he thinks I'm not paying attention like the dirty stalker he is.

I grin at the thought, and he takes it the wrong way.

"They are. Anise is a marvelous tour guide. Why didn't anyone tell me that hellhounds are so wiggly?" I ask, bringing a little humor to the table. "Grim knocked me to the ground and licked my face off."

Killian draws his brows together and turns towards Anise. "She met Grim?"

"Oh, knock it off. You're so boring! Protect this, protect that. Don't let anyone touch my Princess... Grim would never hurt my friend." Anise snaps back.

She's in some kind of mood tonight. I like it. But did she say *my* Princess? Does Killian call me that? By the murderous glare on Lilia's sour face, I'm guessing he has.

I'd like to say that doesn't interest me, but it would be a dirty lie.

Trying to ignore the blades shooting from her Lilia's eyeballs, I address Killian. "I'm assuming you have my backpack. I was wondering if I could have it. There are some clothes and personal things."

I turn to Selene, not wanting to insult her. "I love the dresses, but I have nothing from home."

That sounded pathetic and so not like me. This place makes me nervous, and I still don't know how to act. I've been mostly obedient and meek until this point, sticking to the plan.

A dimple forms on Killian's cheek. "You can have your things, Kitten."

I nod. "And I'd like to train?"

"No," he replies abruptly.

"Why? Afraid I'll kick your ass?" I shouldn't have said that, but it's too late now.

Jagger snorts, and even the twins smirk. Anise claps and bounces, making stabbing motions with a soup spoon. I realize I have eaten nothing yet and pick up a piece of fruit and a cheeseburger? Why are there cheeseburgers here?

I know I should leave it alone and stick to the plan, but my mouth has a mind of its own. "Come on, Killian. It's just a little blood and maybe some flames. You can handle me just fine, can't you?"

"Watch your mouth, you fucking whore! He is the PRINCE!" Lilia blurts out, face twisted in absolute fury.

Before I can open my mouth to put this psycho in her place, Anise flies across the table, grabbing her by the hair, hand poised to stab her in the throat with a spoon! Killian moves fast as lightning, pulling his sister to the side, her arms and legs flailing. He nods at Selene as she comes over and guides a screaming Siren out of the room.

Then he levels a murderous stare at Lilia, all power. The room fills with his dark essence, casting shadows on the walls. *Holy shit.* I've never seen this side of him before. I've also never seen anyone wield shadows in person. "You *will* obey, or you will be removed."

I know I should zip it, but once again my mouth gets ahead of my brain...

"I can fight my own battles. I don't need you to protect me! If she wants to fight the *whore*? I'm right here. Come on then, you miserable bitch." There's that temper that gets me in so much trouble, I knew I couldn't hold it in forever.

Samara flinches at the fury in my voice, Bronwyn smiles, and Lilia doesn't move an inch. I don't know if that's because of Killian's warning. Or if she thought I really was a harmless kitten, and now she's understanding I'm something much more dangerous. Violence thrums in my veins, begging to be set free.

"Enough! I have an announcement to make." Killian speaks over the chatter happening all around the table. "I'll be going away for a time, an important meeting for the future of the realm. I hoped that my court would behave respectfully in my absence."

He's leaving? I mean, I guess that makes sense. He is the ruler of this realm. Although, I haven't seen him do anything remotely 'Princely' since I've been here, so it's a bit of a shock. Why am I a little sad?

You hate him, remember?

Lilia stares at me, sneering as she takes her manicured finger and drags it across her neck, making the 'slit your throat' motion.

I'm not sure how I left my seat and found myself swinging her like a rag doll into the stone pillar? But here I am, holding her off the ground by her neck with one hand, wielding a ball of raging purple flame in the other. My body is lit up like a Glow Worm and ready to end her existence.

"Stand back!" I hear Killian warning Jagger under the loud thump of my pulse and the buzzing in my ears.

Lilia struggles in my grip, flailing and looking to Killian for help. Eyes wide and terrified. Good, it's about time she learns exactly what and who I am. If it were the Earth Realm, she would have been picking those perfect teeth up off the floor the *first* time she disrespected me. Fury rages, burning hotter and hotter. I want to cause damage; I want to inflict pain. I want to burn it all to the ground and dance in the ashes. You can only push someone so far until they break, and I've had enough. I intend to make that crystal fucking clear. To everyone in this room. Rearing back, I aim for her.

"Vivi, can you hear me?" It's Bronwyn. "I know you're mad at me, and I'm so sorry for that, but it was real. My friendship is *real*, and I don't want you to do this."

The fireball flickers, and then rages taller.

"I saved him. I saved Linc for *you*, not for my Prince. And now I'm asking you to save yourself. If you kill her, he will have no choice. He is the ruler. Our punishment for murder is death, Vivi. And it will hurt him to do it. It will hurt *me*."

"And me." Jagger's voice shoves through the buzzing in my head.

I'm shaking now, warring with myself and whatever has been unleashed inside me. "Genevieve, please." Bronwyn whispers, and the killing rage falls away. I release my hand as Lilia drops to the ground, crumpling in on herself, hot tears sliding down her cheeks. Samara rushes to her side as I look up at the stunned faces in the dining hall.

"I think it's time for Princess Genevieve to get some rest." Selene speaks up.

"I'll take her," Lilia spits out reluctantly beneath her sobs.

"You will not set foot inside Genevieve's rooms again. That is an order. I'll be escorting the Princess to her rooms this evening," Killian interjects.

With that bombshell, Lilia breaks into hysterics. "You're a Prince!! It's not how we do things, this isn't proper! Why is she so special? Why does everyone treat her like she's made of gold? Oh, I know. It's because she's...."

Her mouth abruptly closes, and as I search for the reason. I find Killian's hand in the air, glowing blue. He silenced her. What the fuck was she about to say that Killian doesn't want me to hear?

CHAPTER SEVENTEEN

VIVI

SO MUCH FOR BEING docile. We can throw *that* entire plan into the oubliette. I knew it wouldn't last long, but I thought maybe I could make it a little longer than this. Does this fortress even have an oubliette? You know, one of those stone holes with deadly spikes? It is the Netherworld. I bet they have many brutal torture devices hidden somewhere.

Pushing Killian into one seems pretty enticing right about now...

I don't wait for him to escort me before I excuse myself from the table and stomp through the hallway like a fire-breathing wraith. He chases after me, which is surprising. A Dark Prince chasing a naïve idiot in a fancy dress through the halls of Castlevania.

Goddess, I've become a cliché.

"Vivi, stop." Killian is breathless behind me. Power walking isn't his jam, I guess. I ignore him.

"I said, stop!" He repeats the command. Which pisses me off. I'm tired of being ordered about.

Told what to do, how to feel, where I can go, but most of all, I'm tired of being lied to. I whirl on my heels and unleash Hell.

"I thought I made it clear. You're a Prince, but you're not *my* Prince. I don't take commands from you. What are you going to do about it? Lock me in a cell? Oh, wait. You already stood by while Faustus did that! Maybe you helped him? So, what'll it be? Spank me. Silence me. Kill me? Because I'm tired and I'd love to take a bath before I retire to my decorated cage."

Killian smirks, "Are you done yet?"

"Are you fucking her?"

His face goes white, eyes wide. I search his stare and don't like what I see, so I turn away, walking toward my rooms.

"Kitten..." he calls after me.

"Kitten, nothing! That girl hates me, she genuinely *hates* me. There are very few reasons a woman would despise another woman that much, and it always involves a piece of shit who's playing mind games. Are you a lying piece of shit, Killian?" My blood is boiling now, face twisted in absolute fury.

He lowers his head. "It's not like that."

"Oh, it's not like that? Well, that explains everything! Thanks for the clarification, dickhead!" I scream in his face, shoving him backward.

"You are a stubborn, feisty-mouthed, infuriating woman! You make me crazy; you know that?" Killian shouts back.

"How could I know that? You tell me nothing! I don't know why I'm here; I don't know what you were doing at the Academy. I don't know why you're stalking me. You never told me you were a fucking Prince! You didn't tell me you've got yourself some kind of harem in your stupid fancy castle, complete with psychotic demon bitches who live to make everyone miserable! How many more are there? I'm supposed to be one of your concubines, then. Is that it? The big secret family tradition? Fuck that, go stick your dick in that miserable wench."

"I am not FUCKING her!"

"Well, you're not telling me the truth either, so excuse me if I don't trust a word you say. I'm sure she's *cleaning your room* in the middle of the night, too, right? Giggling loud enough for me to hear. Yeah, that makes sense. Why did you touch me and then run as fast as you could? Why did you..." heat fills my cheeks at the thought of his mouth, his hands, all over me. Burning me from the inside out. "Never mind. I don't give a shit."

"Now who's the liar?" he fires back.

"It's not my fault if you can't keep your dick under control around me. That sounds like your problem. Obsessed much? Maybe your bedmates need to up their game. Don't they know any tricks?"

"You are impossible." he grinds his teeth and runs his hands through his dark hair.

"Why are you still following me?"

We round the corner, and he slams me into the wall, pulling my hands above my head and holding my wrists. "Because I can't stop myself."

He breathes into the delicate skin of my neck, lips dangerously close, and I sink into him. This man is my kryptonite. I hate him with the fire of a hundred phoenixes, but when he locks those stormy eyes with mine? I'm consumed by him.

"Because your scent lingers all day long, turning me on, making my dick so hard I can't concentrate. Because I can't even look at you without wondering what you taste like, the noises you would make underneath me. But I can't have you! And it's tearing me apart!"

Whoa, I was not expecting that.

We stand next to my door, both panting. Rage boiling in our eyes, aimed at each other. My hands are bound above me, suspended in the sexiest stare-down of my life. Neither of us moves as the tension increases. It's a tangible thing now, his magic intertwining with mine. Our breaths are hot and angry, mingling together in a firestorm.

And then all sense of control snaps. Desperate and hungry. Our lips crush together, tongues invading one another in a rough, desperate power struggle. His hands hold me in place as his knee spreads between my legs. He sucks in a ragged breath, long and deep, and then releases a moan so erotic my pussy throbs. "You hate me, and you should. I'm a selfish bastard. I tell you pretty lies because I have no other choice. But I can smell your need. I'm going to taste you. And you're going to let me."

Oh, my Goddess. That is the hottest thing I've ever heard come out of someone's mouth. I fucking hate him so much!

Killian moves slowly now, running his tongue along the deep v of my dress. Down, down, all the way to the space between my breasts. I suck in a breath as he lowers himself to a crouch, still holding my wrists above my head with one hand. The other skims the top of the slit in my dress, trailing underneath. He hooks a finger into the side of my panties and rips them free.

The bite of the fabric into my skin as my panties hit the ground sways between pleasure and pain. Killian looks up with those swirling galaxies in his gaze as he slips a finger into my wetness, lingering across my swollen sex. I turn my head and gasp, writhing against him.

"Look at me," he whispers. "I want to watch you come undone."

I turn my eyes back to him as he plunges into me, one finger. Hooking it against the sensitive bundle of nerves and gliding back and forth. I'm out of my mind with need as he slips a second finger into me, mirroring the movement. My body rocks in tune with his rhythm, strangled cries escaping from my lips. But I hold his eyes, letting him see my hatred. He removes his fingers and brings them to his lips, rolling them across the tip of his tongue as a devilish smirk forms on his lips.

He releases my hands and bends down low, wrapping my legs onto his shoulders and lifting me up between the wall and his body. Standing now, six feet in the air with my legs wrapped around his head - he runs his tongue along the slit where his fingers were, and I lose all sanity. His mouth devours the space between my thighs, plunging in and out, licking, sucking. The changes in tempo and intensity pull me out of my body, building an earthquake ready to erupt. "Killian," I breathe huskily, begging.

He groans, moving faster. "Say it again."

"Killian!" I scream as he plunges a finger into me along with his tongue, and I shatter into oblivion. Holy. Shit.

Slowly licking me until the pleasure subsides, he then slides my body down from his shoulders until our eyes are level, and he kisses me softly on the lips, lingering. Until he lets me down on shaky legs and puts his finger into his mouth, tasting me on himself.

"Sleep well, Poison Princess." He smiles devilishly and turns to enter his room in the adjoining doorway.

I WAKE UP ANGRY with myself, again. How did everything get out of control so fast? I need to rethink this *docile* plan. There are other ways to get information, and all it's doing is making me seem weak and easily manipulated. I need to get out of here, but to go where? The same question over and over as I rot in this pretty cage. Where do I go from here, where is my sister, what does Killian really want with me? Why?

I'm pacing the room now. My eyes roam to my backpack waiting on the dresser. Along with my favorite fruits, a latte, more freshly picked larkspur, and another handwritten note that reads -

Stay out of trouble, Kitten. - Prince Charming

I sigh, feeling overwhelmed and confused. I think last night was a hate fuck. Was it something to get me out of his system? I don't know what it was, but I let him touch me again, something I swore I wouldn't do. I'm going to blame it on adrenaline and the physical attraction I can't seem to burn from my foolish body. But I'm not sure about anything anymore. I don't know his game. I don't know what his angle is, and with men like him, there's always an angle. I'm here for a reason, and I'm in the dark on purpose. That's a problem for later, though. If I'm correct, he's already left, and I'm glad of it. I could really use the time to clear my head without this hold he has over me. I have had my fill of Tall, Dark, and Dangerous. Enough for a lifetime of therapy.

Exhilaration takes over as I grab my backpack and rush to the bed, moving the plush blankets over to make more room. Holding the backpack in my arms, I hug it, it smells like home, and I imagine I'm embracing my friends. Silly, I know. But missing them consumes me. What I wouldn't give to have Calypso curled next to me, my sassy little spoon. Holding the bag to my face, I inhale. It calms me, and brings me back to my senses. I promised her I would find my way back to her and I will. I'll find my way back to all of them. Whatever it takes.

Unzipping the front pocket, I reach in and pull out my herbs and candles. Next, I reach into the main section and ease my hands through my clothes, feeling for the box. Relief washes over me when my fingers grasp it, and I pull the intricately carved wooden rectangle into my lap. I don't know what's inside, but it's something important. Life or death, important. I wonder if this room has hidden compartments. Every castle I read about has them somewhere.

I almost shed a tear when my hand brushes the t-shirt fabric and leather. Something I can work with! Screw all these fancy dresses. Can you imagine one in a fight? *Here comes Fluffy, the tulle covered terror, tripping all over her expensive gown onto the battlefield.* Ha! I shake my head at the mental picture.

Pulling on my skintight black leather pants and a white tank top with the red lacy bra, I feel like myself. This is who I am. Vivi, the mother fucking badass. Vivi, the woman who doesn't take shit from anyone. I strap my daggers to my thighs with my makeshift holster. The feel of them against my body, knowing they are with me, gives me a sense of security that settles into my chest. I am Vivi Graves–stop forgetting it.

Now that I'm dressed and have a plan to hidey-hole the box, I realize Lilia and Samara never came to dress me this morning. Thank the universe! But usually, something would happen by now. I'm not supposed to roam the fortress unattended, which isn't a deal breaker for me. I'd do it if I wanted to, but I would not understand where I was going or how to find my way back. I could take another bath, but I'd already taken a quick one last night. Is there a library here? Or a movie theater. Something? I think I'm bored. As soon as the thought crosses my mind, Jagger barges through the door in something that resembles sweatpants. Eating another apple, nonchalant as fuck.

"You really don't know how to knock. Do you?" I sigh. At least he's entertaining company.

He eyes me up and down. "Well, you can't train wearing *that*! My men will lose their gods damned minds, and I'll have a lot of explaining to do when Big Bro gets back."

"My jailer told me I couldn't train at all, remember?" I'm salty about it, whatever.

"Do you see him here?" Jagger pretends to search under my bed, grins, and then tosses me a bundle of clothes. "Change."

He doesn't have to tell me twice. I jump at the opportunity to break some rules. It's been weeks since I've trained, and I feel like I'm losing my edge. I head toward the bathroom and toss a glance across my shoulder. "No offense, Dragon Boy, but I'm going to get naked in here instead."

"Suit yourself," he shrugs.

Minutes later, I'm dressed in more appropriate workout clothes, daggers strapped to my legs, and ready to rock. I know I've complained about it before, but I love to train. My mood lifts thinking about blowing off some of this pent-up steam

"I'm gonna kick your ass today, Little Monster," Jagger teases as he throws me a croissant and a refillable water bottle. I follow him out the door and into the halls.

CHAPTER EIGHTEEN

VIVI

As we navigate corridor after corridor, nerves spring up in my stomach. I barely have time to take in any details of my surroundings, trying to keep up with Jagger's strides, "Hey, Fire Crotch! My legs are short. Wait up."

He slows down enough for me to reach him before resuming a breakneck pace. "Like I said, too much time around humans."

"What is that even supposed to mean?"

"You have magic, you have heightened senses, you have power. I watched you shift at the dinner table and grab Lia's throat before anyone could catch you. And believe me, we are all fast. Yet here you are. Whining." His lip curls in amusement.

Whining? "We weren't allowed to use our elements without supervision! Wards placed all over the city tracked our signatures and alerted the Rune Force to anything larger than party tricks and basic element manipulation. Do you know what the punishment is for unapproved magic? Because I do! I used to carry out the sentences." The only power I could wield at full force was Blood Magic, for obvious reasons. "And you're a judgy twat for saying that to me!"

He chuckles, coming to a two-story-high heavy wooden gate. He smiles over his shoulder and grabs the massive iron shaft that slid behind them as a barrier. When he pushed the heavy gate to the side, I just about pee my leggings. There's a sizable sandpit-type training area surrounded by towering rock and various trees. We're outdoors, in the middle of a forest. But how can that be when we were just in the Fortress?

Jagger watches the wheels spin and the smoke in my head. "There are six sections of The Night Fortress. Three protected by the cliff's edge. Two surrounded by the Forest of Shadows. One heavily guarded main entrance used for visitors from other territories."

So, this place has a name. The Night Fortress, good to know. "And these other territories are who you're fighting?"

"It's complicated. Killian rules over all the Netherworld, but... you know what? You should ask him about the details." He replies, dodging the one thing I wanted to know. Damn. "So, this is where we spar." He points in front of us to a giant sand-filled arena. To the left is for knives, swords, daggers, and archery. "Over here to the right is where we train with magic, whatever elements we possess - see the ward surrounding it? Look closely."

I squint my eyes and turn my head sideways. It's there, like a faint bubble. "Okay, so where do you warm-up?"

Jagger gives me a confused head tilt. "Warm-up?"

Oh, for the love of the goddess. I wave my hand. "Never mind. Where do we start?"

"I told you I was going to kick your ass, Little Monster." Jagger grins like a maniac, headed towards the sparring arena.

WE SPAR UNTIL EVERY muscle in my body is screaming for mercy. Then Jagger tests my skill with the moonstone daggers. After a full day of training, we have good news and bad news. The bad news? I can't spar for shit against a dragon shifter. He kept his word about kicking my ass, and then some, but my dagger throwing skills are *rad* - Jagger's words, not mine.

Too exhausted to dress for dinner, I request for food to be brought to my rooms while I run a hot bath to soak my weary bones. To my surprise, there's no argument. Quite the opposite! Selene had informed me that his Highness had left instructions that said - *let her do what she wants*. Within reason, of course, I still couldn't roam the fortress without an escort.

Sharp pain radiates through my feet when they hit the water. A healer had wrapped them with bandages halfway through our session. When I unwrapped the filthy strips of cloth afterward, blisters and bruises were already formed. My fists weren't in much better shape, blood crusted my knuckles, and I have sand in places I'd rather not discuss. As I sink into the soothing bubble bath, a timid knock sounded on the door.

Probably the food...

"Come in," I call from under the bubbles. The door cracks and a shock of lavender hair attached to ice gray eyes steps through. I guess Bronwyn is done being avoided. I sigh dramatically, not as annoyed as I let on. In reality, even though I didn't know her well, we had a connection, and I'd like to have another ally around here. Goddess knows I could use a few.

Bronwyn is hesitant at first, but she makes her way into the bathroom and grabs the chair from the counter and drags it to the edge of the tub. "So, first, I want to say I'm sorry." The slump of her shoulders makes my heart hurt. "I've been by our Dark Prince's side since I was a youngling. When the Netherworld Fae rose and split factions, my parents chose the Shadowlands. The Dark Fae. They camped us along the forest with some raiders when Killian's forces attacked. I disagreed with what they were doing, you know. My parents. They pillaged and murdered; they deserved their fates. I told him that much, and instead of execution. He took me in. I was a natural spy. I took to the training quickly. So, after several years, Killian started sending me on assignment."

"I was an assignment?" I asked, failing to hide the hurt in my voice.

"He sent me to learn about you, that's all. We had to know your nature. If you had been... corrupted. I had no orders to harm you."

"But you knew who I was the whole time. You knew I was the Bloodgood Heir?"

Bronwyn nodded. "I meant what I said about wanting to be your friend. I told The Dark Prince as much, you're no sorceress. Not an evil one, anyway. He's smitten, you know. It was him that wanted to know all your favorite things."

Smitten with me? Maybe when he's not being bipolar and mysterious. His moods change faster than the hands on a clock. I'd say it's more likely that he's thrilled by the chase and new legs to get between, but I don't express that out loud.

"When your shifter was attacked... I mean Linc. When Linc was attacked, I wasn't supposed to intervene, but you were so broken. I had to help." She admitted.

"Can I ask you a question?"

"Of course, but know that there are certain questions I cannot answer. He's still my Prince, Vivi. I take his orders." She states. The honesty helps, as annoying as it may be.

"Were you punished? For helping me against orders?" my brows crease. I have to know what kind of ruler he is. I have to know if he's cruel and unforgiving. I have to know... I just... I need know what kind of evil I'm dealing with here.

"Gods, no Vivi! Look, I know Killian may seem like the evil beast in this whole mess, but everything he does is for the future of his realm. Everything. It's not my place to tell you his reasons, but he would never hurt me." I sense the truth. She believes it. Whether it's factual? The jury is still out, but her words are somewhat reassuring.

I'm well versed in recon. I saw the raised slab before the throne in the Great Hall on that first night, and I'm not stupid. I know what an execution block looks like. But what I can't figure out is why I hadn't seen or heard anything about him using it. I was confined to my rooms unless escorted. And my nights? Well, I guess I don't know what happens after our awkward family dinners and I'm sent to bed. These are people of the night, maybe Killian punishes his subjects after hours? I wouldn't put it past him.

"I came here to warn you. Don't underestimate Lilia. She puts on a show, but she's far from a simpering victim. She'll be gunning for you, and she can be ruthless. Watch your back while The Prince is away, okay?" Bronwyn appears concerned. "She's been reassigned, but that won't keep you safe. If anything, it makes her more vengeful."

That explains why I saw her lurking about the training arena today, watching me...

"Why does she hate me so much?" I feel a tad vulnerable asking that question, but Bronwyn is the only one I can think of that might give me the answer.

"Because *he* doesn't."

I nod in understanding. There's something between Lilia and Killian. I don't know if it's physical or what it is, but I'm a threat, and I'm puzzling together all the whys. "Thank you for the heads up." I offer Bronwyn a nervous smile.

A petite Brownie walks into the main bedroom as we finish up our conversation, an array of food filling her small, orange-tinted arms. Tacos, potato chips, and ice cream? Bright pink hair falls onto her forehead from her braid as she stumbles with the heavy tray. "I am Maius, here to serve my lady Genevieve," she speaks in a high nasal voice.

Bronwyn and I look at each other, and I crack up, belly laughing. Maius is offended, so I correct her assumption, "We're not laughing at you, I swear. It's just... that's a huge tray of earthling food, more than anyone could eat by themselves, and it looks like a pain in the ass to carry."

Brownies live to serve like I said before. It's their love language, but to offend one? That's never a wise decision. "My Prince has brought a feast that will be more to your liking. You have not been eating enough during your stay." She wrinkles her nose at the tacos. "If I may ask, my lady, what sort of beast is this?"

Ha! This is unbelievable, Marlow and Linc would have a blast looking in on this scene. "Well, I hope it's beef or chicken," I answer, smiling brightly, "And you can call me Vivi."

My skin is shriveling like a raisin, and my stomach growls at the sight of all that delicious food. I've been picking at my plates like a toddler since arriving here. And after such a rigorous training session, I realize I'm starving.

"We'll leave you to get yourself dressed for bed and eat." Bronwyn stands and ushers Maius to follow her from the room. "Get some rest, Vivi... and lock your door."

THESE SHEER NIGHTGOWNS ARE a joke. I mean... why wear pajamas at all? You can see everything but my uterus through them. I'll be asking for some real jammies. No more doorway peep shows for Mr. Stalker, *prince* or not.

It felt amazing to gorge myself on something other than fruit, cheese, and bread for once. With my belly full and my mind spinning, I crawl into bed and wrap the soft blankets around my body. Usually, I would watch television before falling asleep. The silence in this room is pretty deafening without it. Plus, it would be nice to fill my brain with reality TV trash instead of having to lie here and think.

I appreciate Bronwyn's warning. We aren't besties by any means, but I understand a little about feeling loyalty to someone who took you in and gave you a better life. My Sight had told me when we met we had more in common than meets the eye. That's proving to be true so far. Killian is her Deacon, and I can respect that.

As far as the warning? I had suspected as much myself, but it's always helpful to have confirmation. Lilia will not let our confrontation slide without retaliation. She believes herself to be... a girlfriend? Future queen? I'm not sure. But I will have to be extra observant and careful outside these rooms from here on out. I don't know what type of supernatural she is, besides evil as fuck, and that is a disadvantage.

I lay on my side, messing with my amulet, rolling it around in my fingers. I noticed a crack earlier while bathing. Now, I run my fingers across it, wondering what the consequences of that might be? I've always been terrified to allow my magic to be freed. But in my time here, I think my feelings have changed. Being in the training arena, using my Sight freely, it feels right.

I've always had to hide who I am for fear of my life. But I'm understanding that what you accept about yourself can't be used against you. Perhaps embracing your darkness, owning all the parts that never see the light of day - the balance between the light and dark that lives within all of us is the path to being whole.

As I drift off to sleep, a vision strikes me hard and fast.

A young girl with hair of pure white and eyes the color of spring grass sits on a small throne. Beside a larger, more imposing one made of skulls and bones. She fiddles with a doll in her hands. It looks to be handmade. I feel her terror as the vision reveals a chilling man with a handsome yet menacing face. Narrow black eyes, set deep in his sockets, watch the gruesome scene with an air of satisfaction and amusement.

"Kalliope!" his harsh voice calls to the little girl. "You will watch what happens to those who oppose my rule. And if you take your eyes away again? It will be you who takes their place!"

The small girl lays the doll on her lap and peers up through teary eyes as a body is laid before her on a slab of obsidian. A Knight dressed in all black with jagged spikes attached to his knees, elbows, and shoulders flays the skin from its arms. Slowly moving to each finger as he viciously rips claws off the tips and throws them to the ground in a heap of sinew and gore. As the vision moves upward, it's clear that the man-creature has been there quite a while. Although he is still breathing, the top half of his body has been skinned alive. His supernatural healing kicked in at some point, knitting together the mess of flesh that remains. His maimed and disfigured face comes into view. There's a severed tongue on the floor and an eyeball with the slimy trail of veins still attached. Blood drips and pools from the slab as he moans, unable to move his mouth enough to make any actual noise.

Vomit moves up my throat at the sight of the carnage before me. The girl stares at me now as if she feels me there with her. Sadness burrowed deep in those soulful yellow-green eyes.

"Genevieve?"

I jerk awake in a puddle of sweat and panic, the sense of wrongness still embedded in my throat. Tears burn my eyes and streak down my face. She's a child! Like I was.

Kalliope.

CHAPTER NINETEEN

VIVI

I WITNESSED ONE OF my sister's memories, and she knew I was in her mind. Kalliope, her name is Kalliope. I suck in a deep breath, holding back the tears. It's not much, but it's something. A step closer to finding her. She looks like me, but the opposite. Where I have midnight hair and violet eyes, she has stark white hair and yellow-green eyes.

One of Darkness and One of light.

Well, I guess that settles it. I'm darkness, she's light. Emotion swells in my throat at the vision I saw. How she's been raised. How can we have so many similarities? I can't focus on anything but saving her from what must be years and years of torment.

A thought crosses my mind. What if I can hone my Sight to reach her purposely? I need to explore that. As jarring as the vision was, my heart aches. Family. I have a family. I have a sister, and from what I briefly saw, I have a father too, but he doesn't strike me as any kind of father I want to know. No, I just want my sister. I can already feel some of my broken parts mending.

The door creaks as Jagger pops his roguishly handsome head in. He must be my babysitter tonight. "This door is supposed to be locked, remember? I thought I heard something. Are you well?"

Do I tell him? Over the last few weeks, we've bonded, and I'm valuing him as a friend, but he is his brother's confidant. No, for now, I'll keep it to myself: my little secret, my North Star. Guilt scrapes at my deception. He doesn't deserve it, but I don't trust anything or anyone in this fortress. Not until I have answers.

"Just a bad dream," I lie.

"And that happens often?" he prods, but only a little.

"Yeah, I... my childhood wasn't the best. Sometimes I light my bed on fire too, so it could always be worse."

"I know."

He does? Of course he does.

Mr. Stalks-a-Lot probably has an entire file on me hidden somewhere around here. I bet Killian has my school records. Shit, knowing him, I wouldn't be surprised if he knows my entire sexual history from the time that I was seventeen years old, the psycho.

"It's a little early for training. Maius hasn't even brought me a platter full of burgers and fries yet." I smile at what's become something of an inside joke. The trays are ridiculous. I guess Killian takes his captive's eating habits seriously. Malnourished hostages are bad for business, I suppose. Either that, or he has absolutely no idea what witches eat, or in what quantity. Side note: it's the same as humans.

Jagger hesitates like he's going to say something, but closes his mouth. Since when does he *ever* close his mouth? The secrets around here are plentiful.

"If there's something you want to say to me, spit it out." I needle him, hoping it'll loosen his lips a bit.

"You won't like it, but hear me out. I want to bring Bane and Dante in for our last session." He covers his head with his hands as if waiting for me to throw something at him. Which is highly tempting!

"The Silver twins?! Hell no, Dragon Boy. I'm sure somewhere in an alternate universe, they're nice guys, but they freak me out and you know it. What is it they do when it's not dinner time, Jagger? Because that's the only time I see them. Are they off eating babies and sacrificing kittens? They look like the type."

"Hey, those are my brothers you're talking shit about. They're not that bad. You haven't even given them a chance, and they know magic." he wiggles his brow.

Damn, I've been asking for more than combat, but it's such a familiar argument for me I'd given up. I begged for years to learn how to control my magic, and Deacon wouldn't allow it. Linc either. I briefly feel the sting of that truth. It's always been a source of insecurity. They were so hell-bent on protecting me they would never give me the tools to defend myself. *Look where that got us.* I never thought I'd be offered anything more than that. I never thought someone would see the fight in me and find me worthy.

Who would have ever thought I would find a small measure of validation in the "evil" Netherworld among the *monsters*? Goddess, have I been so judgmental? I'm judgmental even now, refusing to work with the twins because they more closely resemble the night creatures I've been taught to hate. I didn't even know they had names because I've never asked. Yeah, I'm a judgy asshole.

"Okay, I'll train with your brothers, but I want to learn fire from you. Deal?"

With a playful glint in his eye, he blows smoke out of his nostrils and claps me on the back. "Get ready then. Let's light some shit up, Little Monster."

BATHED, FED, AND SUITED up. I find Anise fidgeting in my doorway. "What's wrong?" she squirms some more. Stepping into my rooms and looking around.

"I feel danger."

That wasn't what I was expecting at all.

"You feel danger from where, Anise?"

"They won't listen to me; nobody listens to me when Killian is gone. He would believe me. I'm not crazy, you know. Everyone thinks so. Crazy, I mean- they think I'm crazy." She looks at me with expectant eyes. "Are you like them?"

"No, Anise. I'm not." I pat the bed for her to sit. "Can I tell you a story?"

She claps her hands and smiles widely. I'm getting used to the rows of sharp teeth that peek through.

"Back where I'm from, I was a lot like you. People feared me and ran in the other direction when I walked into a room. Even the people I love. They didn't trust me." I was thinking of Deacon and Linc now, the way they handled me with kid gloves and dictated what I could and couldn't do. I know it came from a place of love, but it doesn't hurt any less. I understand how she feels in a way. "Do you want to tell me about the danger?"

Anise plays with my bedspread, weighing the question. "What do you have under your bed?"

Shit! Can she really feel the box my mother entrusted me with under there? I hadn't had time to find a hidey-hole yet. "It's a box from my mother. Is that the danger?"

"No, but you should hide it better. You have enemies here."

"I agree. I don't know where to put it, though. Do you have any ideas where it would be safer?" I didn't think to ask Anise. Maybe I should have.

She jumps up, rushing to the balcony, and I follow, perplexed, but interested in what she may do. "Do you have the box?" She looks at me like I've lost my mind.

"Oh! I'm sorry. I didn't realize you were showing me how to hide it! Hang on." I go back inside and dig the box from the furthest corner under the bed where I'd hidden it behind the post.

She follows her fingers along the outside wall. A pink glow emanates from her fingertips, and then a small door appears. Was that always there? Or did she create it? I assumed her only magic was feeling/influencing the emotions of others. I guess I need to research Sirens. Or maybe...

"Anise, your mother was a Siren, right?" she nods. A familiar irritation washes over her face. "No, I'm not judging you! I'm just wondering. What is your father?"

"A God."

Whoa! The puzzle pieces come together. Jagger told me he was a God, but I thought he was just being Jagger. Cocky, sarcastic, and a pain in my ass. But now? I think I'm understanding. I've been getting clues from all of them, and I've ignored what they were trying to tell me. Their mothers are all different, but their father... they have the same father! And he's a God. Like an actual God? Which makes them Demi-Gods. Oh holy shit! They're Demi-Gods. Killian is a Demi-God, or is he more than that? What is Selene? I think my brain might short circuit.

"Are you going to put the box in here or not?" Anise jars me from my revelation.

"Oh, yes! I'm sorry." I shake my head at myself. I was so mind blown I forgot myself there for a second. *Get it together, Vivi!*

We stash the box, and Anise seals the door, telling me she will bring it to me when I need it. She didn't say *if,* she said *when.* How could she know when I'll need it? Something isn't adding up. Could it be that they can't tell me what I want to know? Like, physically *can't.* Is that part of the curse? Or does she have some sort of ability to predict the future? I decide it's best to leave the rest of the questions for later. I already have more information in the last ten minutes than I've had the whole time I've been in the Netherworld.

"You're training with my brothers today." A statement, not a question. "Now the fun starts. Let's go!"

CHAPTER TWENTY

TRAINING DAY

STANDING AT THE DOME in the training yard, trepidation takes over. I'm scared, although I'll never admit that out loud. I've waited all my life for this moment.

I'm about to unleash my magic.

Excitement builds in my limbs; my hands sing at the thought, and something deep within me comes to life. But it's my mind that needs convincing. What if I hurt someone? I can't handle that, not even one of the twins. I don't know what I'm about to unleash. What if Blood Magic comes pouring out instead of earth, or air, or fire? What if I murder half of this court? I'll be dead meat. Killian will execute me, Bronwyn told me as much. Is this dome strong enough? Or what if it's the opposite?

There's a crowd growing. Curious onlookers, Bronwyn is here. Anise is a Siren's version of a vibrating ball. Even Grim is here—a living volcano-shaped mountain of a dog, prancing about. And Lilia, she thinks I can't see her, but my

Sight is a lot more potent than she realizes. I know she's lurking behind the pillar.

What happens if I crash and burn? I become the laughingstock of The Night Fortress. I'm losing my nerve, but there's a small part of me that wants to be free. Isn't that what I want? I have begged for it. Being able to be myself, to let it flow, to see what happens. Eventually mastering it. I need to do this. I have to prove to *myself* that I can do this.

"Block them out," one of the silver twins comes to stand on my right side.

Fuck, I forgot they're mind readers.

"Which one are you?" I ask him, my voice shaking.

I am Dante.

I turn to him, eyes wide open and mystified. Did he speak *inside* my head?

He did.

The other silver twin comes to stand on my left. Holy fucksticks, this is weird as shit. I try it out, though, thinking to myself, "*You must be Bane?*" He nods.

I don't know if this is super fucking cool or if I'm in a Hitchcock movie. I look them both over. It's the first time I've paid close enough attention to either of them to tell them apart. I've avoided any sort of eye contact, or any other contact, since I saw their serpentine eyes and freaky long silver locks of hair at The Gravestone.

They sort of remind me of the Fae in *Lord of the Rings*, mixed with snakes. That probably sounds insane. Shit!! They know what I'm thinking. Stop it, Vivi. Stop thinking weird shit about them.

Dante has a dimple on his cheek, and Bane? I don't think Bane knows how to act human at all. My veins tremble as I swallow the fear and open my Sight to them, feeling each one separately. When Dante drops his walls and allows me to experience his energy, I am pleasantly surprised. He is gentle, isn't he? A gentle breeze on a spring day. But Bane? His walls remain intact. I don't think that's going to change, but I felt respect. Or something like it.

"You three going to stand around and jerk your cocks all day? Sorry, *lady* cock for you, Princess. Or are you going to get in the dome and do something?" Jagger steps to the side, giving me an aggravating smile.

Our brother told you no because he fears about your safety. Nothing more. He will be angry, but he'll give no repercussion. That was Bane, and coming from him, I relax and nod. Stepping towards the dome of magical protection. Here goes nothing...

Stepping through the barrier feels like a heavy coating on my skin, but as I take my last step, a popping sound reverberates, and there's nothing but silence.

"It's soundproofed here?" I look at them both, questioning.

It is.

I think that's Bane.

"Focus on the earth, feel her vibration. Every drop of water in the blades of grass, the way the trees speak." Dante speaks aloud, and I thank him for it. "Go below the surface, feel the soil, how it calls to you."

I close my eyes and do as he asks, straining to feel anything. Nothing happens.

"You're still thinking about who's watching. Block it out."

Even though I try again, my mind does not seem to empty. This feels like it takes forever, but then... I feel something. This is like a song, like when I found Linc bloody in the street. A seed is nestled under the soil in my mind's eye. It is living. And it has a rhythm. I am entranced by its steady beat. There is someone speaking in the background, but I drown them out. This seed is all that matters. It is beautiful, hypnotic, and all-consuming. There is a rumble in the ground, and I smile. I beckon it to show itself to me.

A terrifying plant-like being knocks me on my ass, and I stare up in horror. Roots with large, spindly tips resemble deformed legs. Each leaf has its own face, and the leaves surrounding it bloom like the mane of a lion. The monstrosity drips fluid from its jagged teeth and then lunges for a bite, and I scramble backward.

"Bane! Put it down!" Jagger orders.

"No," he replies. "She can handle it."

Jagger growls, pacing back and forth. "If anything happens to her, we're fucked, Bro."

"Genevieve, you know what to do." Bane grumbles.

Fanged and misshapen, the monster I created stares back at me. Bane thinks I know what to do, but I'm not so sure. *Think, Vivi, Think! Don't let this giant plant eat your face off.* I know what to do, I know what to do... I just need to repeat it enough to make it stick. Just think! And then I hear a familiar voice, female, the one from my visions.

You are the daughter of Oracles; this is your creation.

My creation. This is *my* creation; I stare into its eyes and shout, "Stop."

The monster stills, eyeing me. "Come to me."

It does. I reach for my creation when it is inches away from me, and it leans towards my outstretched hand, allowing me to stroke its petals. *I'm petting a mother-flipping plant monster!* As I turn my head to gain approval from Dante and Bane, I notice the entire courtyard watching me. There's no way this is going to escape Killian's notice. None.

"What do I do now?" I ask the twins.

"What do you think you should do?" Dante asks.

What should I do? What do I want? Do I want to destroy it? My heart hurts at the thought, No. I won't annihilate a living thing that didn't ask to be put in this situation. I summon it; I won't make it pay for that. I stroke along one of its roots, and it leans down. Nuzzling my leg. It needs a name, I suppose...

"Jagger?" I call out, knowing he crossed the dome barrier when the chaos broke out.

"Right here." He sounds uncertain of what I'm going to do.

"Which gate has the least defenses?"

"I don't understand," he gawks like I've lost my shit, and maybe I have? But I turn my face to him and repeat the question.

"Which. Gate."

"The West section of the *wall*." He grinds out through his teeth; I don't think he was supposed to tell me that.

I once again captured the monster's attention. "You are Yewhusk. That is your name," a high-pitched screech comes from somewhere inside him, like a dinosaur noise, and he bows. "You will protect this fortress at all costs. These people are yours to defend. Killian is your King. Jagger over here..." I point in his direction, "He is your commander. Do what he says."

And with that, Yewhusk moves toward Jagger and bends on spindly roots to match his height, not coming close. I think it's a twisted version of bending the knee, and I see that I've captivated every face in the courtyard. I've never seen so many jaws on the ground at one time.

"He belongs to your forces now. Use him on the West wall." I smile at Jagger, and a calmness overtakes my body and mind.

"Uh, okay?" He's mind-fucked right now.

I can see the wheels turning and envision smoke coming from his ears. I know this is the absolute worst moment to laugh, but a strangled giggle escapes my lips, anyway. I used my magic, and I want more. I want to learn everything. I want to control it, hone it. I want it to belong to *me*.

"Am I in trouble? Or can we proceed?" looking at the twins, I give them a raise of my brow, and they look at Jagger in unison. Indecision splashes across his face, but with my questioning stare, he nods and leads Yewhusk away towards his waiting men and women of the guard.

"So, what's next?" I smile at Dante and Bane.

"I think Anise should assist us with your next task." Bane answers.

———◦———

WE TRAIN FOR HOURS. When my emotions become overwhelming, Anise grabs my hand and helps me direct them. In her own way, she's teaching me what to do with the excess. I raise a tidal wave and then a light misting of rain to cool us off. I create lightning and almost singe the hairs from my arms while doing it, but with their help, I figure out how to direct it. I am a full-fledged, magic-wielding badass. Is it perfect? Definitely not, but I am doing it, and I can't keep the stupid smile off my face.

This has been the best day of my entire life.

After we finish, Dante escorts me back to my room.

"Your daggers. May I see them?"

He wants to hold my blades. My protective instincts kick in, and my hands move to cover them at my thighs.

I have no intention of harming you.

Yikes, that was insulting, wasn't it? After all he'd done for me today. "I'm sorry. Of course, you can. It's just... I got this one from my mother. It's a family heirloom. I didn't mean to offend."

"You have not offended me." his serpentine eyes move to mine, and for once, I don't flinch. Am I? Is this? I think we might be bonding.

As I hand him both daggers, he scrutinizes them. Moving his pale fingers over the hilt, running them across the blades. "These are powerful weapons, Princess."

They're only daggers, suitable for slicing skin and using Blood Magic. What the hell is he talking about, powerful? *Oh, right? He's reading my mind right now...*

"The Gods forged these weapons."

"I'm sorry, what?" just as I was thinking he's not *that* weird, he goes and changes my mind. He stares at me blankly, most likely thinking I'm daft.

Your family heirloom was forged by a God. You have the blood of one in your veins.

"Yeah, I got that part. I'm trying to figure out what drugs you're on," another confounded stare aims in my direction... *Dante, that's sarcasm. It's when you tell a joke, but it seems like it might be serious. You know. Sarcasm? Never mind.*

He hands my daggers back and speaks through my mind. *Rest, I will send Maius with your dinner.*

MY LUXURIOUS TUB HAS never felt so amazing. This isn't the same type of training as combat, but man alive... it still hurts like a bitch! I may not be bleeding this time, but every muscle in my body is screaming in "pissed off." It takes forever to get myself into and out of the tub. By the time I'm done with that, I'm starving and sleepy.

I scarf down some Corn Dogs, chocolate, and potato chips. What in the hell do they think we eat on earth? Junk food and candy only? I'm too tired to care.

As I lay my head down on the pillow, about to zonk the fuck out. I hear voices—furious voices coming from the room adjoining mine. I'm too exhausted to drag my ass over and put my ear to the door like a proper sneak, but I can hear enough.

Killian's back. Jagger is in deep shit, and by the sounds of it? The entire royal line of Demi-Gods and whatever else they are, are all in that room having one hell of a sibling smack down.

Awesome.

CHAPTER TWENTY ONE

KILLIAN

MY MIND IS A raging battlefield, and she invades my every thought. I dig with fists and claws to cut her from under my skin, yet she burrows deeper. If she only knew. Lia is nothing to me. She's my feeder, my subject, nothing more. Born to serve as her mother before her. The noises she makes are a production. She's aware the Princess can hear them. I've contemplated ripping Lia's head clean off to shut her up on more than one occasion, but her father is an old friend of the family. My honor would be called into question. We do not abuse our staff this side of the Netherworld.

The chosen feeder sits at the side of the unwed prince, Genevieve doesn't understand that it's only tradition. She believes I chose Lia to be at my side, that I claim her as mine. That's not the case. If I could feed on Genevieve's essence instead, I'd be the most powerful Incubus the Netherworld has ever known. If I could have her by my side, we could move the stars, but she's not ready. She may never be.

When she displayed awe-inspiring power, my control slipped. Watching her in all her flaming glory, full of vengeance, hell-bent on destroying the woman she thought was a threat to her. I've seen nothing more exquisite in my lifetime. I hoped she would do it, that she would flex that fearsome power and put an end to her enemy.

She didn't know it, but she was fighting for *me*. She showed her dominance. That display of power was a declaration. She doesn't understand her nature, too much time among the humans. Too many lies. I would have refused to execute her. I would have broken my own fucking laws and faced my consequences. I'm sick at the thought. Fuck.

I thought if I could taste her once, it would sate this growing need and I would be done with it. Done with *her*. My kingdom depends on it, but I don't think I can let her go. Rage fills my veins at the thought of Genevieve at the mercy of her father, what he plans to do with her. She'll be an empty shell. She won't survive it. Not her. She's too strong, too feral, too stubborn. She'll fight him, and she's not strong enough to win. Not yet. I envision that fire leaving her eyes and punch my mirror, shredding my knuckles.

"My son." Selene cracks the door.

"Mother." I regard her with the utmost respect.

"You don't have to do this. There is another way." She pleads.

I scoff, "Another way. So, I am to leave the future of this realm to what? Fate?"

My mother frowns. "You have no faith."

"Faith! Don't talk to me of faith, mother. We both know what we've set into motion. And I've already kept her for too long. The attacks are messages, and they grow more insistent each time. My time is up. If I don't bring Mordred his daughter soon, we will be at war. Are you telling me she's worth a war?"

"You're putting words into my mouth. I said, there is another way." She replies while cleaning my wounds.

"Yeah, I know. I just waltz into the Bone Keep and invoke the right of betrothal, without proper claim, and without father's blessing. That betrothal was a farce, a failsafe. The last attempt by a desperate mother to keep her child from the monster she mated with. I have no legitimate claim, mother. Evanora is dead! And father... well, father has been gone a long time. He may never be freed." I flinch at the pain etched on my mother's face. I've gone too far.

"I'm sorry. I know you have hope, and I should never take that from you."

"Curses are made to be broken." She replies. "Yours, my son. My *only* son."

"And if not? Then she dies." I feel the sickness moving up my throat. If not, Genevieve dies, and it will be my fault for believing in my mother's so-called miracles, for not leaving her alone, for caving to my selfish desire to have something that does not belong to me.

"I have to let her go." My shoulders sink with the finality of those words.

"You are making a mistake." Selene hisses through her teeth and exits my suite.

HOURS PASS AS I drink and stew in my misery. I don't need food or drink but I can enjoy them. Enjoy them! I snort. I'm not enjoying this beverage so much as hoping it will numb that anger and anguish that's stuck to my soul. I've run through every scenario, every course of action. None of them are safe, none guarantee her safety *and* protect the future of my realm. It's one or the other. No matter what angle I see it from, I'm gambling with her life. I'm gambling with my kingdom, the people I vowed to protect. I have no recourse here. Mordred is waiting, his impatience grows, and the attacks are more frequent. Before long, he'll arrive in force.

Fate. Fated to break my curse and be my queen. The gods created Genevieve for me. I'm to believe this rubbish? Put my *faith* in it. What has fate ever done for me but torment my mind and destroy my family? But I can't deny the way this woman lights me up from the depths of my corrupted soul. She brightens my world. If I honor this agreement, will Mordred put that glittering light out for good?

"Jagger!" I call out to my brother.

Minutes later, he slides through my door, looking as if he doesn't have a care in the world. If I didn't love him, I'd hate him. The freedom he's afforded because of his lineage. A different mother, a different *fate*.

"What's up, bro?" he bites into an apple, searching my face.

"Gather my guard. I leave for the Bone Keep tonight."

His face remains neutral, but I can feel his judgment. He believes Genevieve can save us all. How can they all believe this with such certainty? "I don't need the judgment."

"I haven't said shit." He replies.

"You don't have to. I can see it on your face."

"Well, since you brought it up. What's the harm in buying some time? Make it a meeting, and negotiate your terms. You have the Princess. He wants the Princess. What's he willing to give you?"

I ponder this for a moment, negotiate my terms... It's brilliant, I admit.

"And what are my terms?" I question my brother and the commander of my forces.

"I dunno," he shrugs, "Make something up."

He's grown attached to her as well, as has Anise. I've never seen my baby sister latch on to another person like she has with Genevieve. She'd tear down armies to keep her safe, and so would the twins. So, this is what it comes down to. gambling with the Universe.

"Ready my guard," I repeat the command.

"And should Selene ready the Princess?" Jagger asks, it's a loaded question and we both know it.

Silence fills the room for what feels like an eternity.

"No." I've decided. "And you'll be staying behind."

Jagger's face contorts, "You're not going into the Shadowlands without backup."

"And Genevieve won't be here without a personal guard. You're staying. End of discussion."

"You're going to invoke the betrothal?" his voice lowers, almost to a whisper.

"I'm going to do what it takes."

I've told the Princess many lies, hidden so much from her. When she finds out the truth, I doubt she'll even have me. This is a suicide mission at best, a declaration of war at worst. Either way, I'm off to seal my *fate*.

CHAPTER TWENTY TWO

VIVI

A HAUNTING FEELING OF being watched startles me awake. As I stretch and wipe the sleep from my eyes, the sensation grows. I don't want to look at the door. My Sight knows what I'll find standing there. I can feel the hostility emanating from him in currents.

"If you're going to yell at me, then get it over with." I roll to my side.

"I will not yell at you." He replies.

"Well, you sure feel like you're going to yell at me. I'm a Seer, remember?"

He crosses the threshold, and my pulse picks up. Curse this stupid body for reacting to him the way it does. He says I'll be *his* undoing. My traitorous heart says otherwise. Killian is standing next to my bed now, tall and imposing. I swallow hard. Waiting for him to say whatever he's found so vital that I needed to wake up for it.

"They could have killed you in that arena." He growls, the line of his strong jaw tenses.

"Do I look dead to you? And you're welcome, by the way. The west wall will be much more difficult to attack now." I grin, and his lip twitches in response.

"You take too many risks with your safety."

Oh, no. Not this again. I've had my fill of dicks and muscles thinking they know what's best for me, to keep me safe. "I don't take enough risks, Killian. Not enough. The council has kept me in the dark, starved of the opportunity to learn from my magic. Umm, hello, kidnapped? And so much more. Don't think because you swaggered back into the fortress, ordering people about and having screaming matches with your siblings, that you control me. As I've said before, you're not *my* Prince and I don't bow to you. I will be training, with or without your permission."

"Is that so?" his jaw ticks.

"Test me. Order Jagger to stop. Order the twins, Anise... and anyone else you can find. I'll resort to training by myself, and if I light this room on fire while doing it? Oh, well. I'm sure you can afford to fix it." I'm sitting up now and realizing my argument would be more convincing if I weren't wearing a see-through nightgown.

His heated gaze lowers to my perky breasts, nipples alert and standing at attention.

"And I want new pajamas! Ones that cover something. It's not negotiable." His eyes lift at that, meeting mine. Defiance written all over them. "Oh, no, sir! Don't you use that sexy mojo on me! I mean it. New. Pajamas. Today. Unless you enjoy Jagger barging into my rooms at all hours of the morning and seeing exactly what you're staring at right now?"

That should do it. Is it fair to use his brother against him? No, but I want the fucking pajamas, and I'm not above blackmail to get them. Sue me.

"Fine, new pajamas. Anything else on your wish list, *Princess*?" his sexy smirk is back.

I don't trust it. What's he up to? I searched his face for... I don't know. Something. And then I can't seem to stop myself from inspecting the rest of his body. My eyes roam from his feet to his legs and then his torso—feeling something "off" in that area. My eyes shoot to his, and I jump out of bed to lift his collared shirt. He chuckles as I raise the shirt away from his magnificent abs, and I let out an audible gasp at what I see there. He's bruised, ugly green and purple splotches cover his stomach, and he's bleeding from his side. Someone's wrapped it already, but I can't stop myself from reacting.

"You're hurt!" I'm moving my feet now, pushing him towards my bathroom, pulling out this and that: bandages and antiseptic herbs.

"I'm fine." Another devilish smirk forms on his lips. "But I will not object if you want to keep pawing at me."

"Get over yourself! I'm not *pawing* at you. This cut is deep." I sneer.

"And I have competent healers to take care of it. If you want my clothes off, Kitten? Just say so."

"Keep wishing!" I yell in frustration. Why is he such an asshole? I could strangle him with my bare hands.

"My lady?" I whip my head into my rooms, where Maius stands, looking unsure of what to do. "My Prince." She bows low, awaiting instruction.

"Thank you, Maius. You may leave our breakfast on the dresser." He smiles at the Brownie, quelling some of my anger. I don't love that he has servants, even knowing that Brownies live to serve. Seeing that he doesn't mistreat them helps a little.

Maius nods and moves to set the tray of oatmeal, Pop Tarts, and Fruit Roll-Ups on the dresser. She pours me a cup of coffee, and I could kiss her! Over the last weeks, Maius and I have come to an understanding. I don't care *what* is on that tray in the mornings, but coffee keeps me alive. *On second thought, I think she might have taken that literally.* Anyway, there's been coffee on my tray ever since, and I love her for it.

"*Our* breakfast?" I glance at Mr. Stalks a Lot, giving him a questioning eye roll.

"Are you too virtuous to share a meal with me?" he questions back.

"Of course not! But I don't trust you. What's your angle? Why aren't you at your big fancy table with your siblings and the redheaded bitch?" I don't feel right about this. It's too intimate. And my track record for keeping my panties where they belong around him is atrocious.

He grins. I'm really loathing that smirk.

"So, the stuffy Prince of the Netherworld is going to drink coffee and eat Pop Tarts?" I'm prodding him now because... well, I guess it's because I enjoy getting a reaction from him? Like I said, I need my head checked.

"The truth is revealed. You think I'm stuffy?" he chuckles.

"And vain, and controlling, and aggravating, and..." My sentence is interrupted by his warm lips pressing to mine, but this time they're gentle. Stirring actual emotion inside my shriveled heart.

Shit! Nope. This isn't happening again. I pull away.

"I'm going to get some clothes." I move as fast as possible without running, throwing my drawers open, and pulling out the leather pants and tank top. He follows me, sitting on the edge of my bed. Okay? So, he's going to watch me change then? Fine. If he likes torture, that's on him.

I drop my nightgown and last night's panties, standing with my back to him in all my naked butt glory. I can feel the lust emanating from behind me, but I refuse to turn around. If I do, it's over with, so I awkwardly get myself dressed, panties and all—while he watches my every move. And when I'm done? I turn to him with a Fruit Roll-Up in my hand, calling his bluff.

As expected, one bite, and he's spitting it into his hand like a toddler. The big baby. Dark Prince of the Netherworld, huh? Okay.

"Are we going to have any interesting conversations? Or am I here to gloat and watch you spit out your food?" I giggle.

"That wasn't food! You want to have conversations with me?" He looks confused.

"Isn't that how you get to know someone? Your tongue has been inside my mouth, Killian. Among other places, but I don't even know what your favorite color is."

"That's a ridiculous question," he waves me off.

"Is it? Then you decide. Tell me something real." I counter.

He sits in contemplation for a moment. "You created a living plant beast. Do you not know how it happened?"

"Don't trust me, huh? The feeling is mutual. But no, for what it's worth, I have no idea. I focused on the earth. There was a seed. I sang to it, and boom. Snarling plant monster." I shrug. I mean, what else can I say?

Killian regards me with a rare, unguarded stare, allowing me to see behind the mask. "You made that decision on your own? To defend my fortress with your creation. Why didn't you attack?"

"Because I didn't want it to hurt my friends," I said it so matter-of-factly that I hadn't realized the weight of what I just admitted. These people, his people, have become my friends and my instinct is to defend them.

* * *

AFTER OUR NOT-SO-AWFUL BREAKFAST, Killian announces that he'll be busy for the day, but Anise has volunteered to be my escort, and I can go wherever I choose within the fortress, *except* his rooms. Really? I could walk into the war room if I wanted. I mean, he didn't specifically say I couldn't.

But I can't go into his bedroom...

If my eyes could roll all the way back into my head and come out the other side, this would be a perfect time. No matter how far I think we've come or what I perceive to be happening between us, I'm still on a leash, and Killian holds the rope. It doesn't matter how I think I may feel about him, or what it means. None of it makes a difference at all because this isn't a relationship, this is control. And I'm *not* that girl.

A ridiculous thought crosses my mind. Back home, I had an all-around sweet guy who messed with me a little but wouldn't hesitate to do anything I wanted. He threw himself at me, offered his soul - bare and ready. And I shot him down. Now? I'm in the Netherworld chasing a ghost, accepting whatever scraps he wants to give me. Yeah, I fight it - but I'm not fooling anyone. Least of all myself.

Maybe girls like me aren't made for happy endings.

The vision of Anise bouncing at my door lifts my mood. She's all smiles and nonsense today. I love the nonsense! It's my favorite mood of hers (and she has many). We decided on a trip to the library for our outing today. I knew there had to be a library here somewhere. With Grim in tow, we walk towards the most mysterious library I've ever seen.

My hand rests on Grim's crackled skin as we walk. He's almost to my chest, so it's an easy feat. I rub my hand across his flank and flakes of volcanic rock fall to the ground, red glowing through the cracks. Wiggly volcano, indeed.

"You miss your animal." Anise blurts, no doubt feeling my unguarded emotions, and my heart splinters.

"I do. Her name is Calypso, she's a shifting cat. My familiar. Witches have animals that bond with their souls... and when we're separated, it's painful." I admit.

"Ahh, Calypso. Goddess of the sea. She was cursed too, you know. Cursed, cursed, everyone's got a curse. But a curse breaker?... Grim likes cats!" she exclaimed, and I grinned. With Anise, you learn to appreciate answers in pieces. Sometimes they fit together later, sometimes they're completely rubbish. May the odds be in your favor.

I let out a sad chuckle. "I'm not sure Calypso would be a good fit for Grim. Something tells me they might not get along." But oh, how I wish I could have her here with me.

"Do you like cakes?" Anise runs her hand through her gorgeous hair, waiting for my response.

On her good days, she is cunning and vicious and brilliant. On her troublesome days, she really likes to talk about cake. I nod my head like I do every time she asks this same question. I mean, who doesn't like cake?

We spend most of the day in one of the most opulent libraries I have ever witnessed. I thought Tanglewood manor had an impressive library, but this? This is a whole new level of awe-inspiring. It's an entire building with a glass-domed ceiling and at least ten stories. Each one was complete with its own balcony and sitting area. A massive chandelier hangs in the middle, glittering like a thousand diamonds in the sun, leaving prisms on every surface.

Today, I'm curious about the stories Selene shared with me. About that maiden and the sorceress. I wish I knew their names; I'd love to read more of their stories. I find a few texts that reference The Night Queen, and I decide to bring those to my rooms for bedtime reading.

I'm positive she's the woman in my visions, and knowing more about her seems essential.

After hours of wandering, I approach Anise and Grim. "Would you mind if I went back to my rooms to nap before dinner? I'm feeling sleepy."

"Sleeping Princess wakes up with a kiss." She sings and prances.

"Do you mean Sleeping Beauty? The earthling fairytale book?" I ask. I love that book.

"Killian reads it to me; the evil witch puts her to sleep. Like father, but he doesn't wake up with kisses." She replies, not even looking in my direction.

The King of the Netherworld is in a magic-induced sleep.

I NAP, PACE THE room, flip through books. Fiddle with my hair. Something about being back at that dinner table tonight has me on edge. My last experience was less than pleasant and although I've seen Lilia lurking about in the dark corners of the fortress, watching me, I have had no direct contact with her since I went full crazy and tried to turn her to ash.

Tonight, I would sit across from her. Watch her paw all over Killian and probably insult me multiple times? I can't say I've missed it. But I am excited to share the table with almost everyone else. I've hidden away for too long. It's time to suck it up and face the music, I suppose. *It's just dinner, Vivi.*

Selene comes to help me dress, and although I put up a small fight on the choice of gown, I

give in. I guess it's a welcome home dinner for
the Dark Prince and considered a formal affair.
So, whatever. I'll play along.

As we walk through the moving pictures in the
corridor, I can't help but admire my gown. A
deep burgundy number that hugs my curves and
pushes my breasts up to an almost obscene level. I
look good. Like, superb. And the satisfaction that
spreads inside me knowing that? Yeah, it's a little
petty. But it seems fitting for the weeks of mean
girl bullshit I've put up with. *Kiss my ass, Lilia.* She
may have the spot by his side, but his eyes will be
all over *me* tonight.

Entering the now-familiar dining room, I
notice the décor has changed. Instead of
burgundy and silver, the room is now decked out
in blacks and golds. It's almost like everything
complimented this dress. I wonder if Selene had
a hand in this? Sometimes I think she's trying
to play matchmaker with her son. I'm probably
crazy, though.

"Princess Genevieve," Selene announces to the
room like I'm esteemed royalty. It never gets
less awkward for me when she does that. I really
prefer plain old Vivi, but Selene is kind and stuck
in her ways. At least they got the memo about
staring.

Well, except Killian. He seems to have missed
it because the way he's staring at me as I walk to
my chair is seriously pornographic. One look at
the stormy turquoise sex traps and you can tell
what's happening inside his head is obscene. Can
he make it *any* more obvious that he's undressing
me in his mind, and doing Goddess knows what
else up there? Which makes me nervous.

"Hey, Little Monster. You're looking good enough to eat!" Jagger breaks the silence with his usual banter.

"Hey!" I smile and wave.

Why did I wave? I'm too awkward for words.

Anise pats the seat next to her; this must be my assigned spot now. It sucks that it is across from Prince Alpha-hole. Trying to avert my eyes all night would be easier if he wasn't right in front of my face, but I feel kind of special that Anise wants me by her side.

When Bronwyn walks in with a gorgeous blue mini dress, looking conflicted, I decide to put my grudges aside and offer the seat next to me. Which she takes.

I'm not even weirded out by the twins anymore. Well... mostly not.

You look well.

That's Dante. I know that because Bane would never compliment me.

That's not true.

Okay, I stand corrected, I guess he would. I look at them both and laugh out loud—amusement glimmers in their beady, snakelike eyes.

"Care to share?" Killian interrupts. "Seems I've missed a lot while I was away, brothers."

Is that jealousy I detect? No, it can't be. Can it? Why does that make my stomach flutter?

I've spent a great deal of energy avoiding Lilia's glare, until this moment I haven't looked in that direction at all, but to address Killian... I sort of have to look at her. And of course, when I do, she's all but peeing on his leg to mark her territory.

"We've come to an understanding," I answered Killian.

"Oh, you have? I'd love to hear about it." There's that sexy fucking smirk again.

"Well, I... I mean, we...." I'm tripping on my words; he looks outstanding tonight, and I'm suddenly feeling too hot. I look at Jagger for a bit of help.

"Our feisty Little Monster agreed to train with the twins, as you already know. It turns out she can hear them mind speak." Jagger shrugs as Killian lifts his brow.

I'm picking at my food, finding this bit of steak extremely interesting. Wow, have you seen the color of these potatoes? Dirt brown. Fascinating.

"And can you mind speak back to them, Kitten?" He rumbles, obviously perturbed.

"Well, no. I figured out that they can read my mind. So, I make my thoughts go loud. The ones I want them to know about, anyway." My cheeks reddened, and I inspected the tablecloth, trying not to get caught in his stormy eyes.

"They can read your mind, you say?" He looks extremely interested in this bit of information. Guess they hadn't shared with the class? I do not know what to say right now, so I decide on nothing.

"She's a badass! She made her own monster, Killian! An enormous and scary one." Anise pipes in, and I wish she hadn't this time. Because the energy in the room changed, and not in a good way.

"It was cool, Vivi, but it was also reckless. You need more control." Jagger adds.

What the fuck? I wasn't expecting that from him, of all people. What a dick! Throwing me under the bus like that. It was *his* idea! I can feel my tongue about to get me in trouble, but I can't stop it from happening.

"Maybe I had an ace up my hole! Err... *in* my hole. No, I mean in my sleeve! I was trying to say Ace in the hole or up my sleeve. I didn't mean in my hole, any hole. No holes!! That's what I meant. I had another plan... Shut up, Vivi!" I cannot believe this is happening.

I'm tripping all over my words and falling face first. My face must be the color of this dress. Why am I like this? I open my mouth around Killian, and filthy nonsensical shit comes tumbling out.

Killian cracks a genuine smile. Eyes lit up like fireflies. I've never seen him smile like that before. Is this what he's like when I'm not around? His shoulders shake, and a booming laugh escapes him. It's an oddly sensual sound. My thighs clench beneath my dress.

"What I wouldn't give to be an ace right about now...." Jagger seizes my moment of mortification to make a joke, a seriously inappropriate and suggestive but hilarious joke.

"Watch it, Jagger." Killian's face is serious again.

"Interesting. If I didn't know better, I'd say someone is feeling possessive? My big brother doesn't want to share his new toy." Jagger needles him further.

I can see the blue flames darken Killian's indigo glare, inky depths becoming darker and darker.

"Oh, fuck off, Jagger! I'm nobody's toy. And *you*." I point at Killian, "Have a sense of humor, would ya? It's a buzzkill."

Anise is smiling wickedly. The entire table, save for Lilia and Samara, looks like they're about to burst into laughter. Even the twins look amused.

"Glad you've all enjoyed the show. I think it's time for me to go to bed." *Before I die of embarrassment.*

"I'll escort you to your rooms." Killian moves from his chair to my side, pulling mine out and giving me his arm.

This is a bad idea. It really is. As we say our goodnights, I notice Lilia giving me an absolute death glare, but I'm over it. Let her glare.

———◇———

KILLIAN AND I START down the hallway, and I'm quiet as a mouse. Still embarrassed by my unfortunate word choices. This walk is one of the most awkward moments we've shared to date. I broke the silence first.

"Was that chivalry back there? Who are you, and what have you done with the alpha-hole who's taken me captive?" It's my attempt to lighten the mood, but I sense it doesn't quite hit the mark.

"You're not a prisoner." His voice has changed. There's an irritated edge to it now. Guess I'm zero for two tonight on tension breakers?

"So, you continue to say, but it seems pretty *you can't escape-ish* around here if you ask me." I look to my left and then to my right as we make our way to my rooms. Making an exaggerated point.

He stops in front of the door and goes still. Turning to face me, he inches closer. My heart races and warmth tingles down my spine. I think he's about to kiss me, and for once I want him to; I lean in to pull him closer...

But instead, he backs away and says, "Do you plan to escape me, Kitten?"

"Goddess, you know how to ruin a moment." I smile. Frustrated, but also amused, "Stay out of my rooms tonight, would ya? I need my beauty sleep."

"Goodnight, my Poison Princess." he chuckles.

CHAPTER TWENTY THREE

VIVI

CLOSING THE DOOR BEHIND me, my breath hitches. What the hell was that? One second, we're about to kiss, and the next? It was a reality check.

Do I plan to escape him? Well, yeah. Eventually. Does he think I'm going to stay locked in this pretty cage forever? Even if he is my fate, which is what I believe Anise and Selene have been hinting at all along. I won't live the rest of my life without my loved ones, and I don't want to be a queen.

A chill snakes across my skin, and my Sight perks up. It feels like I'm being watched again... no, that's silly, there's nobody in my rooms. They get swept for intruders every time I leave and again before I enter. Talk about classic misdirection, Vivi.

Running from yourself again. Conjuring ghosts to avoid what's happening inside you.

Killian dodged me tonight. I stood there, ready. I wanted him to kiss me, and if we're honest? After him being gone and the way he treated me like I was the most precious thing he's ever seen, I wanted more than a kiss, no matter how wrong it may be.

He's under my skin, and I'm not sure I want to pull him back out.

I bathe quickly, and as I come back out into my rooms, I realize there are pajamas on the bed. Real, made of actual fabric pajamas. My heart swelled at the pants, bottles marked poison.

His Poison Princess.

Somehow, this pompous, bipolar, creepy, stalking asshole of a Dark Prince has me twisted like the rope I'm probably going to end up hanging with. I'm screwed.

Curling into my covers, content to listen to him moving around his rooms, hopeful that maybe—even though I told him to stay away, that he would ignore my request. I'm drifting off to sleep when a manicured hand covers my mouth, and I smell the clean scent of larkspur before the acrid taste hits my tongue.

I knew I should have been paying attention. Since when does my Sight alert me for no reason? But no, I'm too busy over here obsessing about Prince Fucking Charming. Men, they *are* bad for your health.

My head pounds as the toxin flows through my veins. *Poison Princess*, what a self-fulfilling prophecy that turned out to be. I'm going numb, beginning with my head. And unfortunately, my mouth. As the red-headed figure comes into view over the top of me, I know I'm screwed.

Lia sneers, one of the most vengeful expressions I've ever seen. "At first, you were a plaything. Something to bide my time with. Tear at your skin to see what's inside. But when he acknowledged you, talked about you when you weren't around, and escorted you to your rooms personally, I knew I'd have to take care of you myself."

I stare at her, willing my limbs to move, wishing I could speak.

"He's cursed, you know. If he allows himself to love you, you'll die a horrific death. Of course, everyone thinks you're the one to break it, with your purple flames and untapped magic. I should let him keep luring you into your own demise and be done with you, but I'm impatient. Plus, someone else wants you to die quicker. Pity." She mocks me with a concerned face as two shadowy figures file into my line of sight behind her.

Why would the shadows be with Lilia? Unless. Ahh, someone has switched teams. Right under Killian's nose. Whoever his enemy is, the one he's fighting? They found someone on the inside. I bet all he had to do was play on her feelings. Poor, discarded, unrequited, Lilia.

Fuck. This is bad.

I'm going to be honest here. I do not know how I'm getting out of this one. Ironic how adamant I'd been that Killian stay out of my space tonight. I can still hear him shuffling around. Unaware of what's happening mere feet from him. My rooms must be cloaked. He can't hear any of this. Which means neither can my guard, who's stationed outside the door. I can't make noise to alert anyone. Shit, why does all the life-threatening stuff happen to me?

"Do you know how hard it is to kill a Blood Witch?" another mocking sadness rolls over Lia's face. "You're part goddess, you know."

My pupils widen, and I'm able to shift my eyeballs a fraction. What is she talking about, part goddess?

"Turns out, the only way to kill you is to remove your blood, and that's only because your true magic is cloaked. Otherwise, I'd have a hell of a time." She sneers as she cuts one of my wrists.

Pain erupts in my arm, and I feel the slickness trickling to the floor. But this is blood. I have blood magic—the idiot! I focus my energy on the opening in my arm, calling to my life force, willing it back inside, but I'm sluggish. It's too slow. It has to be the larkspur. Think, THINK! If I let myself bleed it out, maybe I can get enough that I can move. But I'll have to make fresh blood if I want to stay alive. I've never done it before, another skill I wasn't *allowed* to practice.

Searing discomfort explodes in my other arm as Lilia makes her way to the other side of my useless body. Her satisfied smirk makes me livid. I can feel something stir deep within the core of my magic. I'm believing that anger is my magical catalyst, and I have an idea.

"Oh look, she's going to use her weak magic to save herself. How adorable." She coos at me like I'm a child. Lilia will die for this, she will die, and my smiling face will be the last thing she sees before I rip her to shreds.

She makes an extended cut against my inner thigh. Goddess, she really *is* an evil wench, isn't she? Another pull of the blade across my stomach. Not deep, just painful. Too bad she doesn't know I've endured torture before many times. Faustus Culpepper is a hell of a teacher when he wants you compliant.

My blood is flowing steadily now. I can feel the
sheets soaking with it. I hear the drips falling to
the stones below. Reaching deep into my well
of power, I fumble. Trying to get a grip on my
magic before I lose consciousness... again. I try
not to inner laugh at the absurdity. How many
times would that make now? Seven? Eight? Ha!
Best Blood Seer, ever.

Okay, refocus. Make extra blood. It can't be that
hard, right? I try to isolate a drop, just one drop.
If I can replicate it, that's how I get myself out
of this. I'll pretend the larkspur is still working.
What can I move? My eyeballs. I can judge how
much is gone by my eyeballs. Okay, one drop...
I reach out with my magic, and my heart rate
speeds, pouring more blood onto the bed sheets.
No! The opposite, slow. Slow the heart. One beat,
two, pause... three. That's better.

Just one drop. My brain is moving slower. I'm
becoming confused. One drop. I attempt to find
my song, the song of my blood, and allow my
flames free. Rising to the surface of my skin. As
Lilia comes closer, I realize she was toying with
me. I'm too late. The shadows behind her stir and
buzz. She's going to slit my throat.

Tears well in my eyes as my life flashes before
me. Calypso, will she fade? Will she waste away
until one day she lays down and dies? I've heard
that's what familiars do; I've just never witnessed
it. I hope she knows how much I love her. Actual
fear grips my throat. If my body could move, I'd
be trembling.

Marlow, Linc, Deacon, Rowena... it can't happen
this way. They won't even know where I was, that I
was safe and coming back to them. Huh, *safe*. I felt

safe here. With Killian, Jagger, Anise, and Selene. Even Bronwyn and the twins. The place I never asked to be turned out to be the one place I've ever felt fully alive and accepted. I met myself here. Too bad I never got to meet my sister. I never got to show Killian how I feel.

This is the culmination of my life. A bunch of *almosts* and *could have beens*. I always thought I was meant for more. What a strange twist of fate.

Lilia is face to face with me. The blade she holds glistens in the moonlight. She raises it and smiles, "It was fun while it lasted, whore. Too bad you never got to ask him what he is."

But in those last few seconds when she had to get in the last word. I remembered something.

"DANTE!!!" I scream with all the might inside my head, and as her blade slashes down into my neck. I release my raging flames.

As the abyss takes me, I throw a silent prayer up to the Goddess, Gods, Hades himself, if he'd listen. I hope Dante heard my scream, and if he didn't? I hope I burned that bitch's face off.

CHAPTER TWENTY FOUR

VIVI

I WAS HAVING THE best dream. Calypso was curled next to me, my little spoon. I could almost feel her rumbling purrs and soft fur rubbing against me. I miss her so much And Marlow's voice, her voice is in the dream too...

"Let me in that room or I'll kick your ass!"

"You need to calm down. Calm. Down!"

"Fuck you, calm down! She's in there!"

Wait, Marlow? Loud echoing purrs vibrate my stomach and legs.

Calypso?... I open my weary eyes.

"CALYPSO!!" The tears come fast and furious, racking my chest and dragging heart-wrenching sobs from my throat. I don't know how this is even possible, but Lippy pops her head up from my blanket and whines, making those weird chirping noises I always love. Had she grown since I left her in the mountains? My stomach flips at the thought of that night.

I reach for her as she flops her massive head onto my chest. Who needs to breathe anyway?

My girl is here in the flesh and safe. My fingers are clenched into her sides, as if I'm terrified she'll vanish. With a ragged breath, I throw my face into her fur and ugly sob.

I was so caught up in the moment I had no idea there was a certain Dark Prince in the room. "You called out for her."

"You... you found her for me?" Another strangled cry escapes my lips as I wrap my arms around Lippy's massive frame, hugging her as she nuzzles my neck.

"Bronwyn found her. I only instructed her to do so." Killian replies humbly. "She was with your friends."

My friends. What friends?

I look at Killian. "You let them come here?"

He nods. "You needed your rest. They're waiting to see you. Your wolf is unreasonable and ill-mannered, by the way."

Shit, he was being a pain in the ass.

I moved to get out of my bed and set Lincoln straight when I realized I'm not in my rooms. The bed is enormous, with a deep olive-green bedding, an overly elaborate armoire sits across from me. There are bookshelves across one wall, packed full of hardcovers. I wonder what kinds of books Killian reads. He doesn't strike me as a Stephen King fan. Maybe he reads Poe and Oscar Wilde? Wouldn't it be hilarious if he was a closet Anne Rice groupie? Although, it would make a little sense with the sex haze that rolls off him like overpowering cologne. There's a worn leather reading chair resting in the corner, and a side table with a glass of dark liquid sitting on a coaster. Of course, he uses coasters. He's such a control freak. I bet he'd blow a gasket by spending five minutes in *my* chaotic apartment.

After I finish ogling the bookshelf, and gloating that I'd driven Mr. Perfect to drink, I survey the rest of my surroundings. The bed smells of intoxicating smoke and jasmine... I'm in Killian's room. Giving him an inquiring glance, realization dawns on his face. "Your rooms need to be cleaned."

Okay, but he didn't take me to an infirmary. He put me in his bed...

"Um, thank you. I appreciate it. May... may I see my friends?" I don't know why I sound so fragile or why my asking came out as a plea, but I'm kicking my ass for it. Weakness is for supernaturals who want to be at the bottom of the food chain. Good old Deacon wisdom right there.

"You're still healing. No brawling today." I notice the slight dimple forming on his cheek as if he's trying not to smile. *Uh huh, Mr. Dark One... I'm figuring you out.* He strides over to the door and as soon as he cracks it open, Marlow bursts through, headed straight for me like a freight train.

"Marlow!" A fresh wave of tears hits me like a ton of bricks, and then I'm crushed in her arms. Sobbing, hugging, and sobbing some more. She runs her hand through my midnight hair, checking me over to be sure I'm not a figment of her overactive imagination—I glance past her to Linc, excited to see him, but my excitement is short lived when I see his uninviting expression.

"Linc?" He stands near the edge of the bed, defensive, checking the room for threats. "Lincoln Blackwood! Come over here and hug me, you ass!" That coaxes a smile from him.

"Hello, Warrior Princess. We really have to stop meeting like this." His voice throws me into another fit of tears.

I don't know why I can't stop crying. It's embarrassing enough to be nipped-out in another see through nightgown in Killian's bed. Speaking of. What happened to my *normal* pajamas?

"So, this is the Netherworld, huh? It's nothing like I thought! It's... stunning. I thought it would look like... I don't know. Hell?" Marlow contemplates. She's distracted by the view from Killian's balcony, which is way better than mine! He's been holding out on me in more ways than I can count on my fingers, the bastard; I like waterfalls too.

Calypso adjusts her body as I move, burrowing closer. I hadn't even remembered I was in pain until she moved, and a fresh swell moved through me. I check my wrists... the symbol is still there, with a jagged scar through it. I lift my other wrist and see the same jagged scar. My fear intensifies as my hands travel to my throat.

"Is it bad?" I question them, steeling myself for the worst. I mean, I guess disfigurement isn't the worst. It's better than dead, but a teeny part of me might be a little vain. I admit it.

"You'll have a scar, but Killian assures us that your healer is the finest in all the realms, and she will do her best. Barely noticeable. We met her, Selene. She's like a Goddess come to life!" Marlow casts a beaming smile, Linc scoffs. Not bothering to say a word.

"Yeah, she's astonishing, right? Almost too beautiful to look at straight on." I return Marlow's smile.

Something is off about Linc. He's different. There's something more complex about him, more beastly, brooding. He reeks of violence, which is out of character and hasn't ever been part of his scent before. I can't decide if I like it or not? But I know one thing for sure, this isn't a great place to be throwing around that kind of dominance. There are bigger, badder, and more ruthless beasts in 'Count Dracula's Fortress' than wolf shifters.

"Deacon?" I watch them both, and the pained response is like a reality slap to the face. "What happened to Deacon?"

"We'll have time for this later when we get you the hell out of here and back where you belong." It's Linc who answers me.

"Leaving? Who said I was leaving the Netherworld? My sister is here. Well, not *here* in this fortress, but she's here in the Netherworld. I think she may be in the dark & twisty part. Stop avoiding the question. What happened to Deacon?!"

"My father took him." Marlow whispers. "They took him to The Academy."

"Yeah, and we have to get him out! So, you most definitely ARE leaving here. The sooner, the better." That sounded like an order, and I don't appreciate being controlled by anyone. Linc knows that, but I'm going to choose peace for the moment. Maybe he's feeling defensive. And I get that, but Goddess below... Killian wasn't kidding. Linc's attitude really *is* shit.

"We can figure something out, maybe Jagger and the Twins-"

I'm interrupted before I can even finish my sentence, "So it's true? You've been here fraternizing with Netherlings while the Earth Realm falls to ruin? I guess you aren't the girl I thought you were, after all." He looks at me with disgust. The pot shot lands exactly where Linc intended. Straight through my heart.

Willing the tears to stay in my face this time, I glance at Marlow, questioning in my eyes. *Where's the joyful reunion? What the fuck is his problem?* She gives me a double wink and a wave of her finger. Our secret language as kids. *It's a subject for another time.*

Got it.

The door creaks open as Selene peeks her head through, looking at each of us, all sunbeams and benevolence. "I heard you were awake, Pretty Girl. And what a miracle that is! Do you mind if I check you over? I have some balm to ease your scarring." She looks at Calypso, who's baring her teeth.

Stop it, Lippy, I think she might be a literal angel!

"Of course! Don't mind her. She's protective." I swipe my hands across Lippy's back.

They hurt you. There is danger here.

Although the message is disturbing, the comfortable sound of her voice back in my head clicks one of my missing pieces back together. Another sob threatens to overtake me... home. Calypso is my home.

I nod to Selene to show it's safe to touch me now, and she moves toward the dresser with her cart of herbs and tinctures.

Marlow smiles, heading towards the door, "We've been given 'accommodations for the duration of our stay.' Fancy, right? The prince and his family have been most welcoming *to both of us*..." she glares at Linc, who's still being a silent jerk face. "So, how about we freshen up while you get yourself checked out? You can show us around the place when you're feeling up to it?"

"That sounds amazing. I've missed you guys so much," my heart swells with love, and then Marlow forcefully grabs Linc's arm, directing him out of the room as he grumbles. Closing the door behind her, I can hear them bickering outside the door.

Deacon is in the Halls of Repentance. I'm concerned, but not terribly so. He's a warrior. He'll figure out how to stay alive until rescue can get to him. He trained us for these situations. He's equipped for this. But what about The Gravestone? I'll have to get to the bottom of that later. It sounds like there are many things to discuss later, including whatever the reason is for Linc's hostility and everything that's happened since I was taken.

Speaking of things that happened, "Selene, how long have I been... um, how long has it taken for me to heal?"

"You've been unconscious for the better part of a week. But you wake with glowing eyes. Do you have visions?"

"I do, but I don't always understand or remember."

"Daughter of Oracles..." she muses to herself. There's that title again. I want to know what it means, but I'm not sure now is a good time.

"May I ask you what happened? I mean, I know what happened to me... I know who did this to me. But, how... who..." I'm having trouble forming the correct words for what I want to know.

"You know who did this to you?" Selene's face morphed from the picture of calm serenity to vicious and untamed in a matter of seconds. "I'll fetch Killian." And she rushes out the door. Okay, well, that answers *one* question. They don't know who did this to me. No wonder everyone seems so jumpy.

— ⋅◦⋅ —

THE PREVIOUSLY SPACIOUS ROOM feels far too full; everyone came. And I mean... *everyone*. Killian and Jagger sit on either side of the bed. Bronwyn stands guard at the door. Anise paces the floor like a caged animal. The twins are completely still, Marlow looks concerned, Linc seems pissed, and Calypso? She's standing over the top of me, hissing with her teeth bared.

This isn't what I envisioned when I thought of the two worlds uniting. I'm now part of their meeting with each other. I thought it would be like a semi-awkward dinner situation where someone, probably Jagger, breaks the ice and then everyone is good to go. This is more like a head on collision. They're all wound up tight and staring at me. I might as well pull the 'I'm the one who almost died, so shut up and listen' card while I still have the sympathy vote.

"First, I'm going to need every fucking one of you to chill out. You're making Lippy nervous, and I can't calm her down when there's enough testosterone to drown a kraken in here."

All but Linc heeded my warning and lowered the tension. I'm going to talk with him separately, figure out what he's so bent out of shape about. But for now? He's got a little leeway for asshole-ish-ness. I look around the room at each individual face, wondering how this even happened. How does a foul-mouthed cast away end up here? With this many supernaturals ready to fight. For me? It's mind-boggling.

"Tell us what happened," Killian growls. He's trying to restrain himself. Failing. But trying, nonetheless.

Time to rip off this band-aid?

"It was Lilia. She slit my throat. And she had two shadow beings with her." I recalled the details but didn't get far as a chair flies across the room and smashes into a thousand wooden shards.

Killian is livid, murderous. The room fills with gray shadows as I catch his eyes, drawing them into me. Willing him to come back from the darkness that's overtaking him. As I gape at the raw dark power leaking from every pore, it occurs to me he's been holding out on me. This man is a predator through and through, and there *is* a sinister side lurking behind that facade. I feel my eyes glow, warring with the darkness in him, trying to pull him back from the brink of wherever he was going. Finally, his shoulders relax, and his stormy turquoise eyes return. After that, I explain everything in as much agonizing detail as I could remember. The details could be nothing to me, but even a small word could be a clue to someone who knows Lilia better than I do.

When I get to the part where she slashes down at my throat, Linc leaves the room. I'm unsure if someone should go after him, but it's better to let him blow off some of that shifter steam in the hallways.

"I heard you scream." Dante states frankly, and I smile.

You saved my life.

I breached the spell. Anise saved your life.

My eyes move to Anise, thankful, questioning. "You saved me?"

"I felt your terror. I felt your pain. I couldn't get into the room until you called for Dante." She continues to pace the room, fiddling with her dress. "I opened the box."

My mother's box.

'I need you to put it somewhere safe. Never lose it, Genevieve; it must never leave you. Don't break the seal unless your life is in danger...'

"What happened?" They all know something I don't.

"It released The Goddess of Night into the Netherworld," Killian answers. I can't tell if he's upset about that. Or if he's amazed? Maybe both? "She climbed inside you."

Wait, what?! I let the initial shock sink in before sharing one of my own secrets.

"To heal me, right? I haven't been honest with you, any of you. She's been speaking to me for months through my visions. She calls me Daughter of Oracles a lot. I think she's protecting me. Where did she go?"

"Well, that's the thing. She hasn't come back out." Jagger gives me a somewhat intrigued shrug.

"I have a goddess squatting inside me!?" I've been through a lot of shit over these last few months, but this isn't something I had on my BINGO card. I don't feel her in me. Maybe they're mistaken. She slipped out while nobody was looking. Oh, who am I kidding? I bet Prince Stalkington stared at me the whole time I was out. We'll call it a hunch.

So, she's still inside me. Okay, creepy, but why?

The box belonged to your great - great grandmother. The visions... the seeds... the resemblance. Selene gives me a knowing look, one that says it might not be a good idea to announce that information to the room, not now anyway. But I can see Bane's face shift. He's heard all my thoughts.

It's not my secret to tell.

I release a shaky exhale. It's not that I won't tell them. I just, well, I don't know if it's a good thing or a bad thing. I've already been jailed, beaten, and damn near exsanguinated. I'll tell them on my own time. Selene is right. Now is not that time.

Killian mistakes that shaky exhale for exhaustion and beckons for us all to wrap up the conversation so I can rest. I thank Dante for hearing me and thank them both for trusting my judgment on this. I need to know more about the how's and why's before I go flapping off at the mouth about a dark ancestor who practices necromancy. If I remember correctly.

Anise hugs me tight, peering at Calypso with childlike interest. "Your spirit beast feels like you do. We're going to be good friends! I'll get her some cakes. No, I think honey. Does she like honey?"

I look at Lippy, nodding my head for her to answer. She pads around the bed and slides her sandpaper tongue across Anise's face, which makes her giggle and scratch Lippy's ears. One by one, they file out of the room. The only ones left now are Killian, Marlow, Lippy, and me.

"I love you, bitch." Marlow snorts out.

And I snicker at the ridiculousness of it. "I love you back, hooker. We'll talk later?"

She nods and gives Killian a racy glance. "You going to clear out those cobwebs yet? Or are you waiting for the apocalypse to happen first?"

I nearly suffocate on my tongue, "Marlow Culpepper! Inappropriate!"

She chuckles as she leaves the room, calling for Calypso to follow, making a big production of locking the door behind her "for discretion"... the non-sexually active hussy.

My cheeks blaze red as I turn my head to the Dark Prince of the Netherworld. "I'm so sorry. She really has no filter at all."

As he lifts me into his arms, Killian chuckles, heading toward his massive bathing room, which houses an even more oversized tub than mine. He sets me on the counter, and I'm frozen in place. Is this a trap? Payback? One of those scenarios where he plays mini-Lucifer and bathes in front of me this time? Running warm water and pulling off his shirt, he flashes me one of his infamous smirks.

"You going to bathe fully clothed then, or should we see about those cobwebs?"

CHAPTER TWENTY FIVE

VIVI

I LET MY FEET sink into the enormous oval tub. Black marble, and big enough for a damned orgy. Did Killian have orgies on this thing? Maybe that's not the best thing to ponder now. I'm not sure I want to know the answer to that question. No, I'm positive I don't want to know the answer to that question. But I do have some others I'd love to know about...

Finally, I submerge myself, bringing me much closer to a naked Prince of the Darkside than I was comfortable with, but the hot water welcomes me, soothing my burning muscles. I was out for a week, even with a possibly evil goddess possessing me! It hadn't hit me until now. My arms pebble with goosebumps at the thought of how close I was to death.

Killian slides behind me, and I halt at the jarring contact. Am I really doing this? He must sense my hesitation. He grabs a washcloth and wets it, cleaning the blood and grime from my back, which is even more awkward. I don't know this nurturing Killian. I know broody Killian, infuriating Killian, would-lock-me-in-a-tower Killian. But this version is off-putting.

As he moves the cloth to my shoulders, he speaks, "For the first time in many years, I was afraid."

I don't have a clue what to say to that? So, instead, I allow him to continue bathing me while I scope out the room. I've heard of bathhouses, like the community bathing rooms they have in castles. This room reminds me of one. The walls are made of green tile. They look expensive. Jade, maybe? They're arranged in a symmetrical pattern on the walls. Almost making stars with the intentional placement. Feeling the weight of his stare on my back, I remove a brick from my wall.

"I was afraid, too. I thought I could best her, I thought... with the fire. But she was too fast. I didn't realize she was going to slit my throat until the very end..." I'm shaking now, unable to finish that sentence. Killian's strong hands wrap around me. "I thought of Calypso while my life flashed before me. I mourned for her."

He nods. "I figured as much, the way you called for her."

"Thank you again for bringing my family here. I know it took a lot from you to give up secrets. To trust that those I love won't hurt your people. And I'm sorry for the way Linc is acting. I don't know why he's being so hostile, but I'll talk to him."

He stiffens at the mention of Linc. There's something brewing between them, and I have an idea what it might be. Before I can say anything else, Killian interrupts, "The wolf believes you to be his *mate*."

His WHAT? No, that can't be it. Does he harbor a childhood crush on me? Sure, but we've been over that. He's great, but he's not *mine*. Not in that way. This is what the tension is all about? The Dark Prince of the Netherworld is jealous?

"I'm not his mate, Killian. He's my best friend. He's just protective."

His fingers caress my skin as his breathing grows deeper, more sensual. My heart races at the thought of what is growing harder behind me, brushing up against my lower back. His fingers trail across my shoulders, moving the midnight hair away as he leans closer, trailing kisses across the area he just washed—his breath fanning where the cold air had touched, sending waves of desire through every nerve ending.

I'm not sure what I expect to happen in this tub with The Heir to the Netherworld. I suppose I expected *this*... but the gentleness? The way he's touching me like I am the most precious thing in his world. It's disarming. There goes another brick, tumbling down the cliff.

"I thought about you, too. When I was sure I would die." This could be the dumbest sentence to ever leave my mouth, but it was the truth. I thought of him and how he would never know the things he makes me feel. And now that I have the chance to tell him, I'm losing my nerve.

"And what were you thinking?" He presses the issue.

"You first." I lean back into him and look up at his magnificent face. The steam from the bath is dripping from his dark hair onto his cheeks.

He laughs. I don't think I could ever get sick of that sound. So different from the composed, cloquent, icy Killian he portrays in public. "I was out of my mind with panic. I destroyed your rooms, and I fought my brother."

"Jagger? You fought Jagger?! Why?" my voice grows an octave higher, laced with concern.

"You look at him differently than me. He's earned your trust, your respect. I trusted him to keep you safe. I..."

"So, you were being an asshole?" It's not funny, not really. But it's the truth.

He grins, and it's like witnessing the stars wink into existence. "I was an asshole, yes." He admits.

I exhale shakily at the dark galaxies swirling in his eyes. He doesn't need to say it out loud; I can see it. He feels for me. How much is he capable of feeling? I don't know. But right now, in this room together? It's enough.

Brick by brick by brick, the wall crumbles.

I turn on his lap, facing my body towards his. Inadvertently rubbing against him in the most intimate of places, and it is enormous. My lungs ceased to function, and for a moment, I contemplate sprinting from the room. As if he senses the moment slipping away from him, he grabs my thighs. Gently, but firmly, pulling me as close as we can get, and I can't help myself from looking down between us, my jaw must be about to hit the floor because the next thing that came out of his mouth surprises us both.

"If you keep staring at me like that, this is going to be a lot less enjoyable than either of us intends." He moves his eyes downward, and now we're both looking at his erection, angled dangerously close to my nakedness. Heat flashing in his turquoise eyes. He traces his fingers across the front of my chest, swirling them across my skin in slow, agonizing circles. I can feel him pulsing against my stomach, but he makes no move to take it further. Instead, he traces my breasts with a finger and then with his lips. Looking up into my face, judging my reaction.

And Goddess, help me, this might be the stupidest thing I've *ever* done, and that's saying a lot because I've done some foolish shit in my life. But screw it. I grab his face and kiss him with all I've pent up since the first time he trapped me with those hypnotic eyes. I give in to everything I've fought so hard to deny. I give in to *him*—just this once.

He lifts me, dripping water throughout his bathroom as he walks us toward his bed, his mouth never leaving mine. As he lays me down before him, he breaks the kiss and stares down, taking in my nude form like it might be the last time. And who knows? Maybe it is. This might break me forever. I'm fully aware. Killian isn't the kind of man you walk away from, not after he looks at you like *this*. Touches you like this... but I can't bring myself to care. He leans over; hands splayed on either side of my body. My breath ragged with the need, "Are you wet for me, Kitten?" his hand slides downward, knowing full well the answer to that question. "Do you want me?"

I would have let him do just about anything to me right now, and that's the truth. But I settle for a strangled, "Yes."

"Yes, what?"

"Oh, fucking hell Killian! Yes, I want you. Yes, fuck me. Please. Just... YES." Good Goddess, did I have to spell it out in kindergarten letters? He is enraging!

And then his mouth is on me, and I am burning out of control. We're limbs, mouths, and tongues. Fingers digging into each other's skin, a frenzy of pent-up lust, and holy shit, it's almost too much. I try to catch my breath, but with every inhale, he assaults me with his punishing mouth. He nips my breasts, runs his fingers along my slit, and slides his tongue across the pulse of my neck all at the same time.

I'm moaning now. Writhing in ecstasy. He's an addiction. I can't get enough. I want more. "More!" *Did I say that out loud? Oh shit, I did.* And the raging inferno in his eyes tells me he heard me, loud and clear.

Those dangerous eyes pin me, and I am so fucked.

Literally, figuratively, all the way. Totally fucked.

My knees shake as he positions himself above me, licking across my collar bone as he pushes a finger inside me. Sparks burst behind my eyes at the contact as he moves with ease, rocking his fingers into me with a swaying rhythm as he adds another, stretching me, creating a slick waterfall for only him.

He sinks between my thighs, and I open for him. I watch as he places soft kisses along my inner thighs, and then his hard silken magnificence is moving against my entrance, "You're so fucking beautiful," he growls out before he pushes inside me in one fluid motion burying himself deep, deeper than I thought I could handle. We sit still and silent for a moment, breathing hard

and getting lost in each other's eyes. When
the anticipation is too much for me, I move.
Beckoning him to do the same.

I cried out as he takes me, owns me, possesses
me. He whispers softly as I lose myself to him,
"You're mine."

"Yours," I cry out, the rhythm building into an
inferno that is about to erupt. He moves against
me, rocking my hips, touching every part of
my sensitive core. Just enough to drive me wild,
enough to make me beg. "Please..."

And then he drives into me like a man
possessed. I wrap my legs around his back and
guide him in hard, deep strokes. He pushes
further and further, changing the tempo from
slow and teasing to hard and fast. Tension builds
inside me, about to spill over. I make noises I
didn't know I could make. He catches my mouth
with his own, and he swallows every single one.

My body shakes with the need to explode
as he pulls out just a little, sliding to the
very top of my entrance. Kissing me, waiting,
moving ever so slowly. And when I think I will
go completely mad, he drives into me with
a ferociously possessive thrust—and I shatter
against his perfect shaft. He moves against the
deepest part of me and cries out my name with
his own release, I come undone again.

Stars dance, heavens part, and hell bows to us.

CHAPTER TWENTY SIX

VIVI

I MUST HAVE BEEN exhausted because after Killian and me... well, you know what we did. I fell asleep in his arms: missing dinner and the chance to spend some time with my friends, who I miss so desperately. During the night, he must have let Calypso into the bed because I'm waking up to the *morning aftermath*, and my cat is here, but he isn't.

Don't get all emo about it now, Vivi. You knew what this was, you knew, and you made your choice, I remind as I feel a chink in my armor breaking. The ache between my legs isn't helpful either. No, we will not do this. No, what-ifs. No self-loathing. It was amazing, world flipping, universe-shaking sex. Nothing more, and that's okay because I can't bring myself to regret it, even if that was the only time, even if it all goes to shit. It was worth it. Wasn't it?

"We're not getting all girly over this, right, Calypso?" I run my fingers through her fur, pulling her closer to me. *You're my true love, anyway.* I nuzzle my face into her side and inhale a lungful of her comforting scent.

The door cracks and my heart flips... but it's only Maius, with a huge tray of pancakes, fruit, gummy bears, and coffee. Oh, thank the Goddess for *coffee*!

Behind her, Marlow pops her head in, "Is it safe yet? Or are you two still rearranging the furniture up in here?"

I can't help but bark out an unladylike laugh, snort, and everything. This fantastic creature, she's on a whole different level of dirty bird. Ha! "Enough about my lady bits. Come, eat some of this food! They always give me too much."

Marlow doesn't waste a second, skipping to the tray and grabbing a few pieces of fruit and a couple of pancakes to share. Just as she's about to turn and jump on the bed, no doubt, she stops and picks up a piece of paper. He left me another note. Oh, Goddess. What does it say? Please don't be a *'thanks for the bang'* note or an *'it was fun, but...'*

My heart skips several beats. Please, not in front of Marlow.

"Are you going to share with the class?" I give her an impatient grumble. I'm ready for the letdown. I've done this before. It's fine. She hands the paper to me.

It reads:

I had some pressing business to attend. You were resting, and I didn't want to wake you. Can we talk this evening? I have some truths to share. -Prince Charming.

Some truths to share. Okay, that's not so bad. Now, put it out of your mind, Vivi. And spend the day with your family. "Where's Linc?"

"He's blowing off some steam in the training arena. I think he's made a friend! One of Jagger's men. I think I made a friend too..." she bites her lip. "Jagger is Hella fine."

I smile at that, finding it weird how I compared them...

"Yeah, he's pretty great. If you can get past his dirty mouth."

"That's my favorite part! Hook a girl up, Vivi. This v-card has an expiration date." She fans herself with a sigh. I snort out another giggle. I've missed her, inappropriateness, and all.

"I can't believe you're here! We've got to catch up. Have you met anyone yet?"

"I'm rooming next to Bronwyn. Crazy, huh? Tell me you kicked her ass before you forgave her? Because I like her, I do, but double agent shit is not cool. Oh, and I saw a red-headed girl skipping through the hallways with a hellhound. Calypso didn't seem too impressed with that. Man, this place is a trip!" She sounds mystified. I don't blame her; it was a change for me too.

We're a few pancakes and gummy bears into an old school bed hang-out session when Linc comes in, still pissy-pants. *Bummer.*

"What's the matter, grumpy gills? Come sit! We've got plenty of breakfast to go around." I extend the olive branch, hoping he grabs it.

"I'm good in the chair, thanks." Is all I get in response. Whatever.

CHAPTER TWENTY SEVEN

VIVI

ANISE BOUNCES IN THE doorway, looking over Marlow and Linc. Sizing them up. Apparently, she and Calypso made friends sometime last night? So at least that's one awkward first meeting out of the way.

"What kind of creature are you?" She looks at Marlow, intent on receiving a response. Marlow looks at me questioningly, and I convey the message with my eyes. *She's cool, I'll explain later.*

"I'm half Witch, half human." She smiles at Anise.

"Ew, I don't like humans! Nasty vengeful little worms. They consume and destroy, like a plague." *Oh no. Not today, please let it be a good Anise Day*, "But the Princess loves you?" She squints her eyes as if making an important decision.

"I do. I love them all very much." I reply as Linc rolls his eyes. That's it. We're going to have a conversation the *minute* there are no prying eyes or ears around. He needs an attitude adjustment.

Anise turns her attention back to Marlow. "Can you turn people to stone? My brothers can! But Killian would rather they didn't do that — too many statues, too many questions."

It clicks then, the twins. They're snake-like eyes and odd serpentine movements. They're part Gorgon. I thought Gorgons were only women. I have a lot to learn about this place.

"I can't turn them to stone, no. But you know what I *can* do! I can erase memories, and I can wield the air pretty much any way I want to." Marlow doesn't miss a beat.

"That's so cool! Oh. Yeah, Killian told me to take you for a tour. All of you, and he also said that I must make myself scarce if you need some private time. Do you need private time? Well, too bad you can have it later. Let's go to the garden!" Anise resumes her bouncing, waiting for us to move.

***

We spend the afternoon wandering the fortress. I loved being able to tell Marlow and Linc about the moving pictures on the wall. The story of the Original King of the Netherworld and the twisted love story that made it what it is today, or the parts I know at least. We sit in the gardens for a time, allowing Anise to point out the different plant life and what kind of destruction it could create. Linc seemed to lighten up a bit during that part. We walked past the training area, making it a point to draw attention to the dome. Explaining that here magic is celebrated. Calypso follows us on our meandering walk, clarifying that she will tolerate Grim, but takes swipes at him when he comes too close. Which Anise *loves*! Of course she does.

Throughout our afternoon, I can't say how many times I want to pinch myself. I'm here, and I'm alive. With my childhood best friends and my exasperating but beloved familiar, and they're in the Netherworld mingling with my newfound friends. It feels... right. But I know we need to chat about more pressing matters back home.

As we come to the entrance of the library, I turn to Anise. "Do you suppose you could find us some cakes?"

"Sure!" she smiles and then eyes me warily, "Oh, it's time for privacy?"

I nod, smiling at her like I would my little sister.

As we find a comfortable corner in the fancy fortress library, I look to be sure we're alone... "Spill it, all of it. I don't care who goes first."

Turns out Marlow has a lot to say. When I didn't reappear from The Academy for three days, she knew something was up. So, she spied on Faustus, even used mind magic on him while he slept. It turns out she found more than she bargained for.

Faustus Culpepper is in league with the Shadowfax and always has been. Even worse, the portals were never closed. The lies stack up and just keep stacking. She'd gleaned from using her mind magic that Killian somehow got me out of the Academy, so she and Linc went hunting for a way into the Netherworld. Which was a big old failure, and while they were searching, the Rune Force came for Deacon. Rowena got away with her sprites; nobody knows where they fled to, but they're certain that she's safe.

Meanwhile, Marlow went to Willa and showed her everything she had pulled from Faustus's brain over the last few months. Willa—to

everyone's surprise—was not happy with any of
it. Basically, the Witches are split. Willa and "-
The Resistance," which they now call themselves,
are gathering in an abandoned abbey outside
Thornfall.

Holy. Shit.

It hasn't escaped my notice that Linc hasn't said
a word this entire time, and my irritation with
him is growing by the second. Does he not get it at
all? I am here, in this fucked up situation, having
gone through some unthinkable bullshit because
of *him.* The attack on *him* is what took me to the
gates of The Academy. And no, the rest isn't all
his fault, but you would think a little appreciation
would be in order!

*Hey, I sacrificed myself for you, asshole. You could
have the decency to treat me like we know each other.*

"You don't have much to say." I level my
eyes at Linc, trying my best to manage
my uncontrollable mouth and horrific temper.
Believe it or not? Being here has helped me grow
up a bit.

"You smell like him," the look he gives me is
pure disgust, and it knocks the wind out of me for
a moment. I've never seen that look on Lincoln's
face, ever. And the fact that it's directed at me? I'm
speechless, gutted, heartsick, and fuming.

"What the fuck is your problem, Lincoln?" I
raise my voice, worn-out from whatever this is.
The Scarlet Letter, maybe? But screw that. He
wants a confrontation; I've got one waiting with
his name on it. Yeah, yeah, I said being here
helped me grow up a bit, not that I was a saint...

"What's *my* problem? Oh, that's rich, Viv."
he sneers, "You have a good time flouncing

around the Netherworld, making new friends, and getting to know The Dark Prince's *dick* while our guardian rots in the cells?"

Before I realized it, my fist was in the air, and I decked Lincoln Blackwood halfway to the Moon Realm. He flies off the back of his chair and lands in a pile of pissed-off shifter while I stalk toward him, because I'm not done.

"Don't you EVER speak to me like that again, Lincoln! Never." Tears form in my eyes as I try to keep them from falling. "You have no idea what you're talking about! What I went through, how many times I've almost died to keep you safe! You are a fucking asshole!" The tears are falling in earnest now, and I lift my hands to hit him again, but he blocks me.

"I killed my father for you! I ripped out his throat and spit it on the ground. I went back to that hellhole, and I took *my* pack. So that I could have the power to save you! And when I get here? Imagine my surprise when you didn't need saving at all. Instead, you bagged yourself a Dark Prince."

He did what?!

"Fuck you, Linc!" I try to pull my hands from his grip, and he holds them tighter. "Let me go!" I'm sobbing now, my heart ripped in half, bleeding out.

And that's when I feel his presence. The library fills with shadows, and the blind fury radiating at my back has me legitimately terrified.

"YOU DO NOT TOUCH HER!" Killian bellows, his roaring voice echoing off the walls, creating a loudspeaker effect. No, no, no. This is not what it looks like, or is it? This cannot happen.

Linc lunges for Killian, and I watch in dread as he raises his hand. It glows blue... and with only half a second to spare, I jump in front of Lincoln. Killian's bolt hits me square in the chest, knocking me backward into a bookshelf. Smoke wafting from my ruined clothes.

And that shit hurt!

Calypso lets out an ear-piercing roar and comes to stand between two men that I care deeply for, ready to shred someone to ribbons. While they're both standing slack-jawed, staring down at me like I've grown a tail.

"I'm fine! Thanks for asking. Is anyone going to help me up?" I look purposely at Marlow for that assistance because... no. Just NO. "This is a pissing contest, and I'm not a fucking prize to be won. Figure your shit out on your own and *don't* kill each other!"

I motion to Marlow; we're leaving this library right now. As I turn the corner, Lippy in tow as well—I run into Selene, who must have been coming to see what the commotion was about. *Oh, thank the Goddess, a sane person.*

"Are my rooms fixed yet?" I try my best not to sound cross with her.

"As a matter of fact, they are." She scans the scene, peeking around the corner, and a grin appears on her majestic face. "Boy trouble?"

"Something like that. I want my rooms back, please. Now would be great."

Selene nods and takes us girls to my rooms. On our way, she mentions The Prince has set up a ball for this evening. *In honor of our guests...* I'm guessing that decision was made before he found

Linc and me in a cage match in the middle of his library.

I plan my excuse as Marlow interrupts, "We'd love to attend! But... I have nothing to wear, though." You can see the change of energy plainly on her face. I suspect there's a handsome dragon shifter she wants to look incredible for.

Selene smiles big. "Oh, we have dresses!"

CHAPTER TWENTY EIGHT

VIVI

It's hard not to get excited watching Marlow and Anise prance around my rooms, flinging dresses this way and that. Trying them on and modeling for each other, but something feels lacking. Bronwyn should be here. I think it's time we had proper make-up because in everything I've experienced over the last few months; I realize she *is* my friend.

"Selene," I call to her while she chases two giddy females around, trying to pin them down and do their makeup.

"Yes, my Pretty Girl," she gives me one of those soul-warming smiles. I don't think she ever got to have daughters; my Sight tells me this is her own version of The Elysian Fields.

"I'd like Bronwyn to get ready with us, if that's ok?" a sheepish half-grin crosses my mouth. It comes out as a question rather than a statement.

"I think she would like that very much," she replies as she gets up to fetch the tiny, adorable fae that wormed her way into my heart.

I can't say I'm excited about tonight's festivities. Not exactly, but I'm hopeful. Maybe Killian and Linc have bonded somehow, and there hasn't been an all-out brawl in some unsuspecting Netherlings' foyer.

I hope there hasn't been, but the odds aren't looking great.

Another part of me is nervous. They have stuffed me into frilly dresses and had my boobs and thighs paraded in front of The Dark Prince for weeks now. It shouldn't intimidate me, but he hadn't seen quite so much of me then. Now? It's a different story. I'm trying not to be a girl about it. I am. But I don't know what this is. What *we* are? My lingering hesitation plays with my mind. Lilia said... *you don't even know what he really is yet.*

Granted, that was before she made a stellar effort to kill me, and she was a stage five Killian clinger. So, there's no guarantee that anything she said was true. I *don't* know what he is. Other than a Dark Prince who controls shadows and has some sort of blue magic. Does it matter though? Even if it's the worst-case scenario, if he's an evil overlord or a raging psychopath, would it make a difference to me? I can't answer that because it scares me. I'm not sure it would change how I feel, and that makes me the monster I've always feared I am.

And this supposed curse, I'm not even sure I believe in curses, but when they say I'll die a horrible death... that's slightly concerning. *If he loves me, I'll die.* That sounds like fuckery to me. Everyone around this gothic paradise puts at least a little stock in it, but me? I don't know.

In her own way, Selene said I can break this "curse." I don't know so much about that. I know nothing right now, and when I feel too much? Well, I freeze. Now seems like a good time for emptiness. There's been enough turmoil to last quite a while. Let's have one night.

Selene returns with Bronwyn, who rushes to hug me tight. No words needed. We're good, and then it's a free for all in my closet full of sparkly ball gowns! I've never had a slumber party before. It wasn't something I ever had the luxury of being able to do with the whole *Academy murderer* thing, but this feels like what I imagined a slumber party to be.

Selene comes to stand by my side and whispers, "I have a gift for you."

My eyes expand in surprise. She moves to the far edge of my closet and removes a dress that's shrouded in a dark fabric cover. *Ooh, this must be a fancy one!* When she lays it on the bed and pulls the protective covering, my jaw drops. I may have drooled a little on it. This is the dress of all dresses. Black as pitch, with a flowing empire waist, lace embroidery in all the right places, and woven beads that were so tiny you almost needed a magnifying glass, but the way they shimmer with the effortless movement of the fabric is enchanting.

Selene works to fit my body into it like a glove, then gets working her magic on my hair; loose, inky black curls flow down my back with intricate braids woven into the shape of a crown, inlaid with more tiny jewels. I feel a million unicorns fluttering around in my belly.

These boys do not know what's about to hit them.

CHAPTER TWENTY NINE

VIVI

THE BALLROOM IS A flurry of activity when we make it to the entrance. The hall has been transformed into an abstract rendition of Starry Night. I think some clouds and night-blooming orchids are illusions. It's like a scene out of a fantasy movie. I'm pleasantly surprised to hear some modern music playing, familiar music... Stevie Nicks. Someone really *is* a stalker! And a kiss ass. How did he remember a song on the jukebox while some trashy bartender shook her ass in a miniskirt? On second thought, that's probably exactly how he remembered.

As soon as we enter, Calypso stalks across the shining floor and finds a prime spot to perch on. She wants to be above the fray. I guess it's a cat thing...

There are gowns of every shape and color and more Netherlings than I've seen the whole time I've been here; I wonder where they've all been hiding. Or was it Killian who was hiding from me? I don't want to ponder that any further, instead I go in search of something to drink. I sway with the music over to a Brownie with a platter, and grab a flute of champagne? Oh Hell, it could be ambrosia for all I care right now. My nerves are shot, and I could use a little liquid courage.

I feel him before I see him.

Who am I kidding? I can feel when he's about to enter my space, when he's staring at me and thinks I don't know it, when he's pacing his rooms. He's a force of nature, a natural disaster, a gods' damned catastrophe. Of course, I can *feel* him. He makes a move, and the entire universe feels him. I let my stomach do the flippy flop before it settles again, and then I turn...

Killian in armor? Hot.

Killian in pants and a button-down shirt? Sexy.

Killian in a tailored black suit that matches my dress? Earth shattering.

He whips up that infuriating smirk of his, and my knees tremble—only a little, not enough for him to notice. I think.

"You look devastating." He leans over and murmurs into my ear.

Have you ever seen a deer in the headlights? That's me.

"And have you murdered my friend?" Anything to change the unspoken subject, literally anything! But I am curious if they threw down and fixed the problem, or if I should expect them to mark my legs.

"Kitten," he feigns innocence, "I would never stoop to such a thing."

"Uh, huh?" I give him my best eye roll.

"Remember, we still need to talk. Later?"

Is it me, or does he sound a little nervous? At least I'm not the only one feeling the cosmos shift underneath us.

CHAPTER THIRTY

LET'S DANCE

MARLOW AND I ARE having a blast, dancing, and swaying to the music. Bronwyn and even Anise join in on a few songs, while Selene watches contently from a velvet fainting couch near the royal platform. When the music switches up to a slower pace, one of my favorite songs, #1 *Crush* by Garbage, starts playing. I feel a warm presence that trails shivers up my back. I know before I turn around that it's *him*, and I can't stop my heart from beating too quickly. Memories of our stolen moments over the last few months flash through my mind like they do in the movies, one after another, with the grand finale flashback of his bathroom.

"Miss me, Kitten?" Killian whispers into my ear.

Part of me wants to lean into his chest and show him how much. But we settle for some flirtatious gyrating to the steady beat of the bass instead. The lyrics have a whole new meaning with my body pressed against this man that is The Dark Prince of the Netherworld. He's both simple and complex all at once. Force of nature is what I've called him before and I think it will always apply. Part of me wonders if the song choice was intentional. But if so, he has great taste in music. We sway in time with each other, light brushes of hands and the promise of darker things in the future.

Don't get caught up in him, Vivi. You said you would not do this. But I'm kidding myself, it's too late for that now. One touch, and I'm lost to him.

I'm not sure when the energy shifted, but in the space of a moment, we go from dancing out our desires, and to the next where my chest fills with dread.

I heard her before I saw her. I can hear her melody like it's a mirror to my own. And there's another song too, a more sinister one, like that movie scene where the devil is around the corner, and the victim finds the dead end.

Strong arms lift me in the air and whisk me toward the top of the platform, next to the imposing throne. One minute my feet were on the dance floor, and the next—they're at the base of an onyx seat of supreme authority. I'm scrambling to find my bearings when my eyes land in front of me. The princes (and princess) of the Netherworld have formed a protective line in front of me. Jagger's movements are feral, and Killian? Well, he's impersonating death incarnate with alarming accuracy.

"My sister is here," I whisper. It doesn't matter which one hears me, as long as one of them does - and understands what that means. Because the other song? That one must belong to my father.

I feel sick.

"Killian! Old friend," his voice booms across the spacious room as the music goes silent. My eyes latch on to him—*so this my father?* Short black hair hangs over a strong, menacing face. If his eyes weren't a disturbing shade of red, he'd be handsome, in that evil personified sort of way. He wears a suit of dark blue, with a stitched insignia on his shoulder depicting a skull surrounded by shadows. It disturbs me to my core that I see myself in his features.

"Mordred," Killian's face doesn't soften.

Do they know each other? I glance at Killian, trying to understand. The expression I get drops my stomach into my legs. It's an apology, but an apology for *what*?

"You know good and well what I'm here for. I'm here to collect on my agreement with the Heir of The Netherworld. I believe you are in possession of my daughter. Isn't that correct... *Incubus Prince-*?"

Incubus? As in a sex demon, incubus? My heart hurts. It physically hurts. All the dreams. The visions. Everything we felt, everything I felt... wasn't real? Lilia enters my mind. *Are you ready to feed tonight, my Prince?* What the fuck. I let my walls down for him. I let him in. Did he feed off *me*? Rage simmers in my veins, the fire rushing to my palms. Killian lays a gentle hand on my shoulder. A request. *Don't react.*

The silver twins nod inside my periphery. Affirming his message, I'm in danger. I look at Calypso, using our bond. Stay *where you are*. My eyes scan the room. Recon, find the exits, find vantage points. Where are my friends? I spot Marlow and Linc moving towards the line in front of me. Slowly enough not to be noticed. Good.

"Our agreement has been nullified, as we discussed at our last meeting." Killian's teeth are grinding. Something is going on here. Is that where he's been? He knew where my sister was? And what was the agreement? Questions spin in my mind as I felt faint.

'They have sent me to watch you; it looks like I've arrived in time...' my father sent him to spy on me? Or was he sent to break me, seduce me, and then hand me over?

My eyes flick to Killian's, fury blooming. He doesn't dispute me with it, he only squeezes my shoulder again. *Don't react.* It takes all my concentration, but I manipulate my breath to slow down, calming the pounding in my chest. A coldness steals over my features. No matter what I hear, no matter how fucked it is, I do not want to be captured by the sperm donor. Nope.

Mordred's booming voice fills the room again. "So, you invoke your claim to betrothal? That is most disappointing. You are not a King! Her mother is dead, and your father isn't coming back. The original agreement died with them."

He spits out the word *mother* like it's something foul, and I want to rip the veins from his body and drape them from the rafters like the paper ribbon at children's birthday parties.

"Her rightful place is with me, and Kalliope, at the Bone Keep."

I steal a glance at my sister. So beautiful, so damaged. She feels me too, I know it. She turns her bright yellow-green eyes to mine. I sense the wrongness in her now, the shadows that were not born to her but were forced. In that moment, understanding dawns on me. My sister is brainwashed, and if it comes to a fight, she will obey him. My eyes move back to Mordred, watching him, assessing his body language. I can't stand the thought of the word *father*. He may be the monster who created me, but he'll never be my *father*. How did this happen? What was my mother thinking? Did she know what lurks underneath his skin?

"I have a sponsor," Killian calls out.

What the fuck does that mean? *I have a sponsor...* wait, he said, betrothal. To me? My brain isn't processing. When were we betrothed?

Selene moves to my side and murmurs into my ear, "Trust me."

Well, it doesn't look like I've got many options at my disposal, does it?

She grabs me by the hands, and my soul feels like it's ripping apart. It's not physical pain, but a spiritual pain. It's unmaking, undoing, it's the void, it's true darkness. *I don't understand.* And then my mouth rips open, my jaws come damn near off their hinges—and a black substance rolls from within me, into the air, onto the floor, permeating the surrounding space. The faint taste of cinnamon coats my tongue, and then I understand. The Goddess of Night. Her spirit was within me. *That's* what my mother hid in the box...

She entrapped a Dark Goddess. *The* Dark Goddess. In a box?

I'll need therapy for that. Later...

Rage fills Mordred's eyes as they grow more red, and then the woman from my visions speaks, "I support Killian Morningstar's claim of betrothal."

The fucking Queen of Darkness, The Mother of Witches, The Badass Supreme. She's standing next to me, somehow in the flesh, and I am equal parts freaked out and fascinated. She turns to me smiling, reassurance in her beautifully terrifying face. My skin hums at the power radiating off of her, and something inside me knows I should be afraid of her, but I'm not anymore. The Queen of Darkness is protecting me.

"A misunderstanding, Mordred. My claim is solid and backed by one of the Old Ones. You may remember The Goddess of Night." Killian grins.

Oh, my Goddess, my mother *kidnaped* her! The reality of it hits me all at once. Why would she do that? Is this about the stupid prophecy? I look at my sister, locking eyes, pleading with her. *Let me in.* But he's controlling her.

"Kalliope, be a dear and retrieve your sister," Mordred asks. I can hear the toxin dripping from his words.

If she does this? She dies. I can see it in my mind. Killian, Jagger, Calypso, Linc, The Twins, Anise. They're all ready. She will die right here, right now—and Mordred could not care less. I don't understand. Doesn't he need us both? I can't let this happen.

As I open my Sight wider, trying to find a way out of this predicament, something tugs at me, a vibration. We're not alone. I can feel them outside *his* forces. He brought a legion with him. Mordred has no intention of leaving this fortress without me.

This isn't a fair fight. It's a trap.

"Dante," I think loudly. His eyes move to mine. *"There's a legion outside. I'll buy time."*

My smart mouth has to be good for something, right?

"Hello, father," I smile wide, it's not even remotely sincere, "Pleased to finally meet you! Guess the baby shower invite got lost in the mail. What's it been, twenty-three years? I guess that depends on whether you were at the Bloodgood Manor when my mother died. Were you? At the manor... I mean?" I goad him into a reaction.

I see Jagger shrink away, unnoticed by anyone else. All he needs is a few minutes, time to gather his men.

"Genevieve, you've grown into a stunning young woman. More powerful than I dreamed." *Flattery? Interesting approach, dead beat daddy-*. "Come willingly, and there's no need for bloodshed. Come home to your sister."

What a manipulative piece of shit.

Just another minute...

"I hear the Bone Keep needs a little renovation, fallen on some hard times? I understand, we've all been there, right? But sorry, I'm allergic to dust. I'll have to pass." I smile as I look at Calypso... *when I run, you run.* We need to take this fight outside; we're sitting targets in here. Not enough exits.

A terrifying roar booms in the distance. Jagger's ready.

Mordred shouts to Kalliope again, "Seize her!"

And I run for it, Calypso on my heels. Straight past the pillars and out the front gate into the sprawling field where both forces clash, already in battle. Magic flies in every direction, weapons ring out like nails on a chalkboard. It's chaos; I can't find anyone in the throng of violence.

I rush past Anise, wielding a bow and arrow. When they hit their targets, they drop to the ground. Husks. She's influencing them as she runs past, freezing them in their tracks. Badass! Linc is in full wolf form, monstrous, and tearing it up like a boss. I spy Marlow and Bronwyn working together, mind magic and dark fae magic teamwork.

Killian is shrouded in shadows, and anyone who comes close doesn't come back out. Jagger is in the air. The twins are transformed with silver snakes where their hair used to be, piercing enemies with their venom. Selene is holding a barrier over the innocents. And the Goddess of Night? She's nowhere to be found. But I'm not looking for her right now.

"Kalliope!" I stand in the middle of the carnage and scream. My Sight tells me that Mordred is already hiding behind his guard. Safe and sound, for now. A coward who sends his child to do his dirty work. I will kill him, mark my words. "Kalliope!!"

"I'm right here, Genevieve," I spin, and sure as shit, she's standing behind me.

"Oh, thank the Goddess. Come! Come with me. I can help you." I sigh in relief, offering my hand to her. But she laughs and stalks closer. She's got something behind her back, a weapon, I'm sure. My heart sinks. "Don't do this, please. I don't want to fight you!"

She answers by swinging a curved scythe from behind her back in a wicked arch aimed straight for my head. *What the fuck?* She's not trying to subdue me. She's trying to *kill* me. "You have the mark. He'll capture you, no matter where you are. And when he does, you'll wish you were dead. I'm doing you a favor."

"You don't believe that!" I scream at her as she takes another vicious swipe, and another, and another. *Shit!* I kick with all my might and fling her back to the ground, trying to gain my footing again, but she shoots up like lightning, eyes glowing with electricity. Not the Killian kind, the *authentic kind.* A lightning rod hits me in the torso, and it rocks me to the core. Kalliope aims again and I have seconds before she fries my ass alive.

"FIRE, LITTLE MONSTER! Open wide, let it free. Let go!" Jagger screams from the air.

Let go. Let them be free. I think of every moment in my life, every person I destroyed, every lie, every heartbreak, until I feel it swirling in a mosh pit of destruction underneath my skin. One exhale, and I unleash the well, my violet flames wild and unchecked. Flames and lightning meet in the sky, warring with one another in a battle of lethal beauty. But my sister has had more practice. She's spent her whole life controlling her magic. I could curse Deacon myself right now as the electrified rod whips out and grows closer to my skin.

I struggle to keep my flame lit. I can feel it weakening. One second passes, two seconds pass, three... my fire goes out, and she's beat me fair and square. I'm on the ground. As my sister crouches over the top of me, teeth bared, hands poised, I close my eyes, resigning myself to this fate.

"Genevieve!!!" I hear Killian's strangled scream, and part of me smiles inside. I hate the lying bastard, but in my last moments, I can't deny wanting to hear his voice say my name. Not

Kitten, but Genevieve. I take a deep breath, waiting for oblivion...

And nothing happens.

Opening my eyes, I sense Kalliope's hesitation. Half a second is all I need to decide living is a better idea, so I roll and stumble to my feet. She grabs for me on my way up and catches my amulet—the bite as it tears off my neck is equal parts liberating and horrifying. We both watch as it goes flying into the battlefield, stomped into the blood and muck by the feet of those who remain.

I notice the second she steals her resolve and lifts her hands again; *she's going to do it*. She's going to kill me. I raise my forearm to block the blow, and Calypso jumps...

Time stands still.

I watch in slow motion as Lippy reaches Kalliope, fangs bared, into murder mode. Panic grabs my throat as my sister turns to face Calypso and brings her hand down to her chest. Electricity flows through her and out her ears, mouth, nose. Blood bursts from her muzzle as she crumples to the ground. Unmoving. And I collapse.

"NO!!!" I let out a blood-curdling scream.

Clutching at myself, my chest, my hair. *No.* My soul rips in two. *No.* I'm praying, begging, making promises to every god and goddess I can think of. *No.* I'm shaking and sobbing, rocking back and forth. A pair of solid arms try to hold me while I writhe and shout until my throat bleeds. *No.* She's gone. SHE'S GONE! I beat my hands against the wall of flesh in front of me. Over and over until something inside me rips open and the chains unbind what lurks beneath my skin.

Something that isn't Blood Witch climbs through.

A sweltering rage fills me up to the brim. I raise my head, glowing white hot. I taste ash on my tongue. I feel unrestrained violence inside my soul. And then I spot Mordred standing across the field, with Lilia and Faustus by his side. Smug looks on all their faces.

They think they've won.

I glare at Kalliope, willing the burning rage to end her, my limbs shaking with the urge to do it. To kill her right where she stands, and I know I could. But I can't make myself. Instead, a voice that's not entirely mine comes spilling from my mouth. "Run."

And she does.

With a soul splitting scream, I beat my fists into the ground. The earth beneath us rumbles and shuffles. A fracture opens where my hands meet the soil. It grows and expands. A jagged line separates the legion from the rest of the Netherlings, who are fighting for their Prince. Bodies fall into the cavernous ravine, smacking against the edges, screaming for mercy. But I'm fresh out of that.

Earth Mover. I am an earth mover. I am a Bloodgood, but I'm also Shadowfax... and something else, too. I rise, still glowing. Emptiness where a person used to be. I stroll through a field of blood and flames. Observing the gore squishing between my toes, the stunned faces surrounding me, and the chasm at my back. But I can't find the will to care.

Calypso is dead, and the world can burn.

CHAPTER THIRTY ONE

VIVI

SINCE I HAVEN'T MASTERED the art of opening portals, I've spent the last few hours in my rooms alone. *My rooms*. When did I start calling them mine? None of this is mine. I had one thing in the Universe that was mine, and she's gone. I cover my mouth with my hands in another silent scream... *Calypso*. I think my soul is shattered, damaged beyond repair. And to make everything worse? I feel *him* on the other side of the door. But I can't face anyone in this fortress, especially him.

Marlow appears in the doorway, sorrow rims her eyes, "Are you ready?"

I grab my backpack and head to the hallway; not bothering to glance back at my pretty cage. We walk in silence to the throne room where Linc is waiting, along with my new friends from the Netherworld.

Jagger looks beside himself, holding Anise as she cries. The twins stand statue still, but I can feel the waves of regret rolling off them.

Bronwyn looks devastated, and even Maius stands watching in dismay.

Killian isn't here. I guess 'goodbyes' aren't his thing? A twinge of regret hits my soul. This place, this surprising place, I've felt more real in this gothic castle than I've felt anywhere in my life, but I know what I need to do now.

My amulet is gone.

The monster is free.

And I can't stay here.

Marlow, Linc, and I make our way through the picturesque courtyard to the portal, where Selene waits to let us through, disappointment written all over her exquisite face. I'm sure her mind is running through all that might have been, everything that could be. And I understand, it's the depth of a mother's love.

Some version of me wants to turn around and run to him, to forget everything that's happened and disappear into his arms, but I can't. That Vivi died with Calypso.

Grief drowns me in wave after wave of sorrow and seething rage. I am finally the monster they created me to be. Whether it was my father who schemed and plotted my existence, or Faustus, who helped him mold me into the weapon he thought he could wield, or Killian, who took a piece of my heart despite all my efforts to keep it protected. It doesn't matter. My magic is free, and I have spent all my fucks. I'm going to liberate Deacon, and then I'm going to aid The Resistance in taking The Academy down brick by wicked fucking brick.

Marlow steps through the swirling iridescent gateway back to the Earth Realm, Linc follows behind her, and just as I'm about to put my foot through the portal, I feel him. And curse this stupid useless heart, I can't move any further.

"Genevieve," I turn to him and my stomach dips. He looks awful.

"No."

"Don't do this." he argues.

"It's too late." I hold back a sob for a moment before pulling myself together.

Killian stands in silence, stormy eyes intent on ignoring the rejection.

"Whatever it is? Save it. I've heard it all before. You're no different from any other douchebag who lied his way into my panties, but this time... I wanted you to be."

I can see the shadows radiating on his sharp edges, and I back away. He mirrors my steps until my ass hits the stone wall. It occurs to me that his mother is watching this go down, and a blush of embarrassment crosses my cheeks. I want him. Goddess, I know I shouldn't, but I want him with every jagged piece of my bankrupt soul.

"I won't let you go." He whispers.

"You don't have a choice." I whisper back.

With all that's left of my willpower, I push him away and enter the portal. Closing the door on us in more ways than one. I should cry or scream. I should do *something*. But all I can manage is a cheerless laugh. Everything was a lie, from the moment he stepped into the Gravestone. To the Academy and everything in between. I fell for the enemy. I fell for a man who's not even real.

This is the consequence of daring to hope.

CHAPTER THIRTY TWO

THE TEMPLE OF DUSK

MARLOW AND LINC THINK I'm foolish, but I don't blame Kalliope for Calypso's death. I blame Mordred. I blame him for creating another broken child, one just like me. A little girl who wanted to be loved, and when that love couldn't be found? She settled for pain, and a lifetime of never being enough.

When I'm done with my mission in Thornfall, I'm coming for his head. Then I'll reach my sister, and I'll love her in all her fractured pieces.

Yeah, she tried to kill me.

We all have our moments.

But every epic story needs a wicked witch, or two.

To be continued...

Did you enjoy your reading experience? Please help a girl get the word out and leave a review!

For exclusive content, hilarious memes, a first look at new releases, and fellow bookworms doing bookworm things.

Come to the dark side! Join my author group on Facebook – Darwin's Darklings.

Vivi and her band of Misfits return in Gravestone #2 – Heir of Bone and Shadows

STAY CONNECTED

Darwin's Darklings Discussion Group –
www.facebook.com/groups/darwinsdarklings

Official Website –
www.authoramberdarwin.com
TikTok - @missajwrites
Instagram - @authoramberdarwin

THANK YOU

I HAVE SO MANY PEOPLE to thank, I don't know where to start. This book was a labor of love that took so much teamwork to finish.

To my editor, Sara – I can't thank you enough for all the love and support. Working together on this project has been a dream come true. Literally.

To my PA, Jaime – You are an absolute angel, thank you for putting up with my weird demands and always having my back when I come at you with something off the wall.

To my graphic designer, Ashley Seney – Thank you for all the time and hard work put into my vision. You made it come alive!

To my formatter, Starr Z. Davies – Thank you so much for knowing how to do what I can't and being cool enough to do it! (Also, check out her books available on Amazon)

To my beta readers Keesha, Danielle, Juliet, Jaime, Ange – From Chapter One to the very end, you ladies helped bring this story to life. You are so appreciated!

To my mom and sisters – Thank you for listening to me drone on about characters and making you read all my chapters just to see your reactions. Family is priceless.

To the members of the Darwin's Darklings Facebook Group - you're the first of hopefully many! Thank you for believing in me, and in this series before it was ever released.

And to my husband and my children, I love you beyond words.

About the
Author

AN AUTHOR BY DAY AND a werewolf by night.
Amber is a lover of coffee, books, nature, and all
things dark and witchy. Not necessarily in that
order.
She currently resides in Wisconsin with her rock
band husband, three beastly children and a house
full of familiars.

LEGAL STUFF

Edited by - Sara Berzinski

Formatted by - Starr Z. Davies
Cover Art by - Ashley Seney

Made in United States
Troutdale, OR
09/10/2023

12798082R00209